PARALLEL JOURNEYS

PARALLEL JOURNEYS

Ruth Skrine

HALLMARK PRESS

Published by Hallmark Press International Ltd
34 Lambton Court,
Peterlee,
County Durham
SR8 1NG

Typeset by TW Typesetting, Plymouth, Devon

Printed by CPI Antony Rowe, Eastbourne

ISBN 978 1 906459 07 9

For my daughter

Helen

Acknowledgements

I would like to thank:

Lindsay Clarke for helping me to free my imagination.

All at Schumacher College, Devon for the course
(*Responsible science: from control to participation 2001*)
that stimulated my interest in genetic engineering.

Ruth Skrine is a retired doctor, who was born into a medical family in Chippenham, Wiltshire and was christened Ruth Lister after Lord Lister, a distant relative who was responsible for introducing antiseptic conditions for surgery.

Ruth's career has seen her involved in general practice, family planning and psychosexual medicine. She was a founder member of the National Association of Family Planning Doctors, a precursor of The Faculty of Family Planning and Sexual Health Care at the College of Obstetricians and Gynaecologists.

She has edited a series of books on psychosexual medicine for Chapman and Hall and is a previously published author via *Blocks and Freedoms in Sexual Life* which was published by Radcliffe Medical Press, whose books are aimed at the medical fraternity and allied professions.

In her wide and varied career, Ruth has also served a spell as the chairman of the Institute of Psychosexual Medicine as well as being a leader of various training groups.

Her late husband was a prison governor so most of her married life was spent living close to penal establishments. To sharpen her writing skills she gained an MA in creative writing from Bath Spa University in 2001.

Having spent the last few years writing fiction, she points out that although her stories are never about any particular patient, the stories of sexual unhappiness that she has listened to over the years have lingered on, firing her imagination and helping to colour her characters.

Parallel Journeys is her first novel.

PROLOGUE

2003

Fran stood on a wide heath with the singed ends of Paul's hair rough under her fingers. A smell of burning filled her nostrils. Looking down, she saw a spark in the depths of the brush. It sputtered and a twig exploded into a tongue of yellow light. The dry vegetation above it flared so quickly that she could feel the heat on her face. She turned to flee but discovered her feet wouldn't move. In front of her another blaze erupted as if lit by the touch of a magician's wand. She twisted her head. In every direction small fires sprang up and began to join together until she could see no line of escape. She tried to call Paul's name but her croak was lost in the crackle of the encircling flames.

As she kicked off her duvet she could feel her heart pounding. Turning her pillow, she laid her sweaty head on the cool underside. The fires were nothing but a nightmare; she wasn't going to be incinerated after all. Letting out her breath she felt her muscles soften. Paul hadn't died when they bombed the factory. His desertion was only a dream. She reached out for him but, instead of his warm flesh, her fingers came up against the piping on the narrow mattress.

Her eyes jerked open and she turned onto her back. Staring into the darkness the feeling of relief vanished, leaving her stranded, her skin clammy now, like a jellyfish abandoned by the receding tide. The fire was a vision – but his absence was real. He was dead and she was alone.

Her mind drifted back to her retirement party the previous day. Her boss must have consulted Hazel about her leaving present, a box of oil paints and brushes. Her friend was the only person who knew of her interest in art; though she had no idea that Fran's passion had died many years before.

The smell of burning was still strong. Struggling up, she pulled her dressing gown round her shoulders and felt her way out of the attic, where she'd slept ever since Paul died, and down the stairs. In the sitting room she flicked on the light and saw a black lump lying on the carpet surrounded by a scattering of soot. She knelt down and touched the jackdaw's grey head with her forefinger. It must have fallen down the chimney. One eye opened and the little chest heaved. Oh God, it was still alive.

The body was warm as she cupped her hands and tried to stand it up. The legs had no strength and the wings didn't even twitch. She tried again but as soon as she took her hands away it toppled over. Squeezing her eyes tight shut, and giving herself no time to think, she took the neck between the first finger and thumb of each hand and twisted until she felt the tiny vertebrae grate. Then she dropped the corpse and gazed at her hands in horror.

Paul had always dealt with injured animals. He shouldn't have left her to cope with this one by herself. Bruiser began to snuffle at the bundle of feathers. 'Get away,' she cried, pushing the dog so hard that he staggered back into the soot. She gripped her hands together as she rocked back and forth. 'What have I done?' she whispered.

After a few minutes she picked up the carcass and carried it into the kitchen, where she wrapped it in newspaper. Then she washed her hands several times and filled a glass from the wine box. Feeling detached now, she wondered what she would do with it in the morning. Put the remains in the bin, walk away and sweep it from her mind, like a tide that wipes away the footprints? Or would she bury it in the garden, with a home-made cross and a marker of flowers?

It had been bad enough, after Paul died, not knowing what kind of bread she wanted to buy in the supermarket. The thought that she didn't know whether she was a heartless woman, or an over-sentimental child who'd never grown up, was worse.

She sat at the kitchen table tracing the line of the grain with her finger. One of the self-help books that Hazel had pressed into her hands insisted that grieving was a process of reliving the shared life to unpack every detail. Could she discover who she was by going back over their life together, from the very beginning? She glanced at the kitchen clock that Paul had given her on her last birthday, the one with pictures of herbs round the edges, and refilled her glass. She never drank in the morning, but three-thirty a.m. wasn't yet morning.

Hazel had been solicitous before the party. But when she'd casually mentioned the report Paul had written with Brenda Starling, adding that it had blocked his promotion, the smile on Fran's face had been frozen by a wave of despair. And that slimy man Jackson, who'd badgered her with questions about Paul's papers; why wait till nine months after the funeral to harass her in that way? She emptied her glass, unwilling to admit that she hadn't known everything about her husband's life.

Perhaps it was her fault he'd kept things hidden from her. If she were to separate, drag herself out of his grave, it wouldn't be enough to go back over the good times. She'd have to find the courage to look at the darker corners of their life together.

It might help if she stopped drinking. She'd get through the weekend and start on the wagon from Monday. For now, it wouldn't hurt to have just one more.

ONE

1961

Paul woke on the hard floor of the town hall and felt for the woolly rabbit with bald ears that had been his companion during the air raids of his childhood. Not finding it, he stretched out his hand for the reassurance of a warm body. 'Mother?'

'Get off.'

He recoiled, rolled onto his back and opened his eyes, expecting to see Lizzie and his mother with the other families from the street, huddled on camp beds and lilos, coats pulled hastily over warm underwear, gas masks close by. Instead he found his pile of steaming clothes crushed against him by the bodies of the CND protestors who had invaded his carefully demarcated space. A large group still huddled round the stove at the end of the room. They sang songs, including *Don't you hear the H-bombs thunder*, over and over again.

Sleep evaded him for the rest of the night. His hips felt bruised; no matter how he lay he couldn't get comfortable. Coughs and whispers disturbed the darkness. He was relieved when the noise swelled as if to signal an agreement that the day had started, even before it was light. He struggled back into his wet clothes and started out again.

Plodding on, he stared at the pavement and shivered as another trickle of water ran down his back. It was now the third day of the march. Sometimes the rain had been hard and sharp, then it would ease to a steady drizzle. Once the sun broke through, but it had disappeared after a few minutes, as if it couldn't bear to stay and watch the bedraggled column, over eight miles long, winding slowly through the grey suburbs. The banner at the front read 'Aldermaston to London'.

He had seen nothing of the others from his unit since the first day. Instead, he found himself marching under the banner 'Clydesdale says NO'. Bertrand Russell and his acolytes were far ahead. Paul stepped into the road and tried to quicken his pace. After edging forward through the crush for a few minutes he stopped suddenly.

'Oops!' A young woman collided with him and he almost lost his balance.

'Careful. I nearly trod on it.' He was looking down at something by his feet.

'What is it?'

Glancing up, he saw a curtain of dripping black hair. 'You're not wearing a hat,' he said, without thinking.

She shuffled her feet. He bent quickly and the caterpillar climbed reluctantly onto his finger as he prodded it from behind. Carefully cupping his hands he straightened up. They stood in a pool of stillness as the crowd flowed past them on either side.

'What is it?' she asked again, pushing her hair back from her face. He found himself looking into dark, inquisitive eyes.

'I think it's a Red Underwing.'

'What's that?'

'A moth, or will be. It's one of those that hatch in the spring. I can't think what it's doing here.' Paul raised his head to see where it could have come from. When he looked back the insect was crawling across his palm. His companion was smiling. 'Don't laugh,' he said.

'I'm not laughing. I like butterflies but I don't know much about moths. I thought they were rather dull colours.'

'You only see how beautiful it is when it flies. The bright hind wings are covered when it's resting.'

'What shall we do with it?'

'I'd take it home if I had a container.'

'You can use my sandwich box if you like.' She slipped her rucksack off her shoulders and held it awkwardly in front of her while she rummaged inside. The column of people was still pressing past them, leaving no room to put it on the ground.

'It's good you kept your pack with you. Last year I let them take mine on to the night stop. It took me three hours to find it.'

'There.' She held out an oblong box. He managed to remove the lid with one hand, shake out the crumbs and entice the caterpillar off his finger.

'Now all we need is something for it to eat.' His eyes searched round above the heads of the crowd. 'There must be an oak tree nearby.' They began to walk slowly on with the crowd, looking from side to side. Off to the left there was a patch of green that might have been a park.

'Let's try over there,' Fran said, pointing with one hand as she struggled with her pack.

'We'll get left behind if we leave the route.'

'We can catch them up later.'

They weaved their way through the people and turned down a small side road. The noise of thousands of feet fell away behind them. The rain had stopped and ahead of them a break appeared in the clouds. The smell of wet daffodils rose from the small front gardens.

'What's your name then?' she asked. 'I can't just call you Caterpillar Protector.'

He laughed. 'It's Paul. Paul Ashby. I don't spend all my life collecting caterpillars, you know. What's yours?'

'Fran. Short for Frances. I spotted you last night, but you looked as if you wanted to be alone.'

'Not really. My friends from Bristol must have spent the night somewhere else. I haven't seen any sign of them.'

'I'm from Bristol, too.' Fran looked up at him. 'I'm in my first year at the University doing Chemistry, much to my mother's disgust. She doesn't think it a suitable subject for a girl. I had a real battle over it. She wanted me to go to a ghastly finishing school. If my father hadn't supported me for once, I'd never have got my way.'

Paul felt a stab of envy. 'My father died when I was seven.' He flushed; he'd spoken without thinking.

'Seven? That's awfully young. I can't imagine what it would be like to have no father at home.'

'It does make things difficult.' Paul stared straight in front of him. 'Mothers – whatever we do they aren't satisfied. Mine wanted me to be a doctor but I've always been passionate about animals.' They walked on through the wrought iron gates into the small park. 'Look, there's an oak tree.'

Fran quickened her pace, dropped her pack and unbuttoned her anorak. Throwing it on the ground she reached up to pick some leaves. Paul's eyes lingered for a moment on her body in the damp, chest-hugging sweater. Then he looked up at the sky. The clouds were slipping eastward towards Trafalgar Square, where the climax of the demonstration would take place the next day. The sun emerged from the edge of darkness and stretches of blue expanded and joined together. It was Easter Sunday. Paul was not religious, despite having been exposed to endless services at school, but he felt it the right sort of day for a resurrection.

Fran ran her fingers through her hair. 'I suppose I'd better try and get some of the water out of it. There may still be one or two bits of my towel that aren't soaked.' She reached into her pack and spread out her belongings. Paul was impressed when he saw they had been carefully wrapped in a length of oilcloth. Among the dry clothes were a sketchbook, three pencils and a rubber.

'You're an artist, then?'

'I draw a bit.' She stood with the towel in her hand.

Tentatively, he asked, 'Would you like me to dry your hair?'

'That would be great.'

Standing behind her he rubbed her head, then moved down the long strands. The sun warmed them as Fran took a comb from her pocket and passed it to him. Starting near the bottom he took small handfuls, working gently to remove the tangles.

'Umm, that's nice. You're as good at it as Muriel was.'

'Who was Muriel?' he asked.

'One of our maids. She and Daisy lived in before the war, but Daisy left to work in a munitions factory.'

'Sounds very grand.' Paul's hands faltered. His mother had looked after the two of them with no help, knitting for the troops and doing her share of fire-watching when she could find someone to stay with them. She still lived in the same house she had eventually managed to buy from the council.

'Don't stop.'

He started to comb again with renewed attention. 'Do you still live at home?' he asked.

'Yes, worst luck. I wanted to move into a flat with a couple of friends but my mother wouldn't hear of it. "Perhaps next year," she says. That's her answer to lots of things. They didn't want me to come on the march but for once I took no notice of them.'

'I've just moved into a Hall of Residence on the far side of the downs. I feel guilty about leaving my mother, especially as my sister Lizzie went to London at the end of last year. My mum's alone in the house now.'

'You can't tie yourself to her for ever.' Fran paused, then asked, 'How did your father die? Was it in the war?'

'After the war. He caught a fever. He was in the East. Malaya, to be precise.'

'What was he doing there?'

'He was an engineer. We'd gone out to join him but then the war started.' Paul paused, not sure how much he wanted to tell her. The comb now ran smoothly through the length of her hair. Fran turned towards him, put her hands on his shoulders and kissed his cheek. He was so taken aback that he just stood and looked at her.

She raised her hand to his face and laughed. 'Thank you. That was lovely.' Moving away, she picked up a paper bag with a piece of fruitcake inside. 'Would you like some of this? It's home-made but a bit squashed, I'm afraid.' They perched on their rucksacks to eat the crumbly remains.

Fran wanted to know more. 'Did you spend the war abroad?'

'My mother and I got out before the Japs overran the country. My father was caught in Singapore and interned in Changi gaol. He survived, but when he came home he couldn't settle, so he went back.'

Paul could hardly remember him now, that scarecrow who had walked in through the door and crouched down awkwardly to try and put his arm round Lizzie. She had run off, silly child, but she was only three. Paul had been nearly six and had held out his hand to welcome the stranger. When he'd felt the knobbly bones of his father's fingers he'd wanted to pull his hand away. They reminded him of the rabbit skeleton he'd found on the downs and buried under a tree in a private ceremony. 'It's funny you should ask about him. Last night I dreamed of the toy rabbit he gave me when my mother brought me back to England in 1941. I don't remember Malaya at all, we were home before my second birthday.'

'It must have been awful for you – and your mother.'

'She was pregnant with Lizzie but she didn't know it at the time.'

They sat silent for a moment. Paul felt strange talking to a girl about things that mattered. The easy conversation made him feel good but he knew he mustn't monopolise the conversation. As he tried to think what to say, he realised he was still hungry. He stood up and held out his hand. 'Come on, let's go and find some more food.'

As Fran allowed herself to be pulled to her feet she said, 'We'll never catch up with the others if we do that.'

Paul frowned. The previous year, scuffles had broken out among the people packed into the square. He kept hold of her hand for a moment, wanting to protect her from any harm. 'Would you feel disloyal to the cause if we didn't finish the march?'

Fran looked away. 'What do you think?'

'I've stuck it out to the end before but the walking is the important bit and we've done that.'

She nodded. Although she'd felt so keenly about the march, it now seemed more important to follow her new-found friend. 'Let's get something to eat and see what happens.'

Not far from the park they found a transport café and had a large fry-up. When one of the lorry drivers offered them a lift back to Bristol, Fran agreed to abandon the march.

'You'll have to hang around in Southall for a couple of hours, while I unload,' the driver said. 'Then we'll be off.'

They followed him out to the lorry. Fran had never sat in the cab of a lorry before and she signalled for Paul to get in first so that she could watch how he did it. She passed him their rucksacks and reached for his hand. It was much further up than she expected. At the crucial moment the driver gave her a push from behind and she arrived laughing on the seat. Paul put his arm round her.

'Oh, this is fun,' she said. 'I'll have to ring home at some stage though.'

'We'll find a telephone box when he stops. I'm sorry my caterpillar enticed us off the march, but meeting you has made up for that.' He gave her shoulders a squeeze.

When they reached Southall they sat on the wall by the factory gate, a bag of currant buns between them, kicking their heels against the stones. Paul had filled their water bottles from the drinking tap outside the public toilets while Fran made her phone call. 'What did you tell them?' he asked.

'I said I'd met a friend and we'd got a room in a Youth Hostel.' Fran giggled. 'They wanted to know which friend. I told them she was called Pauline.' She shifted on the cold stone and added, 'I don't usually tell lies.'

'I'm sure you don't.' Paul felt absurdly pleased that she was prepared to deceive her parents in order to be with him. He put his hand on hers where it lay on the wall. 'Sometimes it's necessary if we're to get free without hurting them.'

Fran was silent for a moment. Staring across the road, she watched the cars that streamed past, their occupants lost in their own worlds, faces towards home and the end of the day. Serious now, she asked, 'What do you want to do with your life, Paul?'

'Something useful. I might go abroad. I'd like to work in Africa.' He too looked across the road where he glimpsed, between the passing cars, an old woman pushing a pram loaded with firewood. She was bent over the handles, limping along, one of her shoes tied on with a dirty piece of cloth. It wasn't fair. People shouldn't have to live like that. If there were no more wars the money spent on bombs could be used to help the poor. Those terrible atomic bombs, so many deaths and now the cancers that were inexorably eating into people's bodies, like his caterpillars nibbling leaves, in and out of the veins, up one side of the central strand and down the other until nothing but a flimsy skeleton was left. If his father had lived, his work would have provided food and water for some of the poorest people on earth.

'I want to do what I can make to make the world a better place.' The words sounded feeble. He kept looking straight ahead, not daring to turn towards Fran in case she was laughing at him.

'I know how you feel. That's why I came on the march. There's so little one can do.'

The old woman was trying to cross the road. She had pushed the front wheels of her pram off the pavement. Paul looked up and down but he couldn't see a pedestrian crossing. A motorbike swerved to avoid her and the rider shouted something obscene. Paul jumped off the wall and waited for a small gap in the traffic before walking out to hold up his hand. The advancing stream of cars slowed. He beckoned to her and she wobbled across. He followed behind, sweeping his arm towards the vehicles as he reached the pavement.

A man stuck his head out of the window. 'Who do you think you are? Bloody St Christopher?' Paul shrugged, and went back to sit on the wall. Fran laughed and took his hand.

'Oh Paul, first caterpillars, then old ladies. Whatever next?'

He didn't mind her laughter now.

The journey took several hours. Paul talked to the driver for a while but they had to shout to make themselves heard over the noise of the engine and the rattling of the empty lorry. Fran fell asleep, her head on his shoulder, while he sat as still as he could, until the pain in his arm was so bad that he had to move. She stirred but didn't wake. He ached with longing to care for her.

The driver went slightly off his route so that he could drop them in the centre of Bristol. Paul and Fran didn't feel too guilty, as the streets were empty at that early hour of the morning and he was only delayed by a few minutes. They walked slowly up Park Street, past the closed shops.

'Let's go to the suspension bridge,' Paul said. 'It's lovely up there at night.'

Fran wondered vaguely if they would find anywhere to sleep; but she didn't care if they walked till morning. The warmth of their interlocked fingers flowed through her body and down into her legs, so that each foot lifted with a new spring.

They climbed up the hill to Clifton and swung past the Regency houses. As they reached the observation tower they looked down at the bridge that spanned the gorge. The tide was up, the surface of the water glossy in the moonlight. They walked a little further to where a smooth track had been worn on the rock by generations of sliding children. Two packs hit the ground and they crouched under the fence, first one and then the other, to sit at the top and slither down to the cushion of grass, arms flaying and laughter muted under the stars. After a few turns Fran found herself yawning.

Paul took her hand. 'Come on, let's find a place out of the wind where we can get some sleep.' He led her back to the tower and found a niche inside the doorway. He rummaged in his pack and took out a spare sweater, dry now from the warmth of the lorry, and signalled to her to sit down.

'Thank you, Sir Walter,' she said with a smile. 'What about you?'

'I'll be fine.' He lowered himself beside her and took the remaining two buns out of his pack. They munched in silence for a bit, then finished their water.

'Come on now, lie down and try to get comfy.' Fran did as she was told, reaching out her arms to him. He bent forward and kissed her cheek. 'Will you be warm enough?'

'I will if you snuggle up closer.' As she spoke, Fran sensed his uncertainty. 'I usually go to sleep on my left side. If I turn over you could keep my back warm.'

Paul stretched out behind her and let his arm fall across her waist. Soon her breathing became deep and regular. As he lay along the length of her body he felt at peace. Perhaps this was the girl for whom he had been saving himself. He waited a few minutes and then moved carefully to take off his waterproof and lay it over her. She rolled on to her back but didn't wake. As he sat by her side in the moonlight his eyes traced the lines of her cheekbones, vulnerable below the closed lids.

The following year Paul got a room in an annexe, so that Fran could come and go more easily. She added her own touches with two cushions. The cover of one had a red ant on it, the other a brown frog sitting on a lily leaf. She bought a new saucepan for the gas ring and cooked scrambled eggs that they ate on Marmite toast. After they had made love she tidied the bed and turned down the corner. She had to be in by ten; her parents seemed to believe that chastity could only be breached after that hour.

One day in March Paul travelled to London for an interview. The office was at the top of a steep flight of stairs, the door identified by a small notice, 'Voluntary Service Overseas'. Three people sat squashed behind the desk in the poky room. The man in the centre dominated. He had a round face with ears that stuck out below his short, thinning hair. His nose was hooked above a mouth too small for the rest of his body. 'Please sit down,' he said.

Paul sat, unnerved by the blue eyes that scanned his crumpled suit, the only one he possessed.

'Are you working for an honours degree?'

'Yes. I'm coming to the end of my fourth year.'

'It's a new departure for us to take graduates.' There was a long silence.

Paul looked at his hands in his lap, his nails unusually clean. 'I want to be useful,' he said.

'What do you think you could do? You have no teaching experience.'

'No.' Paul ran two fingers inside his unfamiliar collar. Trying to keep his voice polite he said, 'I can learn. I thought the idea was that Volunteers should learn, as well as teach.'

'You've found out a bit about us then,' the chairman said. The woman on his right shifted as if to add something, then sat back in her chair. The second man gazed into space. Perhaps he was there to see fair play.

'My sister told me about a talk she'd heard at her school. I've read what I can.'

'What do your parents think about you going to Africa?'

'My mother won't stop me. My father's dead.'

The observer leaned forward and made a note on a pad in front of him. Now the woman did speak. 'I'm sorry about your father. When did he die?'

Paul shifted his gaze towards her but was drawn back to the chairman. He had to find a way to penetrate the mask of the man who held the power. 'My father was in Changi gaol when I was little. He died of fever when he went back to the East, soon after the end of the war.' The eyes looked down. Paul leaned forward. 'My particular interest at the moment is insects. I'd like to help the children appreciate the world around them. I'll have to learn what creatures they have in their country, what's poisonous and all that. Once I know which country I'm going to –'

'What about sport?'

The question cut across the table and stopped him short. He grimaced. 'I'm not very good. Never made any of the teams at school. But I like kicking a ball about with my mates.'

'You've plenty of friends, then?'

He wasn't sure how to answer. Since he'd been with Fran he'd seen less of them, but the folk group still met every Friday night in the pub.

'I play the violin a bit. Irish gigs and things.'

'You'll take it with you, of course.' The remark was a statement, not a question.

Then the man who had not said anything finally spoke, as if he needed to justify his presence. 'Life outside the classroom is most important.'

Paul nodded. 'I'd like to learn about African music.'

The chairman shifted and took control again. 'Would you say you're a good mixer?'

Paul knew he had to make use of every possible opportunity to sell himself. 'I do a lot of hitchhiking. I like meeting different people, getting off a lorry with the smell of diesel clinging to my clothes, then straight into an expensive car. I try to fit myself to the person who has given me a lift. Talking is the least I can do to repay their kindness.'

The atmosphere in the room seemed easier when he left. He couldn't help feeling hopeful.

Two weeks latter a letter arrived. He would fly out to Nigeria in August to help build a school and then stay on to teach in it. Details to follow. At last he would be doing something important. He could imagine the rows of black faces turned up towards him.

As he stood with the single sheet of paper in his hands the phone rang. Fran's voice struck the picture from his mind. Was she sure? Couldn't she have made a mistake with the dates? The doctor was in no doubt; she had all the symptoms.

'Can't you get rid of it?'

Fran's voice dropped to a whisper. 'I don't know anyone. It's illegal, you know. Hazel said she knew someone who went to one of those back-street women and died.'

'Don't your parents know a proper doctor who would help?'

'They wouldn't dream of such a thing. They're terribly old-fashioned, you don't know them. Anyway, I couldn't kill it. What am I to do, Paul?' She started to cry.

'Where are you phoning from?'

'The call box on the corner.' Her voice dropped to a whisper. 'Oh my God, my mother is watching me through the glass. She must have trailed me here.'

Paul rubbed his eyes. He couldn't tell her his news now.

'I'm not allowed to see you.' He heard a tapping noise, then her mother's urgent voice in the background. After a while Fran said, 'Did you hear that? I'm to tell you to come and visit them tomorrow afternoon at five-o-clock. To discuss plans. I must go. My mother is signalling to me.'

Paul propped himself against the wall. Fran was only in her first year at university. Although he'd suggested vaguely that she might join him later, the idea had floated in a distant, unreal future.

The meeting with her parents was worse than he could possibly have imagined. Fran was desperate; wide-eyed and rude to them. Paul felt snared by her vulnerability. He couldn't desert her now. The arrangements for the wedding, already under way, closed in round him like a winding-sheet.

When the ordeal was finally over he walked slowly back across the downs. The rain had stopped and it seemed that spring was on the way. One or two trees had swollen buds at the ends of the branches that shimmered in the evening light. Crocuses thrust their blue and yellow knobs through green grass that was replacing the winter brown.

He had been so happy. Fran's enthusiasm for sex had overcome his initial nervousness. For the first time, during his interview, he had known himself to be a real man.

He had no idea how much it cost to keep a wife and a baby. He didn't want to teach, not in an English school, not in the sort of place he had endured, where no one wanted to learn and if you were no good at sport you were no good for anything. It would have been different in Africa. Perhaps he could get something in local government. The idea of a desk job made him wince. A market garden would be better. But plants didn't hold the fascination of animals and such a job wouldn't pay much.

As he trudged on across a playing field, his head bent, he didn't know that he was following the route Fran had taken so often when she wanted to escape from her mother. At the edge of the gorge he found the tide was out. The dark-brown mud matched his humour better than the new colours of spring. He wondered what it would be like to fall and sink slowly into the sludge. He wouldn't struggle, but let it cover him, bit by bit. He could feel the coldness on his knees, sense the weight of his body dragging him down until the slime was in his mouth, covering his eyes and joining over the top of his head with a gurgle.

He drew in a deep breath. If only his father were alive. Paul tried to imagine what advice he might have given, but all that came to his mind was the memory of his mother's voice as she had tried to wake the emaciated man from his nightmares. That first time, Paul had rushed into the bedroom and stood in horror as he watched his father's arms flaying the air to grab at his mother's hair. Paul had tried to unclasp the fingers but their grip was too tight. Reaching for his mother's hand he'd rubbed the rough skin, then turned her wedding ring, round and round as he always did, when he wanted to comfort her. The screaming mouth had closed as his father started to sob and the wild look gradually faded from his eyes.

His mother had pulled her hand away and slipped her arms round her husband to cradle him to her. Lizzie had appeared in the door behind them, clutching her monkey, with her thumb in her mouth. He had taken her back to bed and lain down beside her till the regular breathing told him she was asleep. He remembered the stiffness in his arms and legs as he'd held himself rigid, not daring to move in case he started the screams again.

Standing on the edge of the gorge, he shook himself and turned to walk back to his room. After he was inside, with the door firmly closed, he took up the letter with the offer from VSO and tore it across, again and again. Then he sat down and wrote to say that he had changed his mind. He'd discovered he wasn't the sort of person who could work abroad, after all.

TWO

1962

The figure at the window swivelled round as Paul opened the door of the room set-aside for expectant fathers. The man's shoulders sagged and he walked to the table to grind out the stub of his cigarette in the overfull ashtray.

'Have you been waiting long?' Paul asked.

'The man looked at his watch. 'They sent me out three hours and twenty-two minutes ago.'

'You were with her at the beginning then?'

'Yes. I wanted to stay for the whole thing, but they wouldn't let me.'

Paul flinched. 'I couldn't bear to be in there.'

'Waiting here is worse,' the man said, as he perched on the chair next to Paul, only to spring up again. At that moment a nurse came to fetch him. 'It's a boy,' Paul heard her say, as she led him away.

Through the open door he could hear a woman screaming in the distance. A sharp slap was followed by an angry voice. Then silence. Oh God, surely that couldn't be Fran. Her father, who had lectured him in a tired voice, had been right. It was his fault, he should have controlled himself. If only that durex hadn't broken she wouldn't be suffering, they wouldn't even be married. He might be in Africa right now.

He pushed the thought away. Looking out of the window, he hardly noticed the jumble of rubbish, strewn about the courtyard as if it had been turned over by some scavenging animal. He vowed that if Fran got through this ordeal he would devote the rest of his life to making her happy.

Somehow they had survived the wedding. Fran had been strung so tight he was afraid she might run away. In the end she'd managed to play the part her parents demanded. Wearing the traditional hired suit, Paul had moved through the day as if in a parallel world, invisible to himself. The only thing he remembered clearly was the sound of his own voice repeating the familiar words, 'To have and to hold . . .' At that moment he had became oblivious to the congregation in their silly hats and to the vicar trying not to notice the bump under Fran's dress. She had refused to have the veil over her face, leaving the short end to swing on her shoulders, a billowing frame for her dark eyes that were free to lock with his own as they exchanged their vows.

His mother had given them the upstairs of her house. As soon as he got a job they would look for somewhere else to live, but for the time being the cramped space was better than being apart. Their bed creaked above the room where his mother now slept. At weekends they escaped to the countryside, retracing some of the routes Fran had followed when she had roamed about by herself.

As he paced the room he remembered the day he saw the otter. Afterwards, they'd walked along the river and on to the path leading up through the wood. In about half a mile they came to a clearing. The land formed a shallow bowl with trees round the back and sides, grouped in twos and threes so that the sunlight penetrated between them. The fourth side gave a view out over the valley. At the back of the dell, where low bushes grew, the ground was covered with leaves and occasional stones. It was here that Paul had prepared a place for them to lie, clearing away the stones and collecting the leaves into a soft mattress that he covered with his waterproof cape.

They didn't undress, but he'd slipped his hand under her skirt to draw her pants down. As he did so he felt a sharp kick, and, lifting her clothes, they watched the moving bumps. She lay smiling up at him as she undid his belt and pulled his zip down.

'Will it be all right? I won't hurt the baby, will I?' He had never known anything like the tenderness that welled up inside him as his erection began to subside.

Fran laughed and pulled him towards her. 'Of course not. There's room for the baby and you in there.' She touched him with her fingers, then lifted her head and shoulders for a moment to take him into her mouth. The scent of her talcum powder, mixed with that of last year's damp leaves, made his senses reel as he buried his hands in her hair, letting her take charge. She guided him in and he began to move, slowly and gently. He remembered how careful he'd been to take his weight on his arms, even at the height of his passion. It wasn't easy with the bump in the way. Later, she'd lain on her front with her knees drawn up as he took her from behind, something he had never done before, and would never do again, slipping his hands round to touch her in the way she liked. He knew they had come at the same moment.

Now standing in the dingy hospital room, he shivered. This was no time for such thoughts. Why was it taking so long? Women could die in childbirth; she could be fighting for her life. If she did die it would be his fault for loving her too much, for lusting after her too much.

The door behind him opened and his face flamed as a blue-clad midwife came into the room, rolling down her sleeves.

'Mr Ashby?'

'Yes?'

You've got a daughter.'

'Is she all right?'

'She's lovely. All fingers and toes correct.'

'My wife – she's all right?'

'They're both fine.' The nurse took some starched cuffs from her pocket and pulled them on.

'Thank God for that.' He sat down hard in a chair, hiding his face in his hands. It had been wrong to have sexy thoughts at such a time, terribly wrong. It would serve him right if she had died.

'Do you want to come and see them?'

He looked up, unable to focus his eyes. 'Of course.'

Fran was propped up in bed holding a bundle in her arms. She looked pale, her hair plastered to her head, almost as wet as it had been on the day of the march. He bent down and kissed her gingerly on the cheek. She turned her face up, her lips demanding. Then she pulled away to gaze intently at the baby again.

'Look at our girl,' she said.

The wrinkled face that peeped out of the tightly wound blanket was that of an old woman, the eyes lined. Her nose seemed squashed into her face with a red stain over her forehead and one eye. Paul felt himself sweating. 'What's that mark?'

'Sister says it'll fade in a week or two. It's quite normal.'

Now he had looked at his daughter he couldn't haul his eyes away. He reached out a hesitant finger to touch her cheek.

Fran's smile was kind and slightly patronising. 'D'you want to hold her?'

'I'm not sure . . .'

She held out the bundle and he reached to take it but lost his nerve. 'Perhaps tomorrow, you'd better keep her for now.'

The midwife came bustling into the room to put the baby to the breast. 'It'll stimulate the milk,' she said.

Paul watched. His wife looked awkward as she struggled with her nightdress. Bending over, the nurse helped her to fix the baby on to the dark teat. He blushed as he thought of the times he had kissed that nipple, holding it between his lips while he caressed it with his tongue to make it rise into a small roughened nut. Abruptly he turned away from the bed, remembering that he had to make some phone calls. 'D'you want your parents to visit you today or do you need time to rest?'

'I suppose Mummy will insist on coming. I'd really like to see your mother. She's been so good to me. Lizzie too, she might want to meet her new niece.'

Lizzie was home for a spell between jobs. She was sleeping on the put-u-up in what had been her room, before it was converted into a small sitting room for the newly-weds.

Paul was glad his sister got on with Fran, though there were times when he found the strain of being in the house with the three women almost more than he could bear. He wanted to make them all happy but it was an impossible task. Alone with any one of them, he could change himself to fit the mood of the moment. When they were all together he felt stretched in different directions, pulled out of shape, as if his boundaries were not solid enough to provide him with a form of his own.

As he left the room the baby gave a high-pitched cry. The sound tore into him, making him hover outside the door. He ached to go back, to take the bundle in his arms and rock the noise away. The nurse's voice was calm and reassuring. He sighed as he walked away down the corridor, impotent in the matronly world that had captured his woman.

Two weeks after they took their daughter home, he started work as a laboratory assistant at James, Carter and Smythe, later to become Nonsec.

'Do you really want to work as a technician?' Lizzie asked, as they stood on the platform waiting for the train that was to take her back to London.

'I have to start somewhere. There aren't any jobs for graduates at the moment, and they've taken me on for a three-month trial. If I give satisfaction they'll offer me a contract. I need a regular income, even if it's not very much. We must get a place of our own.'

Lizzie looked along the track, willing the train to delay its arrival. There had been no chance for them to talk in the small house dominated by the demands of a hungry baby. 'I could lend you a bit if you like. I'm making good money now. I'm an efficient secretary, and temping pays well. I'm going to get a bit behind me before I start my nurse training.'

Paul was mortified to feel tears gather in his eyes. He had been up most of the night, happy to take his turn at walking and rocking. He wasn't frightened to hold Sylvia now. When the baby lay peacefully in his arms and the women slept around him in the house, he was filled with a quiet contentment unlike anything he had known before. But the night watch left him exhausted. Now his little sister was offering to help him.

He reached out and took her hand. 'Oh Lizzie, that's such a generous offer, but I have to do it myself. They're my responsibility.'

'I knew you'd say that, it's just like you. ' She pulled her hand away. 'Why do you always have to go it alone?'

'You do so much for me already. It's great that you've agreed to be Sylvia's godmother.'

Lizzie pouted as if she was still a child but her voice was sympathetic as she said 'I'm sorry about Africa.'

'I don't mind. Anyway, I probably wouldn't have been much good in a foreign place.'

But I know you'd set your heart on going.'

'Fran and Sylvia are my life now. They come first.'

Lizzie didn't press the point. 'You're too proud to let me help,' was all she said.

'It's not pride, it's just . . .' Perhaps she was right; but the man did have to provide. He would see it through, not like his father who had deserted them and then died. 'Do you remember Daddy at all?' He looked down at her with a sudden hope that they could talk about him.

'I remember he gave me my monkey. I take it everywhere with me, even now.' She paused. 'He was very thin, wasn't he?'

'Yes.' When she didn't say anything else he had to accept that she knew nothing of those awful nights. He must keep the memories buried inside him, together with his regrets about Africa. If only he had been able to work there, to see something of the reality of a Third World country, he might have been able to make more sense of his father's life.

The train burst into sight and drew up alongside the platform. Lizzie threw her arms round his neck. 'Take care of yourself,' she said.

'You too.'

She hung out of the window to kiss his cheek. He hated partings, those awful truncated moments of waiting for the whistle and the green flag. No time to say anything, yet endless seconds that dragged on for an eternity. He clutched her hands where they lay on the top of the opened window. 'I'm glad I've got a sister.'

'You're daft.' She bent to kiss him again. 'Take care of that daughter of yours.'

The train began to move at last. 'Come again soon,' he called.

She waved her hand, then produced a white handkerchief and continued to wave. Paul watched until the train, a black chain of carriages with a white dot on its side like the identifying mark on a caterpillar, carried her out of sight. His waving hand slowed to a stop, hung motionless for a moment, then dropped to his side.

Once again he remembered the time when, as a seven-year-old boy, he had waved goodbye to his father for the last time. He could hear the splash of hawsers as they dropped off the bollards into the water, the creak of the winches coiling and the sudden three blasts on the ship's siren. The smell of tar and salt filled the air as he watched the slow, widening strip of water. His mother gripped his hand. His father had taken off his light tropical jacket and waved until he blended into the dark blob that was all they could see of the ship that carried him away.

He looked round and realised he was alone on the platform. His legs felt stiff as he walked to the stairs. Outside, he looked back at the Victorian façade of the station, unchanging in the sunlight, and vowed he would never wait to wave anyone goodbye again.

Fran knew from the beginning that the house in Redland was a bad choice. The place smelt damp, the noise of the traffic woke them, even when they were exhausted by the baby, and the only view was of the houses across the street. But she never told Paul how much she hated the place.

When she found Hazel on the doorstep one day, she hid her surprise. 'Come in. We're not straight yet but you're welcome to see round our palatial establishment.' They'd only met occasionally since Fran's marriage. Hazel's chatter of clothes and boyfriends belonged to a world Fran had left behind when her life became dominated by nappies. She soaked them in a bucket before running the new washing machine, their one extravagance. Then she had to hang some of them on the airer in the small kitchen as the line in the garden was too short to take the gauze liners as well as the bulky ones made of terry towelling.

She led Hazel upstairs and they tiptoed round the cot where three-month old Sylvia was sleeping, then poked into the other rooms.

'Has your mother visited you yet?' Hazel asked.

'Not likely. I must get it sorted before I can face her prying eyes scanning every corner. You know what she's like.'

Hazel laughed. 'I've never known anyone so difficult to please. Do you remember the row when you wore jeans for the first time? She thought they were so lower class.'

Fran shuffled her feet. She didn't like anyone else to criticise her mother, but it was true she could do nothing to please her. All hope that the arrival of the baby might soften her attitude had proved unfounded.

In the bathroom a water heater projected over the cold tap like an unexploded bomb. Fran had to steel herself to put a taper to the gas jets, which lit with an explosive bang that made her jump. 'Paul's going to decorate just as soon as he has a moment,' Fran said, 'but he's so busy at work. Most evenings he doesn't get in till after seven and then he's exhausted.'

'How do you manage?' Hazel sounded genuinely interested.

'Looking after Sylvia takes all my time. I walk a lot and we go to the mother and baby group. Not quite the married life we dreamed of, is it? Do you remember how you were going to have a big house in one of those elegant London squares? I wanted a studio in a hot country with a balcony looking out over a bay, where I'd sit and paint all day.' Fran stopped, she didn't want to sound disloyal to Paul. 'What crazy fantasies we had.'

'Let me help you do up this room,' Hazel said, rolling up her sleeves. 'You fetch some hot water and I'll wash it down. Then we can go out and buy some paint. What colour would you like?' She perched on the edge of the bath.

Fran sat on the stool that had been left by the previous owners. 'Sylvia will wake up at any moment.'

'That's all right. You can see to her while I get on with the cleaning. You'll feel much better once we get started.' Hazel leant forward and laid a hand on her knee. 'Honestly, I can come again tomorrow and we could get it finished. I'm on my own this weekend.'

Fran raised her head and saw her friend's eyes sparkling. The prospect of a weekend spent cleaning someone else's bathroom couldn't produce that excitement. 'What's up?'

'I don't know if I should tell you.' Fran knew then that she would. 'I've got some news of my own. I must share it with someone.' So that was why she had come over. 'There's a man at work . . . Paul knows him . . . We've been going out for over two months and I think he's really keen on me. That big house may not be as far away as you think. He's going places, my man.'

Fran stood up and kissed her. 'That's wonderful. Have you any idea when the great day will be?'

'It's not definite yet. Don't tell anyone, it has to be a secret for a while. He hasn't actually asked me, but all the signs point that way.'

'It'll be great. Once you're married we'll see more of each other. What's his name?'

'He's called Geoffrey Protheroe. I think Mrs Protheroe sounds rather posh, don't you?'

Fran smiled at the thought that she might soon be initiating Hazel into the mystery of babygros and mashed carrot.

Sylvia let out a wail. Fran carried her downstairs and put her in a bouncy chair on the kitchen table. Then she fetched some crayons and a large drawing pad. As she drew a house she chatted on about a little girl who lived inside, knowing that Sylvia was far too young to understand, but pulling faces that made her laugh. Without thinking what she was doing, an abstract pattern developed round the edge of the paper suggesting vague animal shapes.

'I'd no idea you could draw like that.' Fran looked up and blinked as Hazel peered over her shoulder at the picture. 'I remember now, you were good at Art in school.'

'I hated the teacher. She made me draw jugs and apples when I wanted to try and discover how to make things look as if they were moving.'

'You should have stuck it out and not let Miss Stinky Bottom lead you astray.'

Fran had forgotten the nickname. 'She may have had a large bum, but at least chemistry was interesting.' She got up with an unexpected burst of energy. 'Let's go and get that paint. If you can do the ceiling I'll manage the walls. I might try a frieze of fishes.

Or frogs,' she added, as she thought of the cushion that lay on their bed upstairs.

Hazel threw her arms round Fran's shoulders. 'What fun this is.'

Fran felt her friend was playing at house and was wondering how she would cope with the reality of a husband and home, when Hazel went on, 'It'll be good practice for when I have my own house. Then you can come and do the pretty bits for me.'

'I'm not good enough for that. I'm probably not good enough to decorate this place, but it's better than sticking around all day wondering how long it will be until Sylvia cuts her first tooth.'

Lying in bed that night she felt happier than she had done since the birth. She put out a hand to Paul, who raised himself up on to one elbow and looked down at her face, illuminated by the street light outside the window.

As she turned her dark eyes towards him he thought she had never looked so beautiful. Leaning over, he kissed her cheek, feeling the beginnings of a lost excitement. She put her arms round his neck and pulled him close. Could she want him? There was no way he could tell what she was thinking as she lay passive in his arms. In the old days she would have started to move against him so that he would have been in no doubt about her wishes. He put his lips to hers but her mouth didn't open. As he brushed his tongue along the groove he felt he was making an unreasonable demand. His head fell back on the pillow but his hand lay on her chest. He began to fiddle with her nipple.

The touch made Fran clench her teeth. If he wanted sex why didn't he get on with it? This time she really would manage it. She shifted her position and his fingers retreated. He was put off so easily. Why couldn't he sense that this was the moment she would like him to take control?

Paul's hand moved back on to her stomach, working its way lower. She tensed as she tried to pull him on top of her. Then she remembered. 'You must wear something.'

Paul scrambled out of bed to fish in his drawer. He managed to get it on. In the old days she would have helped him, turning it into a game, the feel of her fingers increasing his desire. Now she lay still, making no move to come to his assistance.

As he climbed on top of her he remembered the shame that had overwhelmed him as he was waiting for Sylvia to be born. How could any woman want that part of him inside her? His duty was to protect women, not damage them. As the thought came into his head he went soft and rolled away from her.

'I'm sorry,' he said lamely, as he lay at her side.

'It doesn't matter. I don't mind really.' He didn't know if her voice held disappointment or relief.

THREE

2003

Fran put her wineglass on the table by the phone and picked up the telephone directory. If she was to explore those parts of Paul's life that he'd kept hidden she had to start somewhere. She ran her finger down the list of Protheroes, not wanting to ask Hazel for her ex-husband's number. There was a George, a G.G. and several others with G as a second initial.

'Is that Geoffrey?' she asked.

'Who?'

'Geoffrey Protheroe.'

'There's no Geoffrey here. My Dad's Gary and I'm John.'

'Sorry, I've got the wrong number.' She'd have to try the others but she needed another drink first. Going into the kitchen to refill her glass she took two cheesy biscuits from the tin and gave one to Bruiser who had followed her and was looking up expectantly. 'Courage, dog,' she said.

He wagged his tail and lay down at her feet in the hall. She picked up the phone again. A woman's voice answered.

'May I speak to Geoffrey?'

'Who wants him?' She sounded suspicious.

'I'm phoning on behalf of Professor Stein at the University.' Fran blushed. When she had lied to her parents, that time she had stayed out all night with Paul, her love had made her defiant. She hadn't needed the help of alcohol.

'Just a moment, I'll get him.'

'Hello?'

'Hi. Is that Geoffrey Protheroe from Nonsec?'

'That's right. How can I help you?'

'It's Fran speaking. Do you remember? I'm Paul's widow, a friend of Hazel's. I worked for the company till recently.'

'Of course I remember you. There's nothing wrong is there?'

'I'm not ringing about her.'

'You're phoning for the University?'

'Afraid not.'

Fran felt foolish as she resisted the temptation to ring off. She took another swallow of wine and said, 'I wonder if we could meet sometime. I want to talk about Paul but I don't know many of the people he worked with.'

For a moment Geoffrey didn't reply. She could hear the sound of a baby crying in the background. He must have got himself hooked into family life at last.

When he replied his voice sounded as if a mute had been placed over his vocal cords. 'I didn't see much of him once the company acquired the site in Keynsham.' He paused. 'You know, I stayed on in Bristol to expand the work on new foods.'

If he put the receiver down she was lost. Her legs, stretched out in front of her, were still shapely. If only he was standing by her side: he'd fancied her in the old days. With the slightest encouragement . . . but she'd been too bound up with Paul to encourage him. 'Could we meet, anyway?' she said. 'You might be able to put me in touch with someone who worked with him on the new drugs.' Just provided he didn't suggest that man Jackson, she thought.

'When would Professor Stein like to meet me?'

Fran smiled, glad she'd sussed out the situation. 'I could be free any time next week.' She thought quickly. 'Shall we meet at the University entrance?'

'Tuesday at twelve thirty would be fine,' he said.

'I'll see you then.' As she imagined him explaining the appointment to his woman, a twinge of compassion passed through her. But she only wanted to chat about Paul.

She hadn't seen Geoffrey for five years. He was even larger than she remembered. He must dye his hair for it showed no signs of grey at the temples. His mouth was attractive, despite the lower lip that protruded slightly, as if he were uncertain whether to pout or smile. As he reached around her in a large embrace she felt the roughness of his jacket against her cheek. Something had changed. 'You've stopped smoking your pipe.'

His physical presence impinged on those he met, especially women. Paul had been only an inch or two taller than Fran herself. All his movements had been controlled, as if he had to think what muscle he was going to use before he moved. Geoffrey was built on a different scale. He bounced with each step, appearing even taller than his six feet three.

'Alas, tobacco and babies don't mix.' He put his hand under her chin and kissed her lightly on the lips. Fran glowed, pleased she had chosen to wear her favourite pale lipstick. He took her hand and led her to the entrance.

'We're in luck, I got a meter just around the corner. I thought we'd go to the pub on the river. I've booked a table. It's ages since I've had lunch with a pretty woman.'

She hadn't come to flirt: she was on a quest. But that need not stop her enjoying herself. He opened the door of a pale green estate car, motioned her inside and pulled out into the traffic.

'What happened to the Aston Martin?' she asked.

'Life moves on. Babies take up a lot of space and my partner didn't like silver. I insisted on a pale car, it's so much safer. This is a compromise.'

She wouldn't have expected him to give way over one of his precious cars. They crawled through the heavy traffic, down Park Street and round the Centre.

Fran looked at the buses and remembered the freedom of her student days. She would choose one at random, leap on board and travel to the end of the line. Then she would wander about, revelling in the people she met, trying to capture their essence in a collection of pictures in her sketchbook. She was particularly drawn to the faces of middle-aged men: the bus driver or the navvy with a noisy drill. How did they survive their repetitive days?

'You look well,' Geoffrey said. 'How's Sylvia?'

'She's doing OK. Got promoted at work last week. I wish she'd settle down and have a family. She's passed the forty mark, you know.' As she spoke Fran realised that was not the most tactful thing to say.

'It takes some of us longer than others.'

'It's more urgent for a woman. Have you just got the one?'

'She's more than enough. I hadn't realised what it was like. All those disturbed nights . . . She's lovely though. She's called Anna, after my grandmother.'

Fran was startled again. She hadn't seen him as the sort of man who would care about his grandmother. She had imagined him springing fully formed from a line of predatory men. 'Was she your father's mother?'

'No, my maternal grandmother. My mother was killed by a doodlebug before I grew out of my cot.'

He must be older than she thought. What a strain to have a baby so late in life. Fran felt a thrust of jealousy for his new woman.

Geoffrey laid his fingers lightly on her knee, not taking his eyes from the traffic. 'How are you, then?'

'I'm OK,' she replied, lying again.

'Are you still in that lovely house?'

'I've stayed on in the village, though Hazel says I should move back into Bristol.'

'It must be a difficult decision.'

'I love the house but it's too big really.' Hazel gave advice so easily. She'd never understood what a struggle it had been at the beginning. 'I wasn't very happy when we lived in Redland.'

'Why was that?' Although he kept his eyes on the road Geoffrey made her feel that he was really interested. She sat back. The grumble of the traffic, the shouts, the sudden blast of a horn all emphasised the cocoon of silence as he waited for her answer.

'The house was dark, with high ceilings and musty corners.' She screwed up her eyes as she tried to remember. Perhaps it hadn't been so bad after all. Had her mother's scathing views influenced her? Shying away from the idea, she was relieved when Geoffrey broke the silence again.

'I've always admired your lovely place in the country. It would be a shame to leave it. Forgive me asking but . . . is it the money?'

'No. I can manage all right on the two company pensions, if I'm careful. It just seems wrong for one person to take up so much space. Hazel says I could join in more things if I lived in the city.'

'Hazel isn't always right. People have to work things out for themselves.'

Geoffrey drove with confidence, in the same way that he appeared to live his life, even though he left a scattered trail of disappointed women behind him, like socks and pants thrown about the room by an untidy teenager. He had such style and dash, not like Paul, whose loyalty had provided Fran with a security that was essential to her, or so she had believed. Now, as they drove up the hill to the Brislington traffic lights, she wondered if his very devotion had weakened her.

Everything had been so perfect at the beginning. Looking out of the window she saw the place where they had walked down a small cutting between two fields leading to the river. She remembered the Sunday they had discovered the ferry at the end of the path. It had been soon after they had moved in with Paul's mother, when they were looking for secluded places to make love. She had struck the big rusty bell with a piece of iron that hung by the side. A man in a small rowing boat had come across to fetch them. On the far side a pub produced rather stale sandwiches. Not like the smart place upstream where Geoffrey was taking her. Paul had chosen half a pint of lager, typical of his abstemious ways, while she sipped a tomato juice in deference to the child inside her. At that moment he'd seen the otter. Crouching along the bank, he had tracked its course till it disappeared under the opposite bank. She had waited for him at the table, afraid to follow in case the clumsy movements of her swollen body frightened the animal. An unexpected memory of the lovemaking that followed, in the dell at the top of the wood, made her catch her breath.

'You OK?' asked Geoffrey, casting a sideways glance at her.

'I'm fine.'

He led her into the fashionable pub, where a table next to the window had been reserved for them. Now that autumn was well established the bustle at the lock was stilled. A few deserted cabin cruisers lingered along the bank, their curtains drawn. One had been pulled out of the water and was parked under a tree, covered with tarpaulins, as if it were hibernating.

Fran had always longed to own a boat. The notion of gliding under bridges and past fields of lazy cattle had appealed to her but Paul had said it wasn't safe when Sylvia was little. By the time she'd learnt to swim they'd settled into a routine of beach holidays.

Geoffrey touched her hand. 'You're dreaming.'

'I was thinking of Paul.'

Geoffrey took a long swig of his draught bitter and she sipped her second glass of white wine while she waited for him to say something. The silence dragged on, until he eventually took a breath and said, 'He shouldn't have died, he was a good man.'

'D'you think so?'

'Of course. He was devoted to you and Sylvia.'

How could she find the words to ask what she wanted to know? She hadn't formed the questions, even to herself.

She was saved from replying by the arrival of the food. He started to pick out the bones of his fried sole but stopped with a small laugh. 'It's no good, I'll have to use my glasses.' He put on a pair with light, modern frames. They looked incongruous perched like a foreign body on a face where the muscles strained to be eternally youthful. His jaw was beginning to sag into what could only be called a jowl. He'd have to be careful if he were not to get downright obese. Not that Fran could talk. She despaired of the roll of fat that had developed round her middle.

Paul had never gained an ounce of weight; if anything he became leaner as he got older. She frowned at the injustice. He shouldn't have died of heart failure when he'd lived such a healthy life. He didn't have any of the risk factors that she'd learned when she was training to be a drug rep for the company.

He didn't smoke or overeat – and if there had been tensions in his life he'd kept them hidden.

Words bubbled up inside her, loosened by the wine. Once she started to talk she couldn't stop. 'I have to find out more about him. You don't know what it's like, losing the man you've lived with for more than forty years. You can't possibly know, you always moved on to another woman when things got tough. I feel I'm buried up there in the crematorium with his ashes. I don't know who I am or what's left of me.'

She looked down at her plate of ham salad and up at the man sitting opposite her, calmly eating his fish. She had to make him understand. 'Hazel said there was some trouble, but I don't know what it was about. He must have done well enough, we were never short of money. But he changed. When we got married he was passionate about things – poverty, the threat of nuclear weapons – the usual culprits. Once he joined the company he lost all that. What happened to the Paul I used to know, the man who got excited about an otter?' Tears began to drip onto the food she hadn't touched.

Geoffrey took a folded handkerchief from his top pocket and handed it to her in silence. She wiped her eyes and cheeks and looked up to find him smiling at her. Paul would have patted her arm and shushed her, tried to make her feel better. Geoffrey went on eating his meal, not in the least embarrassed.

Fran passed the hanky back and fished in her handbag for a tissue. 'I don't know what's come over me. I never cry in public.' She picked up her fork and pushed some bits of lettuce round her plate before taking a small mouthful. Once she tasted it she realised how hungry she was and began to feel better.

'That's more like it. It doesn't hurt to cry, you know.'

'That's what Hazel always says.'

His heavy shoulders lifted in a small shrug. 'I don't want to echo her platitudes but she does have a point.' He reached across the table to take her hand. 'Can't you just remember the good times you had together?'

'I've been trying to do that ever since he died. I've been so busy with my work . . . I thought I was coming to terms with his death.

It's not true. I'm hollow and empty, I don't understand what happened to us. I can't move on until I find out what made him tick.' She frowned. 'Hazel said something about a report, but he never mentioned it to me.'

'People working on new drugs are even more secretive than we are in the food department. There's so much at stake. If some other company got hold of the research data they could steal our markets. We could lose millions.'

'Is that what Jackson is worried about?'

'Jackson?'

'That bullying man who worked with Paul. He gatecrashed my farewell party and asked if Paul had kept any papers at home. D'you know him?'

Geoffrey frowned. 'He's very ambitious. He wormed his way into Martin Emery's confidence. You know, their boss, who was so badly burned in the fire. But Jackson didn't join the company till ages after the trouble with Brenda.'

Brenda Starling. Hazel had mentioned her and now Geoffrey dragged her in as if she were some trailing weed entangled round the propeller blades of a boat. Fran clenched her fist and banged the table so that the cutlery rattled. 'He should have trusted me, I was his wife. I didn't want to know trade secrets, I wouldn't have gossiped about company business like some I know.' She paused. 'Sorry, but Hazel does chatter.'

'Don't I know it.'

'Come on, tell me. Why didn't he get his own department after so many years? What was this report about?'

'I don't know the details.' Geoffrey looked out of the window and wiped his mouth on his napkin. Then he picked up the menu and started to discuss what they would have for pudding. He chose the Mississippi Mud Pie. Pushing away the thought of the calories, Fran agreed to have that too. When the two slices arrived they were topped with cream, sitting on the plates like brown snails with white shells on their backs. The sweet, rich taste gave her courage.

'Well, do you?'

'Do I what?'

'Know what trouble stopped him rising any higher in the company?'

'Oh that. He was influenced by Brenda – that's all.'

'What did she have to do with it?'

'They worked closely together for a while. The report was signed by both of them.'

Fran frowned and tried to picture the woman. 'I think I met her at a Christmas dance once.'

'We were all there. But she left the company after the row.'

'I'd like to find her.'

Geoffrey looked across the table with a long, searching stare. 'Are you sure you want to do that? You might discover things that are best left alone.'

'If there were problems I want to know about them. Paul always tried to protect me from everything. But now he's gone. He can't protect me from the fact that he's dead.'

'No, he can't do that. But honestly, I don't think it's a good idea to go stirring it all up again. Do let sleeping dogs lie, Fran.'

'Do you know where she lives?'

'She bought herself a house near the lab in Keynsham and I haven't heard that she's moved.' He took a sip of the coffee he had ordered. 'I probably shouldn't have mentioned her, she can be an awkward character. I wish you hadn't pressed me. Don't say I didn't warn you.'

Fran put her hand on his arm and gave it a firm squeeze. 'I shan't blame you. Things can't be worse than they are at the moment. At least if I talk to her I'll be doing something to try and help myself.' She would find Brenda and face the consequences when they came. She smiled at Geoffrey. What kind eyes he had. Now that she had a plan in her mind, however tenuous, she could give him her full attention again. As he helped her on with her coat she turned and kissed him on the cheek. She had meant it as a friendly thank you but he moved his mouth on to hers and turned it into something else.

'Hey . . .' she caught her breath as a softness she had never expected to feel again moved somewhere inside her.

'Sorry, but you're still very beautiful, you know.'

She laughed. 'You have responsibilities now.'

His shoulders drooped. 'I know. I must learn how to be a good boy.' That didn't stop him keeping hold of her hand as they walked to his car, or kissing her again when he dropped her back at the University.

As Fran drove home she took her hand from the steering wheel to touch her lips, remembering the way her body had responded to Geoffrey's kisses. Was it possible, at the age of sixty, to feel again that thrill that she thought had died forever? The bittersweet idea made her blush. She drove in a daze, arriving at her gate before she realised she had left the city. As she swung into the drive she noticed a green car parked against the hedge opposite. She didn't recognise it as belonging to anyone in the village. The front wing was crumpled and for a moment she wondered if there had been an accident. Then she heard it start up behind her, with a flourish of acceleration, and thought no more about it.

Only when she had changed into her old clothes, and the euphoria of the wine had worn off, did she find herself puzzling about Brenda again. As far as she could remember the woman had joined the company some time after Paul had become deputy in Martin's department. At the company party, that first Christmas after they had moved into their new house, Paul had surprised Fran by asking her to dance. He was not much of a dancer; they usually just watched and talked to their friends. But the new disco dancing was all the rage and they'd tried to join in. It was the last dance they ever went to. The strobe lights, which became an essential part of all parties, had triggered Paul's migraine.

Fran poured herself a drink and drifted from room to room as she remembered. At the end of the dance he had led her back to the table they were sharing with Hazel and Geoffrey, saying he must mix and do his duty. She'd caught a fleeting picture of him holding a rather scraggy woman in a dark red dress. As they turned she'd glimpsed their two faces, both looking down at their feet and laughing. The woman was trying to teach him some new steps. When the music stopped he brought her to the table and introduced her as 'My right-hand woman.' Geoffrey immediately asked her to dance and soon afterwards Paul said he had a headache brewing, they must leave.

That was Brenda Starling. Now that she remembered, Fran was surprised how vividly the scene formed in front of her eyes. She could almost smell the wax that had been used on the floor and the over-sweet perfume that she used to dab on her neck and wrists. When they returned home she suggested that Paul should ask Brenda to dinner as she probably didn't know many people yet. At the time he'd agreed. But after Christmas, when she wanted to plan a dinner party, he had been adamant that, as Brenda's boss, he couldn't mix with her socially.

She sighed, remembering how much she had wanted to enter-tain in those days. Looking round her sitting room she thought that if she were to stay on in the house she would need new covers on the three-piece suite and the whole place should be re-decorated. Her eyes lighted on her leaving present, the box of paints, lying on the side table. Surely she'd left it on the desk? She must be getting senile.

Long ago, as she worked to capture the curve of a cheekbone or the shade of sky behind a leafless tree, the voice of her mother had been stilled. As the picture took shape she had known herself to be separate, an individual in her own right. Later, she became once again someone who had to listen to the needs of others: for the cry of her child, for the echo of her husband's shoes on the bare boards. Her one avenue to self-expression had become blocked. Hazel had done her best to encourage her artistic efforts. Fran had been quite pleased with the frieze of dolphins in the bathroom until her mother said they were common.

Impatiently she picked up the telephone directory and found Brenda's number. There was no reply. She couldn't decide if she was disappointed or relieved. She ought to take Bruiser out for a run, but she couldn't be bothered. Or start to go through Paul's clothes. Sylvia had made her promise to sort them out when she retired but it was all too much of an effort.

With a refilled glass in her hand she wandered up into the attic. The original cushions lay on the bed. When they were new the bright eyes of the frog and ant had been privy to their secret joys. Now the details of the creatures had faded. Fran sat on the edge of the bed, emptied her glass and put it on the table by the side. Then she picked up the lumpy cushion with a thin strip of green that marked the edge of the lily leaf where the frog had perched. Clasping it to her chest in silence she rocked forwards and back, struggling to recapture the lift she'd felt under the pressure of Geoffrey's lips.

FOUR

1972

One day, when Paul had been working at Nonsec for nearly ten years, he entered the common room to find Geoffrey sitting in the largest armchair. 'Hi, Paul,' he said, looking up from his newspaper. 'How's things?'

'My licence application is taking an age to write.' Paul couldn't stop his frustration spilling out. 'I'm really fed up with that new technician. He let the drip in cage five run dry this morning. That never happened when I was doing the chores. I hope to God it doesn't invalidate the results – the animals got quite agitated.'

'It's just as well you have such keen eyes.' Geoffrey held out his cup. 'Get me a refill will you, old chap?'

Paul did as he was asked. Geoffrey was a lazy sod. If he sat about reading the paper so early in the morning, no wonder he couldn't keep up with the literature.

'Shut the door and sit down a minute. I want to run some things past you.'

Paul had planned to take his coffee back to his desk but Geoffrey was still a friend of sorts and he could be useful. As head of his section he went in person each month to deliver his report to the board, whereas Paul had to pass on his findings and ideas via his boss, Martin Emery.

Geoffrey put his replenished cup on the table beside him and reached for his pipe. From a different pocket he extracted a special tool and scraped the barrel and stem, then filled it with tobacco and tamped it down, using the flat foot made for the purpose. Paul suspected that the performance made the man feel important.

'Well, what is it?' Paul was afraid he was going to talk about

Hazel. The previous week she had come into his office and started to cry. She seemed to think that, as a friend of his wife, she could interrupt his work whenever she liked. He didn't want to listen to confidences from both sides. He shifted and drained his cup.

'You're a trustworthy chap, aren't you?' Geoffrey asked.

Oh dear, here it comes. 'Probably,' Paul said.

'Have you heard any rumours about the company buying out that firm in Keynsham and taking over their premises?' Paul raised his eyebrows as he tried to hide his surprise. 'There are big plans for expansion ahead. Martin's in the thick of it. I suspect he wants to run the whole show over there. If it comes off.'

'How would that affect you?' Paul asked.

'If I play my cards right I might expand my department here. I'd like you to be part of it.'

Paul wasn't sure that he wanted to work for Geoffrey again. Although Martin was pedantic, he was a conscientious scientist. He'd never patronised Paul for having come up the hard way or for taking so long to get his PhD.

Geoffrey was watching the smoke that he allowed to escape from his mouth in a controlled stream. 'I've heard on the grapevine that Martin is trying to headhunt an assistant for you, someone called Brenda Starling. He's empire building.'

Although Paul had heard nothing about her joining the company the name was familiar. He'd seen a couple of papers co-authored by her recently. 'She might be a great asset,' he said.

'I rather hoped you could slow Martin down a bit. I need help in my department. The modification of foodstuffs is a growing field, a potential money-spinner. We should expand that area more, in preference to endless new drugs. If he must have Brenda he could put her in charge of your lab. Then I could use your talents.'

So that was it. Paul felt himself a pawn in the battle for power between the two men. He said nothing as Geoffrey continued. 'How about it? I could offer you an immediate rise. In a few years time I shall be on the board. Then, who knows, I could put in a good word and wangle you on, too.'

Paul went to get some more coffee and stood stirring in the sugar. His work was far too important to let himself be bought with such a bribe. Doxeril, the latest anti-depressant, had great potential. He reached out for a chocolate biscuit, keeping his back to the room. The man was a manipulative bastard. But the money would be nice. If he became a big success like Fran's father she might warm towards him again. Fuck no, he wouldn't leave his task half-finished – not for anyone, even Fran.

He turned and leaned against the table as he composed his face into friendly lines. Geoffrey would be a dangerous enemy. 'It's a very generous offer, Geoff. But I have to stay with my project until we get Doxeril on the market. We're just about to start clinical trials. I've got a psychiatrist looking for suitable patients already.'

'Well, keep my suggestion in mind. And if you can find out anything about this Starling woman . . .' He let his words hang in the air.

Paul put the rest of his biscuit in his mouth and licked his chocolate-smeared fingers. 'Thanks for thinking of me. I do appreciate it.'

Back in his office he tried to work but his concentration was gone. He'd been more tempted than he realised. It had been easy for Geoffrey, with no family to support and a post-graduate grant at his own university while working for his PhD. He hadn't struggled at night, staying in the department till his eyes hurt and his hands shook with fatigue. He hadn't missed those precious years with a young child.

Paul wasn't sure that Fran understood the struggle it had been for him to reach his present position. After working as a technician for six years, he'd been promoted to research scientist and was now on the second rung of the ladder. He didn't have to resort to power politics to get a bigger mortgage. If he bought the house they had arranged to view on Saturday it would stretch him to the limit. But he would manage somehow. As he sat at his desk, twisting his pen in his fingers, he knew he wouldn't tell Fran about Geoffrey's offer. He had never kept secrets from her before – but he was no longer sure she would understand his scruples.

* * *

A week later the licence application was almost complete. Although he'd rewritten it three times he was still not satisfied. The data held together well enough, but his strong belief in the need for the new drug didn't emerge from what he had written.

His small office led off the lab and from his desk he could see the door that led into the corridor. It opened and Martin's balding head poked in. A slim, bird-like woman followed him into the room. She turned her head quickly from side to side, her eyes behind her gold-rimmed glasses registering everything she saw. Martin introduced her and she held out her hand. Paul liked her firm grip and cool fingers.

'Show Brenda round, will you? I've got another appointment but I won't be more than half an hour. Bring her along to my office then.' He gave a small wave of his hand and left as abruptly as he had come.

'Quite a brainbox, isn't he?' Brenda said.

'He doesn't give much away but he lets me get on without interfering.' Paul led the way to the first cage.

'Don't feel you have to show me everything. I expect some of it is still confidential.'

He looked at her more closely, warmed by her sensitivity. 'It's OK. This stage of the work is almost complete. We go to clinical trials as soon as we get the go-ahead from the ethical committee. Your work is mainly on drugs for psychosis, isn't it? The Phenothiazines? I've seen one or two of your papers.'

'I'm interested in the Tricyclics as well.' She ran her hand along the top of the cage. 'My background's in microbiology. We've hardly begun to use the new genetics flooding the journals.'

Paul couldn't immediately see the relevance to the production of new drugs so he passed on quickly down the line of cages. Number five was empty now. He hoped the dissection of the rats wouldn't reveal any signs of the strain they'd suffered. He was surprised to find himself telling Brenda about the problems with the staff.

'We had the same problem,' she said. 'It's difficult for them if they don't understand the reasons they have to be so meticulous.'

She looked round the room again and added tentatively, 'We introduced staff meetings to try and explain the work and let them air their grievances. As a result we work better as a team.'

Such an idea had never occurred to Paul, there'd been nothing of that kind when he was a technician. He looked at her with growing respect. As she turned to him her gaze was direct and friendly. He took her into the office and showed her the licence application.

'May I?' she asked, as she moved to sit in his chair.

'Of course, make yourself at home.' The space was too small to fit a second chair among the piles of books. Standing by her side, he reached for a journal, not wanting to watch too obviously as she read.

She applied herself with intense concentration, pushing her glasses up on her nose from time to time with a small automatic movement like a muscle twitch. He didn't feel threatened by her; she was not one of those scientific women whom Geoffrey detested, who needed to prove they were more macho than their male colleagues. Her beige dress moved easily over her body, the figure inside outlined with a comfortable degree of vagueness. The patterned scarf at the neck heightened the blue of her eyes. He wondered what she would look like with her glasses off.

'This is really good. You write so clearly. The points that matter grab the attention.'

'I think the data are all right but it doesn't have any emotional punch.'

'I wonder if you've seen the paper in the *Lancet* this month, about the importance of side effects for compliance? That might be a useful quote.'

His spirits rose. She was not only interested, but really up to date. She spoke with a gentle certainty that allowed him to feel grateful, rather than guilty that he hadn't seen the article himself. 'I haven't read this month's copy yet. I've been spending every minute of the day on the application. It sounds just the thing I need. How can I thank you? I might have sent the thing off before I got round to reading it.'

She smiled. 'You could always put in a good word for me with Martin. I think I'd like to work here.'

What an asset she would be. His memory of Geoffrey's attempt at sabotage made him even more determined to support her.

In his office Martin sat neatly behind his desk. Although he wasn't a particularly big man his smart appearance and quiet confidence dominated the room as he started to speak. 'Paul has built up this department almost single-handed. His time as a technician has given him a unique experience of laboratory detail but he hasn't let it blunt his mind. I want to make it quite clear that if you did join us you would be working under him.' His keen eyes moved from one to the other. 'However, I hope that you would spark ideas off each other.'

Brenda slipped Paul a quick look. 'Yes, I understand that.' Turning back to Martin she said, 'I wonder what opportunities there would be for expansion? We might be a bit cramped in the present space.'

Martin pressed his well-shaped lips together. 'I'm working on that. I've got the option on another room.' He looked at Paul. 'The storeroom along the corridor is going to be emptied and the things moved down to the basement. It isn't so convenient for everyone else, they grumbled a lot, but I won.' He gave a tight smile.

Paul felt a power in the man that he'd never seen before. 'That would be for me?' Martin nodded. 'And Brenda would move into my office?'

'Of course. You can't stay there forever. You have to learn to trust someone else to keep an eye on things.'

Paul realised he was being interviewed as well as Brenda. Behind the nice remarks his boss was probing him: his potential for growth, his ability to work with others and to delegate. Martin wasn't sure of him yet. 'We'd still be short of lab space,' he said, thinking of his conversation with Geoffrey.

'I know that.' Martin looked from him to Brenda and back again. 'There are some plans afoot to expand the company. I can't say more at this stage, nothing has been decided. You'll have to trust me to fight your corner as well as I can.' He got up from his chair and walked to the window.

Paul's eyes travelled over the walls, where photographs of mountains in spring, small flowers in the foreground, jostled with snowy vistas. He wondered if they had been taken in the Alps or further afield. He could hear the tick of a clock that stood on the desk between neat piles of papers.

When Martin turned, he seemed to have decided to take them further into his confidence. 'I believe that between us we have the makings of a strong team. Brenda would bring her microbiology expertise, you have your basic biology and all the biochemistry you did for your PhD. If we're going to move ahead in the gene business we must recruit people from other disciplines as well. We have to break down the barriers.' Brenda and Paul exchanged glances as he went on. 'In a few years we may be able to create different strains of organisms that will do much of our work for us. We have to harness nature to our purposes, use living organisms to help us perform our chemistry.'

Brenda took off her glasses and ran her fingers through the front of her hair. 'I'm on, if you'll have me.'

Martin's severe mouth relaxed as if he might be going to smile. 'I'll let you know as soon as I can. I have to take it to the board tomorrow.' He sat down at his desk again and took up a pen. 'Are you on the phone?'

As he drove home through the fading light Paul found himself humming one of the Irish tunes that he used to play on his fiddle. Now he had some news he could share with Fran.

As he opened the door the smell of oil paints hit his nostrils. She came out of the kitchen to meet him in the dark passage that served as a hallway, wiping her hands on her smock. 'You're early,' she said.

'I've got some news.' He put his briefcase on the floor.

'What is it?'

Now he was standing in front of her it didn't seem so marvellous. 'Oh, just that Martin is going to expand the department. I'm going to get a new office.'

'Does that mean you've being promoted?'

'Not immediately.' The bounce left his step as he traipsed after her into the kitchen. 'Where's Sylvia?'

'She's having tea with a friend down the road. I'm going to fetch her at six-thirty.'

Paul saw his wife's paints and brushes spread out on the table where they ate their meals. 'It's great to see you painting again. You've gone back to oils?'

'I'm sorry. I'd have cleared it away if I'd realised the time.'

Paul moved to look at the half-finished picture but she stepped in front of him. 'It's nothing. Just a doodle.'

'Let me look.'

She picked up the sheet by the corners. 'I'll put it upstairs to dry,' she said, taking a step towards the door.

Paul put out his hand. 'Come on. I'd like to see it.'

'No.' With a sudden movement she crumpled the painting between her hands, turned to the bin, put her foot on the pedal and thrust it inside. 'You go and read the paper. I'll clear up, the place needs airing before we eat.'

Paul slumped into a chair. It wasn't long before he heard Fran go out of the front door. When Sylvia burst in he looked up and held out his arms. She came and snuggled into his lap. 'I love you Daddy, I'm so glad you're home.'

Three months later Brenda was settled into her new job. Paul and Fran had moved into their new house in the country and he felt confident enough to take Sylvia to Cornwall on holiday. Fran was going to join them in a few days. After waiting so long she was determined that every detail of her new home would be perfect. She didn't trust the decorators to mix the colours to the exact shade she wanted. The upstairs carpets had to be fitted, curtains for the sitting room were due to be delivered in the middle of the week and the hot water in the main bathroom still ran cold before even one bath had been filled.

Not caring to admit to himself that he was glad she had stayed behind, Paul was pleased with the chance to have his daughter to himself. As he passed over the money for the hired surfboards he realised that he hadn't thought about the lab for at least twenty-four hours.

He followed Sylvia down the steps to the beach and past the line of windbreaks stuck in the sand like flags in a map, marking the position of an advancing army. Beyond, they found an unoccupied rock and claimed it for their own. Sylvia threw off her clothes with staccato movements and ran towards the sea. She led him into the waves, stepping high and holding her wooden board above her head.

Standing beside her, he yelled 'Jump!' as the broken wave approached. She missed it, but caught the second, tucking the end of the board into her groin, lying flat on it as he had shown her. He caught the next one and landed on the sand near the place where she was beached like a small seal, digging her hands into the sand in an ecstasy of excitement.

'I did it, I did it! I went really fast.' She scrambled to her feet and turned to plunge back. Laughing, he matched her, step for step. They caught the next wave together. He turned and raised his hand, but when she tried to wave back, she fell off. He was at her side in a moment, caught her board with one hand and put the other on her shoulder. She coughed.

'OK?'

'Just a bit of sea water gone the wrong way.' She knuckled her eyes and blinked up at him. 'Come on, don't let's miss the next one.'

She learnt quickly. After a while there was no need for him to tell her when to jump. He watched as she matched her start to that of a boy surfing on the other side of her. Paul strode deeper to catch a wave before it broke. This was the best, the sudden acceleration down its slope as he kept just in front of the white water. He could even steer sideways for a few feet like the lads on their big boards. He'd like to try that one day when his daughter was old enough to do it with him.

They stayed in the water too long. Only when he noticed his teeth were chattering did he insist that Sylvia follow him out. She pouted and threatened a tantrum until he spoke more firmly to her than he had ever done before. To his surprise, she followed him meekly up the beach. The goose pimples on his own skin made him look sharply at her. He was responsible for her now. Hurrying her into her clothes, he insisted she put on her long-sleeved shirt. The sun had broken through the early morning haze and the day was threatening to be a scorcher. They went to the café for a tray of drinks and food. Mayonnaise leaked out of their shared baguette and they licked their fingers with no thought of the table manners Fran instilled at home.

When he looked back, Paul knew that week had been the best of his life. Sylvia was still a year or two away from the time when burgeoning adolescence would make her question and judge him. Between their forays into the water they explored the rock pools, then made replicas of the sandcastles they'd built when she was younger.

'Do you remember the one we decorated with feathers?' she asked. They searched the dunes for those with unbroken spines and clear colours. The white and grey ones from seagulls were common. 'Look at this,' Sylvia called, holding up a blue feather with black mottling. Paul thought it had come from a jay. They gave it pride of place at the top of the highest turret.

'Now let's make the one with a bridge.' Paul started to follow her instructions. 'No, it wasn't on that side, it was towards the sea so that the tide could fill the moat when it came in.' Recreating the past, she could play in a way she would otherwise have considered beneath her ten-year-old dignity.

Never before had Paul been able to make another person completely happy. Alone with his daughter he matched his pace to hers, ate when she was hungry, rested when she was tired. A sense of peace spread through him, soothing the jagged memory of his unhappy mother and unsatisfied wife.

When they tired of the beach they took his field glasses and went up on to the cliffs. As the sun moved lower in the sky they perched on the rocks and stared out across the sea. The waves were quieter now, a distant, rhythmic murmur. Behind them the slanted rays flung long shadows from the occasional shrub or small tree, bent sideways by the prevailing wind.

'It's lovely, Daddy, isn't it?' Sylvia slipped her hand into his and they sat on in silence.

When Fran arrived he felt a surge of warmth. Surely their life would be different now. He imagined his happiness to be so strong that it would envelop her in the tranquil world he had created with his daughter.

But inevitably, things changed. Sylvia expected their life to go on just as it had when they were alone. When that didn't happen, she sulked. Fran wanted to visit other beaches and make trips into Penzance. Paul had to rise early to fit in a swim with Sylvia, then stay up late with Fran so they had time alone for adult conversation, as she called it. He tried to take an interest in all she had to tell him but the sagas of cisterns and roller blinds, the shortcomings of the tradesmen, irritated him. He knew he was being unfair. After all, she was trying to create a lovely home where they could be happy together. When he made tentative advances to her in bed she complained that she was tired. He turned away – and the breach between them widened.

As the end of the holiday approached he looked forward to getting back to work, wondering what changes Brenda had made to the lab. He could picture her moving round the room, stopping here to give some encouragement, there to chide gently if she saw something wrong, flicking her glasses in that characteristic way. The technicians were working better since she arrived. Four psychiatrists had started to test the drug and there might be some early results from the trial.

FIVE

2003

Number 3 stood in the middle of the terrace. Fran hadn't planned to call on Brenda, but when repeated phone calls had gone unanswered she'd decided to drive past and get a feel of the place. A van was following close behind her in the one-way street so she couldn't loiter. She drove round a couple of corners to find a place to park the car.

Her senses sharpened as she felt herself propelled back to the house and up the short path. The red front door matched the one beside it, but the shared can of paint must have run out, because the brown undercoat of the bottom right-hand panel hadn't been covered. The window frames were peeling, the exposed wood cracked. Fran felt an urge to rub emollient oil into the parched grain, as she rubbed Nivea cream into her hands after gardening. Through the ground floor window she could see a computer playing its screen-saving patterns. Papers and books were scattered on the table beside it and a chair stood at an angle as if it had been hurriedly discarded. Fran lifted the tarnished knocker, made in the shape of a fish.

The door opened and her memory jerked as she looked at the woman in front of her. Intense blue eyes stared out under pale eyebrows. The woman wore a cream-coloured smock and baggy blue jeans, very different from the smart red dress she was wearing when she had laughed up at Paul more than thirty years before.

'Yes?'

'I'm Fran Ashby.'

'Paul's wife . . . widow?' Fran nodded. 'What do you want?' Her voice was hostile.

Fran wished she were safely back in her own house. 'Can I come in for a moment?'

Brenda didn't answer but led the way through into the back where a surprisingly big room acted as both kitchen and dining room. She waved a hand towards the chairs neatly pushed in under the square pine table. 'I can't stop long, I've got to get to grips with two papers that arrived this morning.'

Fran pulled out a chair and perched on the edge. 'What are you working on?'

'The usual; yet another attempt to plant a modified crop. A friend in high places sends me copies of the applications for experimental planting. I have to scrutinise them for methodology and flaws in the data. It takes me hours.'

Fran couldn't think of anything to say. She put her handbag on the floor and looked around. At first glance the kitchen seemed as messy as she'd expected from the outside of the house. Then she realised it was the surface untidiness of a busy person. Dirty crockery was stacked neatly on the draining board, newspapers filled two cardboard boxes in the corner. The blue and white china displayed on the Welsh dresser was interspersed with bowls of paper clips and pens. A bunch of letters stuck out at the end, held in place by a lurid, painted dog, quite out of keeping with the traditional elegance of the rest of the china.

Brenda reached for two mugs from a cupboard above the stove. 'Real or decaff?'

On the far side Fran could see a tin of fair-trade coffee, some packets of herb tea and a row of glass jars with beans, lentils and bulgar wheat all labelled in a spidery hand. 'Whatever is easiest.'

'I'm a bit of a caffeine addict.'

A German dictionary lay at the top of a pile of books, a notebook by the side with a well-sharpened pencil sticking out between the pages. A large tabby cat was curled up on the only easy chair in the room and a dish of uneaten cat food sat on the floor by the French window that led out to the small back garden.

'You've got a cat,' Fran said.

'Yes. I shouldn't have because I'm away so much. But my neighbour is very good to him. He's old now. Paul named him Tibbles when he was a kitten. Such a silly name.'

Fran gripped her hands together. How could Paul have been in this room, with a tabby kitten, without her knowing? A void in front of her seemed to widen, but she would not be drawn into it. 'He was good at silly names. My friend Hazel was asking how Bruiser got his name. That's my retriever, you know. I expect he mentioned his dog when you were working together.'

Brenda said nothing as the kettle sang in the silence. She spooned the coffee granules into the mugs. Fran longed to escape. She wished, not for the first time, that she had finished her degree and been a proper scientist, not just a hack sales-person. Brenda put two small mats on the table and plonked the mugs down, followed by a plate of biscuits.

Taking a deep breath, Fran said, 'You're still working then, even though you're not with the company?'

'Goodness, yes. It's ten years since I left, you know, I'm tied up with all sorts of international negotiations now.'

'What do you do?'

'I work with the NGOs, acting as an intermediary between them and governments. Several Third World countries trust me now and use me to help them.'

Fran had heard Sylvia and her friends talking about Non-Governmental Organisations, but she wasn't quite sure what they were. 'Do you mean the World Wildlife Fund and things like that?'

'The ones I work with are fighting against big businesses and the awful effects they have on the lives of people in developing countries. I'm especially interested in the introduction of new crops that haven't been properly tested.'

Fran was out of her depth. 'My daughter, Sylvia, has taken part in some of the demonstrations.'

A smile transformed Brenda's face. 'I've met her, more than once. How is she?' Fran relaxed a bit as she heard a new warmth in Brenda's voice, but she hadn't come to talk about her daughter.

'She's fine.' How could she move the conversation forward? 'You've got lovely china. That's willow pattern isn't it?'

'Some of it. I've been collecting for years but I've no time to go round the second hand shops now. I used to find good bargains.'

Fran sipped her coffee. 'Why did you leave the company?' as soon as the words were out of her mouth, she regretted them. Geoffrey had warned her to leave the past alone, she should have led up to the question more carefully.

Brenda got up to fetch a bowl of sugar and put two spoonfuls into her coffee, then bit into a biscuit. Fran refused to take one, annoyed that the woman could snack with such abandon and stay so thin.

'Don't you know anything about it?' Brenda asked.

'Paul never discussed his work at home.'

'Maybe it's not for me to enlighten you, then.' Brenda ran her fingers through the front of her hair, which settled back with accustomed ease into its short waves. She shifted in her chair as her eyes strayed to an article on the table.

Fran felt trapped by the stronger will of the woman in front of her, held in an iron grip like that of her mother. She was afraid that as soon as their coffee was finished she would be firmly dismissed. The woman was totally in charge: of her burgeoning papers, her elderly cat – and the past.

Damn it, Fran thought. She'd been married and widowed, held down an adequate job, even wrung the neck of a jackdaw. She'd raised a child, for god's sake. 'Have you any children?' she asked.

'No.'

'Did you know Paul well?' Again, she wished she hadn't asked, and again Brenda Starling didn't reply. She picked up a pencil and started to draw an elaborate doodle on the cover of her notebook. It began with a large swirl in the middle and moved out towards one of the corners, swirls within swirls, interlocking and changing to circles and ovals. Fran squinted at it but could see none of the hidden life she had tried to put into her own drawings. The pencil in Brenda's hand was just a mechanical diversion, like an executive toy. Fran wanted to shake her. 'I tried to ask Geoffrey Protheroe about him but he was no help.'

The doodle had developed kinks that sharpened till they echoed the right-angled corner of the paper. They reached the edge and Brenda moved the pencil down to start filling in the opposite quarter of the page. Fran stretched out and covered the moving fingers, forcing them to be still. 'Please tell me.' She felt the hand beneath her own contract with such force that the pencil broke.

'He should have resigned when I did. It would have been the honourable thing to do.' She looked up into Fran's face. 'Then he could have lived with himself.' Draining her coffee, she got up to carry the mugs to the sink. With her back turned she began to speak, her words slicing through the space between them.

'We had to try and stop the work after the Tryptophan affair. I don't suppose you know about that.' She didn't allow any time for a response. 'A study in America linked a new disease to the food supplement. Although we were developing a different drug we were using a similar technique. I was always afraid the method was dangerous, that using genetically engineered organisms might produce toxic impurities. Paul agreed that our methods were faulty, so we talked to Martin Emery, our immediate boss. He was interested at first but nothing happened for weeks. We went on with the work, there didn't seem to be much else to do, but when we raised the subject again Martin was evasive, so we wrote a strong paper to the director. When he took no notice, I circulated it to the whole board. All hell broke loose.'

She walked back to the table and stood looking down at Fran. 'I think you'd better read the research yourself, the stuff that made us so worried about our work. Come with me.' Leading the way into the front room, she hunted through one pile of papers after another till she found what she was looking for. The large photocopier standing in the corner was the sort you found in libraries, not private houses.

Fran clutched at the name she recognised. 'I met Martin and his wife once, before the fire. Paul asked them to supper.'

Brenda gave a small shrug of her shoulders. Fran remembered the night of the bomb, the horror of it and her certainty that Paul had been in the building. She could hardly believe it when his voice had come over the phone, pitched higher than normal, but still his own voice. Thank goodness he had left the building early. She could never understand how the animal rights people could care more for a few rats than for human life. 'Poor Martin, that bomb was a terrible experience.'

'His luck ran out.'

'He never came for another meal. Paul asked him several times but he always refused. I suppose his scars made him too self-conscious.'

Brenda was silent. Fran wondered if she was hurt because they had never invited her. Paul had been so definite about it, but surely she could have come with one of the other couples. Perhaps Brenda thought he had been sucking up to his superiors. Fran felt herself blushing. He never tried to pull strings, he'd got as far as he had by hard work – only she knew just how hard.

The sheets were flying out of the copier. Brenda collected them together and reached for the stapler. 'I have to get back to work now, but come again when you've read this, if you want to. Give me a ring first and I'll try to make a bit of time.'

Fran couldn't leave it. 'Was your paper the reason you were fired?'

'I wasn't fired,' Brenda snapped. 'I resigned. We had already signed a company pledge about confidentiality but we were asked to sign another. We were not to publish anything without the written approval of the company. Although our results weren't complete we had enough to be suspicious. How could we keep it secret, if the drug was dangerous? It wasn't ethical. Scientific discoveries must be freely circulated so that others can confirm or refute them.' She walked towards the door of the room as if she couldn't get Fran out quickly enough. Then she turned. 'That's the only way the truth can emerge, slowly and safely. I refuse to work in any other way.' Her hands were trembling so that the pages shook. 'We were offered better positions in the food department if we would sign. Paul said he would resign with me. Then he chickened out. I never thought he could be such a coward.' She was almost shouting now, her eyes a deeper blue. Gone was the cool scientist. In her place an exploding ball of anger that reminded Fran of a kitten, its fur raised as it spat and clawed at some inquisitive animal.

The storm subsided as quickly as it had come. 'I'm sorry. He was your husband. I'm not really angry with him, he had to think of you and Sylvia. It's the company, the power, the absolute power of these huge organisations. They do so much damage, they're not responsible to anyone, interested only in profit, profit, profit. They spew out their poisonous products, untested and untried, polluting the world and messing up ecosystems that have worked for thousands of years. We can do so little about it.'

She held out the paper again and gave Fran a small, closed smile. 'See what you think. This is the report of the original work – ours was never published.'

'Thank you.'

Fran found herself on the road outside without quite realising how she had got there. She looked back to see Brenda already sitting at the table, immersed in her work.

When she reached into her bag for the car keys she was surprised to see she still carried the article in her hand. It felt like a parasite, attached to her body against her will, waiting to force its way deeply into her flesh like a burrowing worm. She put the pages on the front sill of the car. Those few sheets held the key to the trouble. They had stopped Paul getting his promotion and caused Brenda to lose her job. Fran wondered how difficult it had been for him to withstand her pressure.

Picking up the paper again, she looked at the date on the top. 1990, thirteen years before. Sylvia had finished at university and was supporting herself. Of course, at that time the mortgage on the house still wasn't paid off; it would have been difficult if he'd been out of work for any length of time. But they could have managed. She had become a fully trained rep for the company by then and could have increased her hours.

Her hands rested on the steering wheel, and her head lay on her hands. A deep pain gnawed inside her. Would he have talked to her if she'd shown more interest in his work?

She sighed and started the engine. The journey from Keynsham took about twenty minutes but she was so preoccupied that she was past the village shop sooner than she expected. Four years before, they had all fought to keep it open. Now it was run by a Sikh man and his wife, the only people who were prepared to work hard enough to make it a profitable concern. The green car with the battered wing was parked outside. Perhaps they had family staying. As she turned into the drive and saw her 1920s house standing solid in the faded light she felt a sense of relief. Inside, the walls surrounded her like a soft stole, keeping her safe from the world outside.

With a drink in her hand, she realised that she must have done something very wrong if Paul couldn't trust her: his wife. As she paced about she thought, for the first time, that he might have been irritated by her efforts to make the house so perfect. Perhaps he preferred going to work rather than being with her.

She finished her glass. Brenda said that if he had resigned he could have lived with himself. Had he regretted his decision, been left to carry a sense of failure for the rest of his life? It was unbearable to think that her husband had been disloyal to his principles for her sake, without even consulting her.

Walking to the French windows to let Bruiser out, she caught sight of the photo of her mother. It was standing on the top of her desk, next to the one of the three of them at Sylvia's graduation. With painful clarity she realised how much of her enthusiasm for the house had been an effort to regain her parents' respect, lost so completely when she'd got pregnant before she was married.

Fran picked up the photo and took it to the window. The eyes, unlike her own dark ones that she had inherited from her father, were narrow and jealous. With a spurt of her old rebellion Fran tore the photo from the frame, dragged open the bottom drawer of the desk and thrust the picture inside. It had been absurd to worry about what her mother thought when Paul was in trouble.

The desk looked empty without her mother's disapproving presence. She went upstairs to look for a replacement and found a snapshot of Sylvia on her pony. In the background Paul was leaning on the gate watching her, one hand shading his eyes. She carried it downstairs. That was better. Looking round the room she knew she didn't want to leave, whatever Hazel said. The place held such vivid memories. It was here that she had nursed Paul during his last illness, bringing his bed down and turning the place into a sick room. She sat on the sofa and sipped another glass of wine as she relived those last weeks.

He had been off work, very ill with the swollen ankles and breathlessness that were the most obvious signs of his heart failure. Every nerve of his body had rebelled as Fran helped him on to the commode. She would retreat outside the door to listen in case he fell. When he was well enough he wrote notes in the file he kept by his bed, locked in a briefcase. When she tried to dissuade him, asking what was so urgent that it couldn't wait, he said he must get his records straight. It had made her furious to watch him pushing himself so hard.

'If you wear yourself out with those beastly papers I'll take them away and hide them in the attic. You won't be able to climb the stairs, you haven't the breath.' Even such brutal remarks hadn't dissuaded him.

After a few weeks of treatment he'd begun to improve. One day he managed to walk round the garden, supported by her arm. When he was back in bed, exhausted but triumphant, he said he must go to his office.

'Surely it can wait a week or two?' she said. 'You really aren't fit enough to make such a journey.'

'It's something I have to do.'

Since his death Fran had been haunted by the thought that the outing had hastened his end. As time passed she'd managed to push the guilt to the back of her mind.

She could see him again, almost as vividly as in those rare dreams. He was lying on the bed, one foot crossed over the other as if to show off the fact that the anklebones were visible again. He had reached out and pulled her to sit on the bed beside him. As she searched his features she'd been struck by some new power that seemed to fill his ruined body. Under a surface transparency he'd looked distinguished in a way she'd never noticed before.

'This is something I have to do, Fran. I have to do it for myself and I need you to help me.'

She couldn't remember him asking for her support in that blunt way during the whole of their married life. So often it had been he who had sustained her. She had looked at his hand in hers, how frail it was, the length of the fingers exaggerated by the wasted muscles, the skin marked by new brown patches. She had rubbed them gently with her thumb, not aware of what she did.

'You know, I've not talked much about my work . . .' He looked around the room, as if to savour all the details. 'For some reason I've had to keep my home and my work separate.' His free hand smoothed the briefcase lying on his bed.

Fran had the unfamiliar feeling that he was talking to her as an equal. He'd always been so attentive, as if he believed she could not exist outside the shadow of his protective arm.

He'd pointed to the family photo in its usual place on her desk and asked her to bring it to his bed. Running his fingers over Sylvia's face he asked, 'What do you think of this new boyfriend, Richard? Could he be the one for her?'

'I don't know. It's early days yet, they've been together for less than a year.'

'I'd like to see her settled.'

'I'm sure you will. She just needs a bit more time.'

He hadn't replied, his uncertain future hanging in the air between them. Then he put the photo down and took her hand again. His grip was firm, not in panic, but containing a force she hadn't been aware of for years. She herself had felt strangely powerful. With the unaccustomed sensation had come a longing to hold his body to her, to give herself to him. But he was sick; you couldn't seduce a sick man. She'd leant forward and kissed his cheek. She wouldn't let him down. If he wanted to go to the office she'd get him there somehow.

* * *

Jumping up from the sofa, she nearly toppled over. She felt her way to the wine box and walked into the garden, the refilled glass in her hands. Bruiser followed her, sniffing his way down the path. The small pond, where the variegated fish crowded into the corner, was overgrown with blanket weed. She liked them best as they changed colour. Noses and underbellies turned first in individual patterns, then later the rest of the body, leaving a rim of black to linger along the edge of the dorsal fin. Once they'd turned a uniform gold they were just part of the crowd, like the strangers she passed in the street.

The evenings were drawing in and it wouldn't be long before the clocks went back. Then she would be faced with the long dark evenings alone. She should be used to it; she had been alone so often when Paul was alive. But she'd always known that sooner or later the garage door would rumble and she would hear his key grate in the lock.

She looked at her drink with disgust. Was she going to spend the rest of her life in a maudlin alcoholic haze? In a sudden fury she hurled the glass against the low wall round the pond. It smashed on the concrete paving slabs. The shattered remains sprayed out in all directions and the stone took on a dark stain. Bruiser trotted along to investigate. Oh God, his feet. She seized him by the collar and put her arms under his heavy body but it was too late. Blood dripped from one paw and fell on to her trouser leg making a stain she would never get out.

'Oh, Bruiser, I'm so sorry.' She staggered under his weight as she took him to the kitchen and pressed on the small cut until the bleeding had stopped. It wasn't very deep, so she dabbed at it with weak disinfectant while feeding him two cream biscuits. 'You'll have to stay inside till I've cleared it up,' she said.

She took a broom out of the cupboard and swept up what glass was visible in the dusky light. It would have to be done again in the morning. Perched back on the seat she shivered, not so much because of the cold as the unexpected spasm of temper. Above her she saw the first stars in the sky and a crescent moon low on the horizon. She'd never lost control in that way before. As she absorbed the shock, she found she could think more clearly.

First, she really would stop drinking. In the absence of anyone else, she vowed to the fish in the pond that she would do so. She would study the paper Brenda had given her until she understood. She might not have a fancy degree but she knew that, when she was sober, she was far from stupid.

Back in the kitchen Fran saw the wine box sitting on the table, the square corners making it look like a surprise present. One glass wouldn't hurt. She watched her fingers as they dismantled the cardboard and removed the foil container. Cutting one corner with the kitchen scissors, she tipped it up over the sink. The red liquid gurgled down the plug. With it went her determination. She was so alone. She leaned against the draining board, propping the weight of her body on her hands. Through clenched teeth she said aloud, 'I will manage, by myself.'

The stairs creaked as she climbed slowly up to bed. Under the blankets she hugged her hot water bottle to her stomach. When she was warm she let her hand drop on to Bruiser's soft back where he lay in the basket beside her. The muscles moved as he wagged his tail, though it made no sound against his soft rugs. As she closed her eyes the picture of a large tabby cat, curled up in a chair, forced its way into her mind.

SIX

2003

After swallowing three paracetamol tablets Fran sat at the kitchen table trying to get to grips with the article Brenda had given her the day before. When she got to the end, for the second time, she understood that the new disease, eosinophilia-myalgia syndrome – what a mouthful – had been caused by a particular batch of Tryptophan, made in Japan. They had used a new strain of bacteria for the fermentation, presumably genetically modified, but also less powdered carbon to purify the drug. The authors didn't seem to know which factor was responsible for the illness.

Fran rubbed her eyes. She couldn't see how a food supplement, made in a distant country, could possibly have been relevant to Paul's work on drugs.

Standing up, she reached for the wicker shopping basket, one of her mother's belongings she still enjoyed using. Before going out she took an onion tart from the deep freeze and checked on Bruiser's paw. The cut was healing well.

As she entered the shop, which was also a small post office, Mr Singh looked up. Ever since Paul's death he and his wife had been particularly kind to Fran. Their direct way of expressing sympathy, without asking questions or invading her privacy, had soothed her. They took more time to comment on the weather, ask after her dog and commiserate about the cost of postage to New Zealand, where she had distant cousins. She picked up some fresh vegetables and reached for her purse.

Mr Singh looked worried as he passed over her change. 'I'm not sure if I should tell you. We don't like to gossip but I think you should know. A man was asking about you yesterday.'

'A man?'

'At first he enquired how long you had lived in the village. I said you were here when we arrived, so I didn't know. Then he wanted to know about your husband and if you had many visitors . . . In the end I had to tell him that I do not spy on my neighbours.'

Fran gripped one of the parsnips she'd put in her basket. She felt hollow, as if her guts had been scooped out, leaving her heart to echo in an empty space. 'What was he like?'

'A square sort of man, older than you would expect with his close cropped-hair.' He paused as he noticed Fran's stillness. 'Do you know him perhaps?'

'I think I do.' It must be Jackson. 'Yesterday, you said? Was he driving a green car?'

Mr Singh nodded. 'An Alpha Romeo, with a dented wing.'

Fran hadn't noticed the make but it was obviously the same car. 'He was parked outside my house a few days ago.' He must have been snooping around. Could he have got inside? No one in the village had ever been burgled so she didn't lock up very carefully. Her fingers went to her throat, leaving brown streaks from the soil-streaked parsnips.

Mr Singh looked concerned. 'Do you want me to tell the police, if he comes in again?'

Her headache returned, gripping her temples like one of the iron rings round the barrel on her front doorstep, the one she filled with annuals each year. If Paul had been involved in something shady . . . 'I have to deal with this myself. But thanks, all the same.'

The shopkeeper nodded. 'I understand. If you ever need help we are always here. Pick up the phone and I'll come at once. Day or night.'

'You're very kind.' His offer only increased her fears. She turned to leave.

'Mrs Ashby . . .'

'Yes?'

'We are your friends you know. You can trust us . . .'

'I know. I'm so grateful to you for everything.'

Letting herself back into the house, she looked around. The familiar rooms threatened her now. As she unpacked the shopping, her hands were shaking. It was no good, despite all her resolutions and her vow to the goldfish: she couldn't face Sylvia without a drink.

After downing a double gin her courage began to return. She forced herself to walk through the ground floor, scanning her belongings and looking behind the doors. Her mouth twitched as she remembered playing hide-and-seek with Sylvia, knowing all along where she was but delaying the moment of discovery.

Everything seemed to be in the right place ... but those letters on the desk – had she left them piled so tidily? Taking a deep breath she climbed the stairs and stopped outside the door to the main bedroom. Impulsively, she opened it and went inside.

Cobwebs hung in the corners by the window. She'd hardly been in the room since Paul's death. If she were to move back she'd have to throw out his clothes and reorganise the furniture. But she might feel safer in the room where his spirit still seemed to linger. She opened the top drawer of his chest and saw socks neatly rolled by the side of his underwear. He had always put the newly washed pants at the bottom of the pile so that every pair was worn in turn.

In a rush of impatience she strode downstairs to fetch a couple of black dustbin bags. It was daft to wait in the hope of finding a good home for his things; nobody would want second-hand underwear.

Once the chest was empty she turned to the built-in cupboard. His suits and jackets, old grey flannels and more recent jeans hung in a reproachful row. On the floor two pairs of white cricket trousers lay abandoned in the dust, relics from his undergraduate days. As she gazed at them she heard a door bang downstairs.

'Hi, old cock, how's things?'

Fran wished her daughter wouldn't talk to the dog like that. 'Hello, darling,' she called, 'I'll be right down.' Sylvia would be pleased with the bags that stood by the door, their necks tied tight as if to ensure that the remains of the departed life could not escape.

She was standing in the kitchen looking at the photocopied article on the table. Giving her mother a quick kiss, she moved away. Even as a small child with a grazed knee, she hadn't wanted to be hugged for long and Fran had learnt to let her go at the first hint of tension.

'What's this?' Sylvia asked.

'I got it from Brenda Starling. I don't see why she wanted me to read it. She resigned, you know. She said that Dad should have resigned with her. That he would have been happier if he'd done so.' She was startled by the small sob that escaped from her throat.

Sylvia searched her mother's face. 'You went to see her?' Fran nodded. 'Oh Mum, why ever did you do that?'

'Why not? She worked closely with Dad and must have known what he was doing. But I don't understand why this paper was so important.'

Sylvia turned towards the patio doors. 'It's lovely outside, surprisingly warm. Shall we sit in the garden for a bit? Bruiser would like that, wouldn't you, old cock?'

'Don't call him that.'

'Sorry.'

They moved out into the late sunshine and sat on the wooden seat Paul had found in a second-hand market in Clifton. He had produced it as a house-warming present the day after they moved in. They had sat together watching Sylvia catching newts with her holiday fishing net. Fran could see her ten-year-old daughter bending over the edge, feel the pressure of Paul's thigh against her own.

Turning to her daughter, she said, 'I've bagged up all the things from his drawers.'

'Well done. Can I help?'

'I haven't been able to face his study yet.' In her mind she saw his papers thrown about, ransacked by that odious man. She wondered if she should warn her daughter that someone had been in the house. 'I've never been through his desk and I don't know what to do about all his books.'

'Do you have to do anything with them? Are you going to move?'

'I'm not sure. Hazel says I should move back into Bristol.' Now her house felt so unsafe the idea was more attractive. 'How would you feel if I did?'

Sylvia's eyes swept round the garden. 'I don't know.' The bird table stood where it had always been, outside the dining-room window, the wood rotting. Broken boards hung in the sycamore tree at the end, the remains of the tree house her father had built for her. The fork in the branches, where she used to put her left foot at the start of her climb, was covered with moss. 'It's not the same without Dad. You might feel better in a new place.'

'I suppose so. We had so many good times here.'

Sylvia felt the tug of her own memories. She had arrived home the day after her father died to find her mother too dazed to take decisions. Feeling important, Sylvia had chosen the music for the funeral service and organised the tea afterwards. For the first time she had been the adult, her mother the child who had to be looked after. By the time she left, ten days later, her mother was back in charge. As she had begun to feel the depth of her own loss, visiting her old home had become an effort. She looked at the fish and was surprised by a feeling of desolation. It sounded as if her mother were seriously considering moving away.

'I would miss the place. But you must do what's right for you.'

Fran longed to say that it would be different if there were grandchildren. 'How's Richard?'

'Oh, he's fine,' Sylvia said.

That told her nothing. 'Perhaps he'd understand the significance of that paper. He knows about genes and things, doesn't he?'

Sylvia sighed. 'I wish you'd leave it, Mum. Brenda is a real extremist.'

'She certainly was over the top at times. She gave me coffee,' Fran added, as if to soften the criticism.

'She can be kind. She once said that Dad would have been proud of me.'

'So he would. You've done incredibly well, and now this recent promotion –'

'She wasn't talking about my career. She meant the demonstration. I'd just cut my hand on a sharp stalk and was feeling a bit upset.'

Fran winced, fixing her eyes on the fish circling in the pool. She could see the woman bending over her daughter, offering words of comfort, even being allowed to put an arm round her shoulders. 'Perhaps I should come with you on the next one,' she said.

Sylvia jumped up from the bench. 'Oh Mum, it's not your sort of thing, you'd hate it. You have to live your own life and for God's sake let me live mine in my own way.'

Fran sat rigid. She'd only wanted to offer support, to try and make up for her lack of interest in Paul's world. She watched Sylvia walk towards the end of the garden and the fears, that she'd held at bay while throwing out his clothes and talking to her daughter, gripped her with renewed force.

Sylvia looking up through the leaves. They were drooping, as if poised to fall with the next strong wind. She squeezed her eyelids shut, trying to banish the hurt look that had swept over her mother's face. If only she would shout back sometimes. What could a mere daughter do about the empty bottles of gin that lurked at the back of the garage? By meddling with the past her mother was only risking further unhappiness. There must have been good reasons for her father to be so secretive about his work. Sylvia frowned as she went inside, determined to behave better.

They were careful of each other over lunch. Sylvia's praise of the onion tart was exaggerated and Fran knew she'd annoyed her daughter. However tactful she tried to be, she could feel the tact itself creating a distance between them. If she didn't care so much it would be easier for them both. She poured some red wine from her last bottle and the tension began to ease.

After lunch they loaded the contents of the hanging cupboard into the back of the car, ready for her to take to the Oxfam shop in the morning. Then they went down to Paul's study. Fran, glad to have Sylvia by her side, looked round quickly as she entered. Everything seemed to be in its right place in the tidy room. They worked through the drawers in his desk and found nothing but scrap paper, some old data sheets and a brochure for lab equipment, dated 1991.

Sylvia began to examine the books. 'I didn't know Dad was interested in parasites.'

'He was keen on all living creatures. When I first knew him, his great love was insects.'

'Shall I see if there's anything Richard might like? Even if I only took one or two it would leave a bit more room on the shelves.'

'Would he want any of them?'

'He might, he's into parasitology. Especially in fish.'

Sylvia settled herself on the floor, drawing her knees close to her chest as she turned the pages of a small book with a worn leather cover. 'This seems to be a biography of some Australian. Dad's marked several passages with a pencil.'

Fran moved to her side and looked down. Paul never wrote in his books, regarding it as a terrible sacrilege; some previous owner must have done it.

'Goodness, this man infected himself with a tapeworm to study its natural history.'

Fran worked her way along the shelves, looking at the titles more closely than she'd ever done before. She'd assumed she wouldn't understand the technical ones. Only now could she admit to herself that insects bored her. Sylvia was right, there were several about parasites of one sort or another, as well as those on chemistry, molecular biology and the collection of first editions of the *New Naturalist* that he had treasured so much. What would she do with them all? Unbidden, the image of Brenda Starling rose between her and the shelves. They'd worked so closely together, she should have something of his to keep. The idea was less disturbing than to imagine the books in the care of a man who might not be a permanent member of the family. However, she forced herself to say, 'Maybe Richard should come and choose for himself.'

'He'd like that.' Sylvia looked up. 'He's not very settled where he is. He wants to specialise. He believes we must develop fish farming if the world is going to feed itself. The industry will need more specialist vets. Only if he does . . .' she hesitated, 'it will mean years more study and we won't be financially stable for ages.' She looked down at the book in her hand, adding, 'I do want a baby, Mum.'

Fran stood still and gazed at the top of her daughter's hair, shaped by what must have been a very expensive cut. Words cascaded through her mind – you don't have to get everything perfect before you start – I'll help – you could live here and I'll look after the baby while you go out to work . . . With a sigh she realised that wouldn't do. They only got on well together when there was plenty of space between them. She straightened her back. 'You mustn't leave it too late. You'd manage somehow. You can't control everything in life and your chance of getting pregnant is less as you get older.'

'Don't I know it. But I can't hold him back, can I, if that's what he really wants to do?' Her eyes, turned up to her mother, were pleading.

For once it didn't matter if Sylvia snapped and hurt her. Fran knew it was more important to speak out. 'There's no reason why you can't do both. You don't need all the things you think are essential – expensive holidays and cars. You could manage on much less –' she had a sudden doubt '– if you really love each other.'

'How do you know if you love each other enough?'

That was the question Fran had asked herself, so many times. She had been thrust into marriage with Paul too early in her life. At least Sylvia's baby would be planned, if she could find the courage to plan it. 'Perhaps you can never know for certain. Trust your guts – and jump.'

Sylvia shifted on the floor. Fran knew they couldn't go on with the conversation without the risk of spoiling the rare moment of contact. 'Come on, let's take Bruiser out for a walk, I'm sure he's feeling neglected. You can stay for a quick cup of tea?'

'I'll do that.' Sylvia got up from the floor. 'Thanks, Mum,' she muttered, as she led the way back up the stairs.

* * *

After her daughter had left, Fran went automatically to the wine rack, forgetting they had finished the last bottle. Gin then, or whisky? She tightened her jaw as she began to shake, feeling the sweat start on her forehead. Collecting every bottle of alcohol in the house, she went down into the basement again and put them into the cupboard by Paul's desk. The door had a lock. After turning the key she took her coat, put Bruiser on the lead and headed across the fields towards the river. He was putting all four feet to the ground with only a suggestion of a limp. The gash on his foot must be healing.

From beneath the branches of a willow tree she looked into the murky depths, torn between two choices. She could throw herself in, escape forever from her loneliness and panic. Or she could find the courage to face cold turkey and whatever nastiness Jackson had in store for her. At the top of the bank she hesitated, fingering the key in her pocket. As she shifted on her feet the ground gave way. She began to slide towards the water. Reaching out she grabbed at the root of a tree. The key dropped from her fingers. She watched it disappear under the surface, before pulling herself back on to solid ground to wipe her muddy hand on the grass. Fate had played his card. With a shaky laugh she said to the dog, 'Well, old cock. I'm damned if we'll give in now. Neither Jackson nor anyone else is going to stop me. Come on home and help me through the next days; they are going to be murder.' Bruiser rubbed against her legs and set off eagerly to show her the way towards his dinner. The blasted dog thought of nothing but himself.

That night Fran was woken by a recurrence of the nightmare in which she was trapped by a ring of fire. Paul's pyjamas, the only bit of his clothing she'd decided to keep and use, were so wet they clung to her skin as she lay stiff, her muscles clenched against the fear. The stairs creaked. Someone was hovering outside her room. She turned her head on the pillow and thought the door opened. Cowering away, she put her arm across her face and waited for the blow that never came.

A plaintive whine from Bruiser convinced her that someone was walking towards her bed. Only when she heard the dog scrabbling at the door could she believe it was shut. She ran her tongue over her dry lips and forced herself to reach out for the bedside light. The room was empty.

The morning took a lifetime to arrive. At last she saw that dawn was breaking behind the curtains, so she went downstairs and brewed some coffee. The smell made her retch. She put a piece of bread in the toaster, hoping it would settle her stomach, but when it popped up she took it outside to scatter for the birds.

Going into the sitting room, she turned on the television. From time to time the inanities of the chat show made her turn it off and pick up a newspaper, but reading was impossible and she would throw it on the floor. Whenever she went into the kitchen and opened the fridge she felt nauseated. At one moment she had a fleeting idea that the doctor might be able to help her, but she couldn't bring herself to admit to him that she might be an alcoholic.

The hours wore on so slowly that she kept phoning to check the time, convinced that her clocks had all gone wrong. She tuned her radio to Classic FM but the music hurt her ears and made her head worse. By six-o-clock she took herself back to bed. Lying with her fingers clenched, every cell in her body cried out for a drink. Tossing in the bed she determined to get a bottle at the shop as soon as it opened.

She slept fitfully. In the morning she decided she couldn't face Mr Singh with her face all blotchy and her hands shaking. In his kind way he would ask her what was wrong and want to help. No one could help; she had to do this on her own.

By teatime that day, almost forty-eight hours after her last drink, she reached the nadir of her suffering. Collecting every key she could find she went down to her store of drink. None of them fitted the lock. In fury she beat on the doors, then fell sobbing to the ground.

After a time she struggled to her feet and took Bruiser across the fields, in the vain hope that she might be able to dredge the key from the bottom of the river. When she reached the bank she realised it was a futile idea. Leaning against the willow tree, she felt the cool air on her cheeks and a vestige of courage returned. She walked slowly back to the house and forced herself to eat a plate of cornflakes. Holding out her hands in front of her, she realised the shaking was a bit less marked.

On each of the following three days she made herself walk for half an hour in the morning and again in the afternoon. If she were in danger of passing anyone she knew her head lowered and she turned in the opposite direction.

On the morning of the fifth day she woke feeling hungry. After scrambling some eggs she sat down to read the scientific paper once more. She could make no more sense of it than she had before. She would have to talk to Brenda again.

The problem was how to arrange a meeting. If Fran invited her for a meal she would have the advantage of being on home ground. She couldn't believe that Paul had promised to resign with her and then broken his word. He was an honourable man. If he had not been he wouldn't have married her, when all he really wanted to do was to go abroad.

The unwanted thought made her squirm, but as she sat gazing across the kitchen she couldn't stop another scene replaying in her head. She saw again the excitement on his face as he pleaded with her to help him to the office that last time. It had reminded her of the young Paul, who had been filled with passion to travel and make a difference in the world. She'd been prompted to ask, 'Were you ever offered that job with VSO?'

He'd raised his eyebrows. 'Whatever makes you think of that just now?'

Ignoring his question, she said, 'I think you were, but you never told me.'

'You never asked.'

In the misery of the wedding and the uncertainties of new motherhood she hadn't wanted to know. 'I'm sorry,' she said.

'Don't be. I've had a good life. I wouldn't change it now.'

'Don't talk as if it's over. You're getting better.'

'Of course.' The response had been automatic.

Only now, with the energy of an alcohol-free body, could Fran allow herself to remember the conversation. If she hadn't seduced him and fallen pregnant with Sylvia, he could have followed his plans. Then his inner hunger might have been satisfied. It was her fault that he had spent all his life in a job he didn't want. If he'd failed, she must accept some of the responsibility.

With a resolute movement she stood up from the table. She would jolly well make Brenda tell her everything. The old hope, that careful hospitality would provide the setting in which she could wangle whatever she wanted, surged up inside her.

But it might not be as easy as that. She would have to entice the woman with the promise of Paul's books. As she remembered her daughter sitting on the floor of his study, she smiled. One day there might be grandchildren. Opening the telephone directory, she ran her finger down the list of phone numbers and knew she would not let Jackson, or anyone else, drive her out of her home.

SEVEN

2003

The room was crowded when Fran slipped in at the back. For a moment she could see nowhere to sit. Then a willowy man beckoned her with the microphone he was holding. He moved the people along the bench under the window to make a space at the end. His lapel badge announced 'Steward, OUT GM CROPS'. Her neighbours all sported OUT badges, miniature replicas of the banner that was strung behind the platform. Fran felt overdressed in her slogan-free suit, too tidy among the jeans and T-shirts, a throwback to a time when smart clothes assured you some standing in the world. Those who were not in jeans wore black from head to toe.

The man gave her a wide smile. His curly brown hair reached below his ears, balancing his elongated face. 'Would you like a sticker?' Not waiting for a reply he pushed one on to her lapel, smoothing it with sensuous fingers. 'I haven't seen you at one of these meetings before.'

'It's my first time,' she said.

'Great to have you here. The cause is so important.'

Fran was warmed by his friendliness. He wasn't deterred by her inappropriate dress but she felt a bit patronised. 'I've met the lecturer but I haven't heard her in public.'

Brenda had refused her invitation to lunch, though she had seemed quite interested in Paul's books. She would try to visit soon. Meanwhile she had suggested Fran might like to come to the meeting, so they could have a bit of time together afterwards.

'She's very inspiring,' the guide said, walking away as he called through his microphone for people to move up and make room for latecomers. Fran watched him working with the other stewards to chivvy the audience into the few remaining seats.

The murmur of voices rose, then fell away as the Chairman of the local group led Brenda up the steps and on to the rostrum. Also in black, she held her notes loosely in her hand, placing them nonchalantly on the lectern as she passed. She tucked her handbag under the table and while she waited for the introduction to finish she scanned the audience, her head turning from side to side, challenging and confident. Fran envied the composure of the woman, who looked as comfortable in the large hall as she had been in her own kitchen.

'... distinguished worker in the field of international agreements ... prominent at Rio ... important part in drawing up the Kyoto protocol ... works with the Third World Network ...' No wonder she could draw crowds of the converted.

Despite herself, Fran was impressed by the lecture. Brenda presided over her material, and her audience, with easy grace. Her slides were professional, the words carefully pruned to give one simple message on each, with their white letters on a blue background, accentuated with sparse touches of yellow. Before she retired Fran had become a tutor to the trainee drug reps and she could find no fault with the visual aids that were flashing up in a steady stream to punctuate the speaker's words at exactly the right time.

Brenda spoke about the half-truths that were used by the biotech companies to try to allay the public's fears. Their claim, that only one gene was transferred, did not make sense. For each transfer there had to be a promoter and a terminator, plus an antibiotic selection marker, whatever that was. Viruses were used as promoters, like CaMV 35S, the cauliflower virus. Fran took out a pencil and noted the number on the back of an unpaid bill. The speaker continued to explain that, of course, we eat more of this virus in cauliflower and broccoli than we do in GM foods. She paused dramatically, took a sip of water, and delivered her punch line. 'When we eat it in naturally occurring food, the DNA has a protein coat. In GM foods it is naked.'

Fran had an image of a microscopic creature waiting to sink sharp teeth into the lining of her stomach. This creature could escape to other crops by 'horizontal transfer'. That must depend on the range that fertilising insects could travel, she thought, and the strength and direction of the wind. It seemed that nobody knew what distance was needed for the safe isolation of the new crops. In Brenda's view no government had done the necessary research. New organisms, new DNA, new proteins that had never existed in the world before, had been let loose without proper tests. Deadly substances lurked to poison us. Or if not us, then our children.

The audience sat silent. Fran was surprised to hear no cries of encouragement or chanted slogans to punctuate the speech. This crowd didn't sing songs as they had done on the CND march. When it was time for questions they didn't heckle. A uniform sense of outrage seemed to cover a deep despair. The questions were all about what could be done. Governments and peoples must be influenced somehow; but what could individuals do?

The room slowly cleared as Fran waited by the door. Walking down between the chairs Brenda continued to talk to the admirers who pressed around her. Looking up, she caught sight of Fran and waved for her to join them. On the doorstep she took her arm with a gesture that dismissed her followers. 'Come on, we'll go and get a cup of tea.'

Fran felt privileged to have been singled out by the goddess of the rostrum. Brenda ordered Earl Grey tea with lemon. Fran's own cup of Darjeeling, made pallid by the milk she added, was conventional and boring. She would have liked a cake but was inhibited by the ascetic woman across the table. When she saw the woman ladle two spoonfuls of sugar into her tea she was reminded of the digestive biscuits she had devoured in her own kitchen. Signalling to the waitress, Fran ordered a piece of buttered toast; a reasonable compromise.

'I enjoyed your lecture,' she said. The remark fell, inadequate, into the murmur that filled the café.

Brenda flashed her surprising smile. 'Thank you. I think it went well enough.'

'What is the Third World Network?' Fran asked.

'It's an alliance of undeveloped countries that want to defend themselves from the ravages of big business, forced on them by the Western World. They sometimes ask me to help with their negotiations.'

'Gosh, you are important.'

Brenda looked down as she stirred her tea. For the first time Fran noticed dark rings under her eyes. Her face seemed to have collapsed, as if the elastic that had held it up when she was on the platform had perished and allowed the skin to sag in loose folds.

'I do what I can. It's so important.'

'D'you really think we're going to poison the world?' Fran found it hard to believe that so many scientists, all those working at Nonsec and the other big companies, could be wrong. It must be right to try and develop better crops to feed the world, better drugs to cure illnesses. She had been proud when she talking to doctors about new drugs and heard that they worked. At least for some patients.

'I don't say we should stop all experiments. One day we may have a safe way of modifying the genetic make-up of living organisms. The trouble is that we are going too fast. Look at Dolly the sheep. She was the result of nearly three hundred attempts. Because they did succeed, eventually, we have the possibility of creating cloned humans beings. That is horrific.'

'Just because something can be done, it doesn't mean it will be.' Fran was struggling to keep her thoughts rational, to hang on to her belief in the basic decency of those who held power in the world.

'I don't have your faith in human nature,' Brenda said. 'It wouldn't be so bad if the research was funded properly by the government. At the moment, the companies are the driving force. In their search for quick profits they cut corners, don't do adequate safety tests, spend their money chasing rainbows instead of doing those things that we know would help the poor. Why can't they put their resources into providing clean water and basic health care? I'll tell you why not, it's because there's no money in those things.' She paused, as if she realised her tone of voice was more suited to the platform than to a small tea table and an audience of one. She seemed to shrivel into herself as she added, 'I have to keep fighting them, with every ounce of energy that I have left, even if it kills me.' She looked across at Fran. 'It's such lonely work. It was different when Paul was alive . . .'

Fran put her triangle of toast down on her plate. It lay there, the bitten corner indented with tooth marks. She chewed on the piece in her mouth, each movement a supreme effort of her muscles. Her tongue changed the bolus from one side of her mouth to the other. It wouldn't go down. Outside the confines of her skin the world retreated. With a final effort she swallowed. Her hand went out to raise her cup. The hot liquid burned her throat. 'You were having an affair with him,' she spluttered. It was a statement, not a question. She knew in every cranny of her being that it was true. Geoffrey had tried to warn her. Hazel wanted to protect her from something. Even Sylvia . . . oh God, perhaps even her daughter knew that she had been betrayed.

How could she have been so blind? Fran didn't look at the woman opposite, wanting only to run from the room. But she couldn't run from the knowledge that was deep inside her, hollowing out the centre of her being. She looked at her hands, the nails clean and neat as befitted an ex-drug rep, the joints no more swollen that those of any other woman of her age. Her suit covered her body, an egg-cosy hiding a shell, the inside eaten away. If she sat very still she might delay her disintegration for a few moments.

Brenda's voice reached her from far away. 'I'm sorry. Did you never suspect?'

Fran glanced up and looked down again. This woman had nothing to do with her. Not now. When, oh when, did Paul leave her? His body was there, coming into the house and going out again, but his soul was somewhere else. The memory of his hands as he had dried her hair that first day in the park came flooding back. He was with her then. Those weeks after Sylvia was born, surely he was still devoted to her. And later: on the beach, in the new house, at Sylvia's graduation. Didn't he belong to them then? He had seemed to be there but he wasn't. He was playing with someone else's kitten.

Brenda was speaking again. 'I've lost him too, you know.' She lifted her cup and drank. 'He was never really mine, always it was you. You and Sylvia. That was why he wouldn't resign with me. He said he couldn't hurt you. He dishonoured himself for your sake.'

Fran shook her head. She didn't want to hear.

'Once I resigned it was different. I was so angry that he had betrayed our work, I kicked him out of my bed. But he was still supportive, he visited occasionally and encouraged me to continue the fight.'

Something in her voice made Fran look up. Two tears quivered on the pale cheeks. She had no right to cry; Paul was not her husband. Her claim to be bereaved was out of order. Fran wanted to tip the table up and send the cheap metal teapot flying into her lap. If the water still held enough heat it would scald her, scald those thighs and run down to blister those parts that had held her man. She wound her fingers together to stop them escaping from her control. 'How could you?'

Brenda gave a small shrug of her shoulders. 'These things aren't planned. They happen. He cared so passionately about the things I cared about . . .'

So that was where his passion had gone. Despite herself, Fran thought of the article that Brenda had given her. It was lying folded, a foreign body wedged between the familiar contents of her handbag. She reached down and handed it across the table. 'I don't understand why you gave me this. It doesn't prove the genetically modified organisms caused the illness – it might as easily have been the filtration process.' The words could be coming from someone else's mouth. For the first time in her life Fran didn't apologise for her scientific ignorance. It no longer mattered if she wasn't clever enough. Nothing mattered any more.

Brenda took the photocopied sheets and laid them on the table. 'I realised after I'd given this to you that it might not make much sense. I was so startled when you called . . .' You could have fooled me, Fran thought, '. . . I hoped that if I started at the beginning of our troubles you might understand. We were using the same process. 37 people died, you know.'

'The paper said nothing about any deaths.'

'They happened after it was written. We were in danger of causing the illness, of killing people in the same way, if we went ahead with the clinical trials.' She raised the sheets and shook them in front of Fran's face. 'This paper started our suspicions about the use of GM organisms. We've been proved right. The Soya bean showed the desperate dangers of such meddling.'

Fran wasn't interested, but it was easier to ask what had happened rather than try to think.

'They introduced a gene from the Brazil nut, and people who were allergic to those nuts had severe reactions to the Soya. That's why we have to fight for detailed labelling of everything. That's why we should stop mixing the species, playing God with nature.'

Tiredness swept over Fran like a tsunami. She put her elbows on the table and covered her face with her hands. It didn't matter to her now. Her life had been a fraud. He hadn't loved her, he'd loved this obsessional, dried-up stick of a woman, with her pale skin and her strong, evangelistic voice.

The arguments battered her; she didn't know what to believe. That nice man who had found her a seat was gentle, just as Paul had been. If he, and all those young people, believed what Brenda said, perhaps she was right. 'I must go. Maybe we can talk again another day. I'll try to understand, but it's all too much for me now.' She put three one-pound coins on the table. They looked unreal, as if their chocolate centres were covered with yellow foil. Standing up she resisted the temptation to take them back. 'That should cover my tea.'

Brenda put out her hand. 'Don't go just yet. There's something I have to say.'

Fran sat down again, on the edge of her chair. She needed to disentangle herself and get home. She wanted to cry or throw things or lock herself in the garage with the engine running. She'd block up the cracks and drink a bottle of whisky so she could fall asleep forever. She would have to make sure Bruiser was nowhere near; he mustn't get gassed. She cared nothing about genes or the poor of the world: but she did care about her dog.

Looking across the table, she longed to leave the woman to her secrets and her passions. But the recollection, that her home was no longer the safe place it had been, helped to keep her on her seat. 'What is it?'

'I don't know how to say this.'

'If you want to say you're sorry, don't. Sorry is not an adequate word.'

'It's not that. I am sorry, of course. I know that can't help. No . . .' She paused. 'I think I want to ask for your help. Help in trying to find out what really happened to Paul.'

'Whatever do you mean? He died . . . of cardiomyopathy and heart failure.'

'I know.' She paused. 'Cardiomyopathy is a funny thing. The muscles swell and soften so that the heart enlarges –'

'I was with him all the time. We had oxygen at home, but in the end they took him to hospital and connected him to some machine. His breathing got worse and they had to sedate him. He became unconscious and died.' She had been there and done what a wife could do. He'd clung to her and looked into her eyes for a brief moment. Surely he'd loved her then.

Brenda broke into her reverie. 'D'you think his heart was weakened in some way?'

'I don't know what you're suggesting. If you think he died of a broken heart, just because you wouldn't let him into your bed any more, you're mad. You may have been important to him – but not so important that he would die for love of you. Of that I'm quite sure.'

'No, no, I didn't mean that.' Brenda withdrew into herself again. 'I expect I'm wrong. It was just that . . . I don't know. He no longer told me what he was doing at work. I fear it was something . . . unorthodox, against company policy. That wouldn't be safe.'

The memory of the green car parked in her village prompted Fran to ask one last question. 'What do you know about a chap called Jackson? I think he joined the company after you left.'

'I've heard the name. He became a great favourite with Martin, I believe. Why do you ask?'

'Oh, nothing. He seems to be interested in the work Paul was doing before he died. That's all.'

Brenda leaned forward. 'Do you know what Paul was doing?'

Fran didn't want to confess her ignorance to her rival. 'He never brought his work home.' The fact that he had changed his routine in the last weeks of his life was no business of hers. Brenda was obviously as much in the dark as she was. 'I must go, my dog will be getting desperate.'

'Take care.'

Fran blundered out of the shop and down the street. Not focusing her eyes properly she bumped into two young men who shouted at her. 'Sorry,' she said automatically, even though they hadn't been looking where they were going either.

'Silly cow,' one said to the other, with a scornful laugh. Yes, she was a silly cow, silly to have been so trusting of her husband. She was furious now, not with the woman she had just left, but with the man who had deceived her all those years. Serve him right if he had died too young.

When she reached the car Bruiser jumped up to welcome her. A small patch of grass proved inadequate for his needs. Fran looked up, hoping no one was watching as the yellow liquid trickled into the road. She hurried him back into the car before he had time to produce anything worse. As she climbed into the driving seat she found she was shaking again. Oh God, for just one drink. A pub sign advertising *The Ship* hung over the road. In her state she was unfit to drive anyway, so just one glass with a sandwich could do no harm. She got out again, locked the car door and walked towards the entrance. As she did so the bells in the tower of St Mary Redcliffe rang out in an incongruous peal of joy, that made her cover her ears. Without any conscious decision her feet changed their direction.

As she entered the church a priest was standing near the door, talking to a middle-aged woman. He smiled at her but said nothing, for which she was grateful. She wasn't a religious person and hadn't been inside a place of worship since she had stood in the chapel at the crematorium, watching Paul's coffin disappear behind the discreet, blue curtains.

Sitting in one of the St Mary's pews, she remembered that Brenda hadn't been at the short service. Perhaps she was afraid of meeting people from the company that had fired her. Sylvia had clasped Fran's right hand while Hazel had held her arm on the other side. The pressure had been irritating, for she had known she would not let herself collapse. She'd repeated her Father's old-fashioned words, fortitude and courage, over and over again, to keep erect. Afterwards, from within her numbness, she had found something to say to each person who shook her hand and mouthed faltering words of comfort.

Now, as she sat at the back of the church, the same feeling of deadness enveloped her. She couldn't think why she had gone in. Perhaps she'd hoped that the soaring arches, the history of troubles held and soothed over the centuries, might offer her comfort and keep her from entering the pub. But she felt nothing. No rescue descended from the lofty spaces to absorb her pain into that of a larger, suffering humanity.

She got up to fetch one of the pamphlets that described the features of the church. Holding it in her hand to ward off strangers, she wandering down the north isle, behind the altar and back the other side. Nothing grabbed her attention. Only as she made her way towards the exit did she notice the model of the *Matthew* in a niche above the door. The ship, replicated a few years earlier, had taken Cabot on his voyage to the Americas. She looked down at the leaflet in her hand and read that sailors through the ages had used the church for blessings before they set out on their voyages. Bristol, where she had been born, was first and foremost a port, a place where journeys began and to which those with luck were able to return.

Walking back towards her car she knew herself to be travelling on a different kind of journey. She lifted her chin and allowed herself to face what she had been denying all those years. Her marriage had been a sham. But even as she looked at that truth she had to accept another. There must have been some reason he'd returned home night after night, week after week. If the marriage held nothing for him, surely, once Sylvia had left home, he would have moved out.

Brenda had hinted he was doing something dangerous. Fran couldn't get her head round that idea. He was such a cautious person. When Sylvia was little he was the one who saw bumps in the ground where she might trip; and he always seized her hand to cross a road. He never took her on a boat until she could swim, even in a life jacket. The man she'd married didn't take risks.

The engine of her car started with its usual ease. As she nosed into the rush hour traffic a picture of Paul, on the day they had met, flashed into her mind. She saw him stepping out to stop the lorries, so that the old woman could cross the road. That had been a risk and his eyes had sparkled. She'd seen the same expression on his face near the end of his life. Something had rekindled his passion. But Brenda had no more idea what had set him alight than she had. The knowledge was both a consolation and a disappointment.

If Brenda didn't know the answer to her questions she would have to go back to Geoffrey. The prospect was not unpleasant. When an unknown woman in the car next to her at the traffic lights turned and smiled, Fran found herself smiling back.

EIGHT

1973

Paul walked along the corridor and knocked on Martin's door. The clipped 'Come in,' made him smile. Of all the men he knew, Martin was the most consistent. His voice, clothes and movements were always spare and functional, as if his past experience in the mountains had taught him to live with a minimum of fuss.

'Good holiday?' he asked.

'Wonderful.' The trip to the seaside was now a fixture in Paul's calendar. 'Sylvia had a great time. She learnt to surf last year and is really confident now.' Too late, Paul remembered that Martin's only child had died of leukaemia. Paul didn't even know if he was still with his wife. There had been no other children, he'd learned that much from the office grapevine.

Martin didn't seem to notice his discomfort as he took up a memo from his desk. 'Things are moving fast,' he said. 'After more than a year, and every snag you could imagine, the two boards are meeting today. If all goes well the merger will be announced this evening. The company shares are rising rapidly.' His keen eyes bored into Paul's face. 'You don't have any, do you?' Paul shook his head. 'Thank goodness for that.' Martin let out a small sigh. 'I want no one from my department making a fortune by insider trading.' He paused, then asked, 'Have you seen Brenda yet?'

'No. I've looked at her summary of the preliminary report of the trial. So far so good.'

'She's making no claims yet, which is sensible, seeing there isn't enough evidence to go on. She's got a level head on those shoulders.' He looked down at the paper in his hands. 'If there are no more hitches we might be in the new building soon after

Christmas. Then the two of you can really get things moving. The journey will be easier for you then.'

Through a crack in the professional crust Paul glimpsed what might be human warmth. Or maybe his boss was only interested in getting his staff to work in good time. Paul flinched; he should have come even earlier and visited the lab before he presented himself.

Martin stood up from his desk. 'I'll try and let you know the answer tonight, before you leave. Then you and Brenda can give your minds to future plans.'

As he went along the corridor to the lab, Paul's step lightened with pleasant expectation. The first thing he saw was Brenda's back where she sat at a table she had moved under the window. Only one technician worked with her, cleaning the cages with disinfectant. The others had taken their holidays while the programme was between batches of animals. For a moment he stood imagining her face, as it had been when he last saw her. She sensed his gaze and turned, taking off her glasses to smile up at him. Her blue eyes shone with warmth. He took her proffered hand in both of his.

'I'm so glad you're back,' she said. Then, as if to justify her enthusiasm, she added, 'There's a lot of work piling up.'

In her office he perched on a corner of the desk while she filled him in. The next compound they were going to try was undergoing purity tests and would be ready for the first rat trial in a few weeks. 'Could we manage with half the number for this preliminary study?' Brenda asked.

Paul frowned. 'I doubt it.' What an odd thing to ask. She must know the numbers had to be big enough for rigorous statistical analysis. 'What made you suggest that?'

'I know I'm stupid but I just hate to see so many of them suffering.' She ran her hand through her hair in the gesture Paul knew so well. 'I wish we had a different method to study the toxicology of the drugs. Is it right that other species should endure so much for the benefit of human beings?'

It was the first time Paul had heard a proper scientist voice such an idea. He'd come to accept the use of animals as a matter of course – he took the greatest care of them. 'Surely they have as good a life as they would in the wild. Nature isn't so kind.'

Brenda sighed. 'You're right, of course. I just want to check, each time we design a study, to make sure we don't use more than we have to. Is that OK by you?'

He nodded and turned to look at her profile as she gazed through the door into the lab. Her nose turned up just a fraction at the end. 'Absolutely all right.' After a moment he went on, 'It's difficult to plan, not knowing when we're going to move.'

'It's not just the space. If we set up the new batch of animals here, and then have to shift them to another building, they'll be thoroughly unsettled. The results will be useless.'

As so often during the time she'd worked with him, Paul wanted to put his arm round her thin shoulders. 'I think it's all coming to a head between the companies.' He wouldn't raise her hopes by telling her it was decision day, in case it fell through. She'd done such a good job, she deserved the room to develop her own ideas: under his protection, of course. 'You haven't moved out of your rented room yet?'

'No.' She made a face. 'I must buy my own house and settle down. But there's no point till we're sure of the move.'

'You've never had your own place?'

'I didn't want to be tied down. My father was in the army and I quite enjoyed moving about as a child.' Paul knew that both her parents were dead and that she had no siblings. 'I'm used to being on my own but I need a base now.'

Her voice held no trace of self-pity; she was just giving him the facts. For the first time he sensed that he was in the company of a woman who might feel patronised if he gave in to his impulse to cherish and protect her. 'I'd better try and catch up on the journals,' he said. ' I've probably missed a lot while I've been away.'

'I've jotted down a few references that you might find interesting. There's some basic stuff in *Nature* on the genome that caught my eye, and Smith and Ague have a trial with a drug very similar to ours. Just two radicles in different positions.'

'Thanks, I'll start with those. You OK here?'

'Fine. The clean up is going well. I'll visit the animal house later to make sure there are enough when we need them.' She looked anxious as she added, 'I won't let my squeamishness interfere with our work.'

'I never thought you would.' He gave her a reassuring smile but felt a twinge of envy. So often now she seemed to be a step in front of him. With no family to worry about, she was free to devote all her energies to her science.

Back in his own office he immersed himself in his reading. At lunch he went to the cafeteria. An expectant air hung over the metal trays and chipped china so that the usual buzz of conversation was subdued. The table at the end, used exclusively by senior management, was empty. The fact that senior management was busy elsewhere was obvious to the restless staff, whose hopes and fears for the future of their jobs flitted across their faces. Brenda would have picked up the vibes – he'd been stupid to try to keep the news from her.

He was still sitting in his office when she popped her head round the door to say she was going home, and he was grateful she didn't ask what time he planned to leave. Determined to wait for Martin's return, he phoned Fran to warn her he would be later than expected. She said, with a sigh, that she'd keep his meal hot. The disappointment in her voice grated. When she added that it would be too dark for him to help Sylvia build some jumps for her pony, he recognised the implied blackmail. If he wouldn't go home for her, perhaps he would make the effort for his precious daughter.

After replacing the phone he tried to concentrate on the paper in front of him but it was useless. He threw it down on the desk. No one moved in the building and he felt so alone. If only he'd asked Brenda to wait with him; her absence was a sore that chafed his side.

By the time he heard footsteps, the windows were dark. Martin closed the door behind him before saying, 'It's all settled.'

Paul pulled the second chair up to his desk. His boss looked exhausted.

'Once the agreement was signed and the publicity boys went to prepare their press statements, the department heads had to wade in and try to agree a strategy. Geoffrey was difficult. I had to argue hard but I got my way in the end.' He looked up, his thin smile conspiratorial. 'We'll be moving to Keynsham.'

'That's wonderful,' Paul said.

'Yes.' Martin was silent for a moment as he gazed at Paul's bare walls as if clothing them with his own images. 'No climbing for me this year.'

'I didn't know you still climbed?'

'I haven't for ages. Recently, my wife's developed an interest in garden history. She's going with a group to Italy. I had hoped to spend that time in Switzerland with a friend. Thought I might try the Jungfrau . . . one of the easier routes, of course.' He seemed to sink lower into his chair. 'Have to put it off again.' He sighed. 'I miss the mountains.'

Paul's admiration for mountaineers bordered on idolatry. Climbers fought nature, testing the limits of their strength, as he had wanted to do in Africa. No wonder Martin had the guts to outwit someone like Geoffrey. As the older man pulled himself out of the chair, Paul felt a surge of warmth. They would do all right as a team. Together they might even create a breakthrough drug that would really make a difference in the world.

When he eventually reached home Paul found Sylvia grooming her grey pony by the light of a lantern. He leaned on the stable door and watched her working over the animal with firm, knowledgeable hands. She lifted each hoof with confidence, cleaning out the mud and stones with the special tool he'd given her. She'd grown fast during the year they'd owned the creature; her body was developing the curves of a young woman.

Paul smiled to himself as the fumes from a new pile of dung reached his nose. He had managed to set his family up in the style he'd planned for them, without losing his integrity. If all went well he would have his own department in a few years. He might even aspire to a seat on the board, gained by his own efforts, not Geoffrey's patronage.

As he turned away from the stable and walked towards the back door he composed his face into the smile with which he habitually greeted his wife. 'How's things?' he asked as he kissed her cheek, noticing some yellow paint on her fingers. 'You've been busy upstairs?'

'Just dabbling.'

'I'd like to see what you've done.'

'It's nothing. Not worth showing you.' She twisted away from him and went on stirring the fried onions. The smell made him hungry. He glanced at his watch. Fran looked up and frowned. 'I'm sorry, the meal's not ready yet. I got carried away.'

'I'm glad you were enjoying yourself. Sylvia is still messing about with the pony. I'll have a packet of crisps to keep me going. What's for supper?'

'Only the remains of the joint –'

You know that's one of my favourite dishes. Can I do anything to help? Lay the table?'

'It's done. I won't be long. Get yourself a drink.'

Paul would have liked to stay with her. His hope that they might become intimate again when they moved into the new house had come to nothing. He couldn't understand what he'd done wrong, for he still loved her, with a deep commitment that he thought could withstand the wintry shroud of their almost non-existent sex life. On the rare occasions when he felt able to approach her he was tolerated, nothing more.

The books told him that the woman wanted cuddles and reassurance after the act of love. In his marital bed it was he who lay listening to her regular breathing, feeling he had forced himself on her and been accepted as a gesture of charity. Then he was supposed to feel grateful, his carnal needs satisfied for the next few months.

As he poured himself a sherry he remembered the look on her face, in the days when she had wanted him. The only time he caught a glimpse of that passion was when she emerged from the little room at the top of the house, after a session with her paints.

With a swift step he climbed the stairs, his glass in his hand. He had to see what it was that could satisfy her when he could not. Several canvases were propped up, facing into the walls. In front of the window her easel supported a picture that was a tumult of colour. At the bottom left-hand corner a grey patch invaded the blues and reds, sending out disturbing, octopus-like fingers. The yellow splashes at the top could have been stylised birds or lizards. He turned his head to the side and half closed his eyes. Was it an underwater scene?

A gasp from the door made him jump. Fran pushed past him and dragged the canvas from the stand. 'Don't look. I told you not to.' She reached for a palate knife and began to slash at the picture.

'Hey, stop that.' He tried to wrest it from her hands but her grip was too tight. 'It's great, don't spoil it.'

'It's private. No good anyway.' She threw it across the room and turned to him. 'This is my place, I don't want you up here. You've got your study downstairs, go to your books and leave me to my messes.'

Paul looked at her contorted face, hardly recognising the wife he thought he knew. 'I'm sorry.' As he retreated down the stairs he found he was shaking, aware that he had breached some invisible barrier.

He didn't often spend much time in the room that Fran had prepared for him with so much care, preferring to do his reading in the lab where he had access to the library. Now as he sat at his desk and surveyed his books he tried to calm himself.

He looked up as Sylvia came through the door. 'What's up with Mummy?' she asked.

Paul pulled a face. 'It was my fault. I went upstairs to look as the painting she's doing. She hates anyone to see her work.'

'Poor Mummy.' Sylvia sounded older that her years. She came and leant against him as if she would like to snuggle into his lap as she had done when she was younger. He put his arm round her. 'I'll tell you a secret Daddy. I sometimes creep up and look when I know she's busy in the kitchen. Is that very wicked?'

'Just don't let her catch you.'

'I'll be careful.' She paused. 'Some of them are a bit strange, aren't they? I wish she'd paint things I could recognise.'

'Yes, I know, but it takes time to learn to look at paintings so you can find your own pictures inside them. I don't understand them either.' For a moment Paul was tempted to tell her how excluded he felt, but he reminded himself she was still only a child. 'We all need our own space. Tell me about your plans for Silver. Are you going to ride him at the next gymkhana?'

'We're going to enter several races. Will you help me put up some jumps in the paddock at the weekend? We need to practise.'

'I'll enjoy that.' Paul was soothed by the knowledge that he could be of some use.

Fran made an effort to be cheerful over supper. Sylvia regaled them with details of the hand and leg controls needed to get her pony over a jump in good style. Her parents felt ignorant, but proud.

In bed that night Fran apologised for her temper. 'I know it's silly of me to be so sensitive. I don't understand what I'm doing when I try to paint. All I know is that it never turns out as I want. Even if no one else looks at them, I have an urge to destroy what I have created.'

'I promise I'll never go up to your room again, unless you invite me.' Paul put his hand on her thigh and wondered if he dared to move closer. Fran lay stiff but put her hand over his as she said, 'Thanks. That makes me feel safer.'

Then she turned on her side with a brief goodnight, as if the day could not end soon enough.

Strobe lights illuminated the firm party that Christmas for the first time. Paul made an effort to be more sociable than usual. He managed to get round the dance floor with a couple of the secretaries, then asked Fran to take a turn with him. After he'd led her back to the table, where Geoffrey was buying another round of drinks, he went across the room to Brenda. Her red dress shivered over her body as she encouraged his feet into steps they had never tried before. She tilted her head, eyes playful as she looked up at him. Her smile broke into laughter. He hadn't heard the sound before – she didn't laugh in the lab. He'd known their minds were in tune but the experience, of two bodies moving as one, was a revelation. And a terror. Her fingers entwined with his for a moment as the music stopped.

He had to get away. He pleaded a headache and almost dragged Fran from the room.

That night his wife did allow him to make love to her. As he moved he tried desperately to keep the details of her face behind his closed lids. All he could see were deep blue pools in a pale skin, tinged pink with excitement. He finished quickly, it had been a long time. Fran turned away from him with a sigh.

On Christmas morning he went to see to the animals. He never asked the technicians to work during their Christmas break – he could do the jobs quickly and get back in time for the family meal. Fran's parents were coming and she was anxious to show that she could provide the traditional food to her mother's high standards.

The evening before, he had helped with the sprouts and peeled all the chestnuts, almost scalding his fingers as he took them from the boiling water. Fran had passed him her kitchen gloves, continuing to stuff the turkey with her bare hands. Sylvia had been upstairs in her room, preparing some secret. This is how it should be, he'd thought. We are a happy family.

Going straight to the lab, he stopped short when he saw Brenda adjusting the drip feed to one of the cages.

She looked up as he entered. 'I won't bite,' she said, as he stood frozen by the door.

'I d-didn't expect you to come in today.'

'I wanted to see you.'

'Did you?'

She nodded, her eyes on his face. He moved to her side as the attraction that had sparked between them on the dance floor returned with overpowering force. His arms went round her shoulders as he hugged her to him. Then she raised her head so he could press his lips against hers. 'Did you really want to see me?' he asked, as he released her.

'Of course.' She pulled herself against him and they kissed with a passion that swept them both into a place apart, oblivious to anything outside the boundary of their own bodies. They sank to the floor, fumbling with clothes, driven by a blinding sense of urgency. Paul was engulfed by the joy of being wanted. He opened his eyes and found her smiling at him. 'Take your time. Enjoy me as much as I am enjoying you.'

'Is it all right? I'm not hurting you?' With Fran, even at moments of heightened tension, he was always afraid of thrusting too hard and damaging something deep inside her.

Brenda gurgled. 'Hurting me? It's wonderful, I've wanted you so much.'

He moved, then stopped. 'The floor must be awfully hard, are you really OK?' He couldn't believe how easy it was to talk and he had no fear of losing his erection. As the thought came into his mind he felt himself going soft. 'Oops' he said, and knew the loss was unimportant; it would come again and she would understand.

'I can think of more comfortable places, but needs must . . .' she laughed. The sound carried him back to that moment at the party and they began to move together as if they were dancing again. He had forgotten it could be like this. Over the years with Fran he had gained some control, but as the distance between them had grown, his fear of doing something wrong had made him clumsy: and quick. Now there was a natural rhythm that joined them, as if the facets of each separate being were perfectly designed to fit the other, like the ball and socket of a hip joint.

After a while she moved on top of him. 'It's your turn to suffer the floor,' she said, and he let her take charge, revelling in her confidence.

Afterwards he lay by her side, beyond thought or words, knowing only that he was fulfilled in a way he had never been before. His desire was not, after all, something dangerous. This woman enjoyed his passion. The very core of his being had been loved.

Gradually he came to realise where he was. And where he was supposed to be. 'I have to get back for lunch. What about you?'

'I've got plans. I'm OK.'

He sat up and rubbed a hand across his forehead. 'That shouldn't have happened.' Even to his own ears, it didn't sound convincing. The feeling of comfort between them was so strong, it was difficult to feel guilty.

'I know. You're a married man. My mother warned me not to mess with them. But I won't make trouble, I promise.'

Paul couldn't think. Driving home he floated in a limbo of contentment that filled him with new confidence. As the rituals of the season were negotiated he had no difficulty being polite to his in-laws, gentle with Fran and loving towards his daughter. The memory of the morning lubricated his day.

It was not until he was lying in bed that night that he began to wonder what he was going to do. Would Brenda want some commitment from him? There was no way he would leave Fran, ever. For him 'till death do us part' meant just that. If she really hated sex so much perhaps she wouldn't mind if he saw Brenda occasionally? Even as that thought came into his mind, he rejected it. Women were possessive creatures; she would be so hurt she would never forgive him.

The consolations of confession and absolution were not for him. He must find the strength to hold it inside him, a secret like the magpies in the child's rhyme. 'One for sorrow, two for joy ... seven for a secret that's never been told'. He must push it down into that other part of him, where he mourned for the trip to Africa, and for the father he never had. Just for a moment, as he had merged with Brenda on the floor, those pains had been eased.

A few days later they walked along the path by the river, both aware that their hands were not touching. It was one of those still, winter afternoons, the surface of the water glassy in the mild air. The trees stood silent along the bank on the far side, each individual twig etched against the sky. The world waited, held its breath, neither in the grip of frost nor yet with any expectation of spring. Paul drew the air into his nostrils but found no lingering trace of autumn smoke, nothing to identify a season of any sort. With his senses heightened it was as if time itself had paused on his skin. He shortened his stride, to match his step to hers.

He hated to break the silence but it had to be done. 'I can't leave my wife, you know.'

'I wouldn't want you to.'

'How can we go on working together?'

'This need make no difference,' she said.

He walked on for several minutes, before he broke the silence. 'I don't see how it can fail to change things. We can't let it happen again.'

'If that's what you want.'

Of course he didn't want to deny himself, or her, but he had to be strong. He wasn't the sort of person who could dissemble for long. He was too honest; at least, he thought he was. Little did he know that this was the beginning of a falsehood that would last for the rest of his life, one he would learn to wear with some semblance of ease. If only the two women could merge into one, like the pictures on two sides of a coin. He longed to feel again the ease of his first months with Fran, the lift when he felt she wanted him, lusted after him. Then he would be able to renounce the joy that Brenda had so unexpectedly provided.

They resisted temptation till the day Brenda moved into her terrace house. Paul helped her transport her belongings from her room, loading his estate car with her television, books and the cooking utensils she had been collecting. She threw open the doors from the kitchen into the small back garden. 'What do you think of it?' she asked

Before he could reply there was a ring at the door. A van had pulled up on to the pavement. The new furniture she'd ordered was carried in and it didn't take long for the pieces to be spread out between the few rooms of the house. As soon as the men had gone Brenda rummaged in one of the carrier bags and extracted two mugs and a kettle.

'I'll just run to the shop on the corner and get some milk.' Despite the piles of boxes and books, Paul felt comfortable. As they sat drinking their tea, Brenda said, 'I think I'll get a cat. I've always wanted one but I've never had a home till now.'

It seemed natural for Paul to reach across and take her hand. He led her upstairs to her new bed, where she hastily threw a towel over the bare mattress. Their love-making flowed smoothly, reaching a simultaneous climax that transported them both and released them into peace.

From that time it was easy for Paul to visit her on his way home. He didn't go very often for their union never held quite the same magic for him as it had on those first two occasions. Each meeting was clouded by thoughts of Fran and Sylvia, who flitted, vulnerable, at the back of his mind, making him meticulously careful never to risk a scandal.

Over the months he began to feel Brenda's boundaries hardening, as if she were developing a carapace to protect herself from his repeated departures. She still responded to him in bed, apparently grateful, but she would sometimes hurry him out of the house, even before he needed to leave.

She never asked for more than his occasional visits, aware that they were all he could spare for her. Nevertheless, he sensed that a part of her was unfulfilled. He worried that he was standing in the way of her finding a partner who could give her more, although she reassured him that she had never wanted children. But as he took the long way back along the river, to the deserted park where he left his car, he dreamed of raising a boy with her. Despite her denials, when he watched her playing with the young Tibbles he saw a yearning in her face that made his heart contract. His inability to satisfy more than her immediate sexual needs re-opened old wounds. He saw his mother, her face haunted by a melancholy he could never chase away. He threw himself into his work.

NINE

1975

A searing flash lit the sky and the windows of Brenda's house rattled in the powerful blast. Paul leapt out of her bed. 'What in Christ's name is that?' Throwing himself at the curtains, he dragged them aside. A cloud of smoke was lit from below by an orange glow. 'My God, the labs.' He seized his clothes.

'I'm coming with you,' Brenda said.

'No, don't. We mustn't be seen together.' Even as he forced his legs into his trousers, he couldn't forget that their meetings had to be kept secret. He had left his car in the usual place. Normally he walked to and from the house by a variety of circuitous routes, not just to evade inquisitive eyes but as if to throw off the detective that was his conscience. Now he ran straight, started the engine, drove off and within minutes was turning into the gates. A fire engine already stood in front of the building and another swung into the courtyard behind him, ringing its bell. Men were running about shouting as they dragged hoses towards the fire. He left his car against the perimeter fence and strode up to the front door.

A policeman stopped him. 'You can't go in, sir. It's not safe.'

'But I work here, I must see about the rats.' In his mind Paul saw their bodies smoking and charred, some still writhing in agony, not quite dead, others choking in their cages as they desperately tried to escape the smoke.

A fireman hurried past. 'Anyone likely to be inside?' he asked.

Horror made Paul clutch his chest. His mind had been so set on the rats, he'd forgotten about his boss. An hour before he'd called a cheery 'goodnight' to Martin, who had been sitting at his desk, visible through the half-open door. Grabbing at the fireman's jacket, Paul said, 'Possibly. I'll show you.' He evaded the policeman's arm and was in at the door and up the stairs. The smoke got thicker. He began to cough and couldn't stop. The door to his office was off its hinges and a blast of heat coming down the corridor forced him to the floor, where he crouched on his knees, gasping for breath.

A man running past raised the mask of his breathing apparatus to call out, 'Go back. This is our job.'

Paul pointed down the corridor. 'On the right,' he choked, as he felt arms lifting him to his feet. 'Don't worry about me . . . he's still in there.'

Outside, he collapsed on the ground, coughing and retching. His eyes streamed, so that the men moving around him became blurred shapes, decorated by stars projected from behind his lids. He rubbed his hand across them and felt a searing pain, made worse when he blinked. Tottering to his feet, he took a few steps, swerving from side to side. He must let Fran know he was all right, get to her before she heard about the explosion from someone else. She would think he was still in the building – he'd phoned her earlier in the evening to say he would be working late.

Someone was coming out of the building with a shape draped over his shoulders. Paul knew without asking that it was Martin. The fire was a punishment, a judgement, not on his own head where it belonged, but on that of the person he most admired. He followed the men and reached the ambulance just as the doors were closing.

'Out of the way, please, sir,' one of the men said. How could they be so polite in the face of such horror?

Paul turned to the man nearest to him. 'Is he all right?'

'Burned, I'm afraid. Difficult to tell how badly.' The man put a hand on his shoulder. 'Friend of yours?'

'My boss.' No, not just his boss, he was a friend. 'I must go to him.' Paul tried to pull away.

'You can't do anything at the moment. Leave it to the professionals. You'd better come along to the hospital for a check-up, yourself. You got a lot of smoke in there.'

He allowed himself to be led into another ambulance, where he subsided on to the stretcher. After a minute he stood and tried to wipe the black marks off the pristine sheets. The grime that covered his hands only made them worse. 'What a mess,' he said to the ambulance man who sat opposite him.

'No matter. We're used to it.'

Paul realised he was being foolish but he felt responsible. For the first time he wondered how the fire had started. In his haste to reach Brenda's house he could have left the gas to the Bunsen burners turned on at the main. He frowned and felt the skin of his forehead stiff, as if it had a crust over the surface. 'D'you know what happened?' he asked.

'Not for certain. It might be those animal rights people. They're getting cheeky these days. I wouldn't put it past them to do something like this. You do work with animals in there, don't you, sir?'

Animal rights ... At least it wouldn't be his fault if there had been a bomb or something. How could anyone risk human life for the sake of a few rats? Anyway, the rats were far worse off now in their burnt cages. He tried not to think what it must be like in the building but he couldn't shut out the picture of Martin, sitting at his desk, his outline disappearing in drifts of smoke as flames sputtered at the door.

In the casualty department at the hospital he gave his details to the receptionist. She warned that there would be a wait to see the doctor. His question about Martin was met by a disinterested stare. Trudging across to the door, he repeated his question to a porter, who shook his head. 'Sorry, mate, they don't tell us anything.'

He found his way to the gents' and washed some of the dirt off his hands and face. The middle finger of his right hand was sore where a blister had formed. He couldn't find any other signs of damage but when he looked in the mirror, bloodshot eyes stared out at him below singed eyebrows.

Standing in the long queue for the public telephone his knees began to shake. He couldn't sit down or he would lose his place.

When he finally got through to Fran she was so distraught he hardly recognised her voice.

'Is that really you, Paul? Are you all right?'

He said he was fine, that he was only in the hospital for a check-up because of the smoke. She burst into tears. He explained that he'd just started home when he heard the explosion and had turned straight back. The lie came easily. 'It's Martin who's copped it. I think he's badly burned but no one will tell me.'

'Oh God. Hazel said someone had been hurt. I thought it was you.'

'No, really. I'm OK. Just a bit dazed.'

' I'll get back to Hazel. Geoffrey must see if Martin's wife knows.' Fran's voice was stronger now.

Paul felt he should have contacted her himself but what could he have said about that bundle, carried on a shoulder like a sack of coals? At the desk he badgered the receptionist again until she made a phone call. When she eventually put the receiver down she told him that his boss had been taken straight to the burns unit at Frenchay hospital and that his wife was on her way there.

Paul slumped into a chair and waited for what seemed like hours, feeling hot and cold in turns. If Martin had to die it should have been in the frozen heights of his beloved mountains, not suffocated and charred, a victim of fanatical bigotry.

When the doctor did at last reach the cubicle, he listened to Paul's chest and called a nurse to dress his hand. After putting drops in his eyes to see if the cornea was damaged, he said they were only inflamed. Both doctor and nurse tried to persuade him to stay in for observation but Paul shook his head dumbly. All he wanted was to get home. His car . . . where was his car?

The doctor fiddled impatiently with his stethoscope while Paul tried to solve the impossible problem. As he pulled himself to his feet, swaying slightly, the nurse drew back the drapes, exposing him to the main hall – and there was Fran, weaving her way towards him through the casualties.

Blinking his sore eyes, he realised he'd never been so glad to see her. She took hold of his undamaged hand and turned firmly to the doctor. She would take care of him and bring him back at once, if he wasn't well. The man moved away, apparently satisfied, and they went out to find the small car that she now had for her own use. Despite her new-found independence he was astonished that she had come. He would have expected her to wait for him to tell her what to do. Instead, she'd responded by herself to the crisis, materialising at the moment when he needed her most.

Stiffly, he climbed into the passenger seat. She slipped in behind the wheel and turned to touch his face before starting the engine. 'You need a bath. Let's get you home.' He leaned back and closed his eyes.

A week passed before he was fit enough to return to work. From the gate he could see the remains of the wing that had held the whole of his division. The roof was missing in places, the walls blackened. Clearly, the inside had been gutted.

Two uniformed officers flanked the regular doorman who was at his post. He told Paul that the whole place had been shut for several days while the police made extensive enquiries. Only the heads of department had been allowed into the undamaged parts of the building, escorted at all times by a policeman, to feed their animals and make the observations that were essential to their experiments.

Paul wondered who had been in charge of his section. Each day he'd rung the hospital to ask about Martin, and was told he'd suffered extensive burns that needed many skin grafts. That morning he had, at last, been taken off 'the critical list'.

Paul made his way towards the administration block. A hand-written notice propped on a chair told all members of staff belonging to his division to report to Room 87. When he got there a small queue had formed. Technicians and secretaries were talking in hushed voices. As he approached they moved aside and a silence fell.

Then a voice asked, 'You all right now, Mr Ashby?'

'Yes, thank you. Who's in charge here?'

'Someone's come over from the food division in Clifton.'

At that moment the door in front of him opened and Geoffrey put his head out. 'Paul. Glad you've made it. Come in.'

Casting an apologetic glance at the people waiting, he followed Geoffrey into the room. Mr Bennett, an influential member of the board, was perched behind a desk too small for his corporate bulk. Geoffrey sat himself alongside and waved towards the chair opposite.

'We're delighted you're here.' Mr Bennett scrutinised him from below his bushy eyebrows. 'Not too badly hurt, I hope?'

'I'm fine. I've tried to phone several times but the number was always engaged. I came as soon as I could – the doctor wouldn't let me leave the house till today. What's happening?'

Geoffrey answered. 'We're going to deploy your staff between the other sections. This is the first day they've been allowed inside. The police have been a real nuisance.' He leaned back in his chair, thoroughly in command.

Paul tried to keep his voice level as he asked, 'What are you doing here? Since we moved into this building you know nothing of our operations.'

Mr Bennett intervened. 'With Martin so badly damaged, and not knowing when you would be back, we had to move somebody in to organise the staff. The department won't be able to operate for a while. As you must have seen, the whole wing is destroyed. The rebuilding will be extensive.'

Paul stood up. If Geoffrey thought he could dismantle his department without even consulting him, he could think again. 'We must re-start our work immediately. We need an office and at least a rudimentary laboratory where we can redo the experiments that have been interrupted. Surely some space can be found for us in the other wings? We've two major drugs in the pipeline.' He stopped as he realised he hadn't seen Brenda outside. 'Where's my assistant?'

The two men exchanged glances. 'The police are still investigating her. That was another reason Geoffrey had to come and help with the restructuring.'

'Investigating her? Whatever for?'

'They say she has contacts with animal rights sympathisers. She's still helping them with their enquiries.'

'That's absurd.' Paul felt himself colouring as he remembered her remarks about not using more rats than necessary. But she would never do anything violent to jeopardise the work she loved so passionately. He moved forward and thumped the desk. 'We must fight to get her back immediately. She's essential to our team.' Mr Bennett's eyes narrowed as if he were seeing Paul for the first time. Geoffrey moved in his seat.

Paul examined the faces of both men. 'She is totally devoted to the work we are doing.' There was only one way he could make them understand. 'These drugs are potential money-spinners. If we stop now the company will lose thousands, if not millions, of pounds.'

'What do you suggest?' Mr Bennett asked.

'Find me some space and leave me my whole team. I can put the technicians to work at once. We must scrounge what equipment we can and buy replacements where necessary. The outlay will be minimal in comparison with future profits.'

Geoffrey sat forward. 'You won't need your clerical staff for a few weeks. I've drawn up plans for their redistribution. We can certainly use one of them in my own department – we're always so hard pressed. Besides, we owe it to them to provide continuous employment.'

His look of magnanimous concern infuriated Paul further. 'Of course we need them. All our papers have gone. Thank goodness the central library is intact. Our early results are stored in the archives, but there are several ongoing bits of work that will have to be rewritten. Brenda will oversee all that, she'll need every pair of hands she can get.'

'If they let her come back,' said Geoffrey.

Not deigning to look at him, Paul leant over towards Mr Bennett. 'You can use your influence to insist that each department vacate at least one room for us. We'll manage, even if we're scattered. Let's go now.' He turned and started to walk towards the door. To his relief he heard Mr Bennett get out of his chair. For a heavy man he could move quickly. By the time Paul had reached the door he was beside him. Geoffrey trailed behind.

Outside, Paul stopped to speak to the men and women who were waiting patiently. 'Has anyone else been hurt?' he asked. Heads were shaken and a murmur of sympathy spread along the line. Paul held up his hand and explained that they were going to find temporary accommodation. 'Go and find yourselves a snack or something.' He looked at his watch. 'I'll be back here at midday and I'll speak to you all then.'

Geoffrey hesitated as if he wanted to contradict him but Mr Bennett was already striding down the corridor. Paul hurried after him.

By eleven-thirty they had secured a small office, the promise of two rooms that could be used as labs and the possibility of a section in the basement for the secretaries. Paul worried about the artificial light and the grime of the accumulated years, but when he discussed it with the girls they said it would be fine, once they had scrubbed the place out. They went off to borrow aprons, buckets and scrubbing brushes from the domestic staff, who rallied round and offered to stay on to help.

As Paul moved around the corridors each person he passed gave him a smile and asked if he'd recovered. Some of the women eyed him in a way that gave him the uncomfortable feeling he had become some sort of hero. Martin deserved their admiration and sympathy, not a two-timing bastard like himself.

Geoffrey slunk off before they'd finished, pleading pressure of work. Mr Bennett gave a cursory nod towards his departing back. With Paul by his side he visited every remaining corner of the factory, before leading the way back to Room 87.

'This place is fairly central. Make it your office.' He waved his hand towards the chair behind the desk that he had been occupying when Paul first entered the room. 'I'm not going to breathe down your neck,' he continued. 'Do what has to be done. Put the development of those drugs back on track. I'll phone the police about your assistant.' He paused, noticing the fatigue that still hit Paul from time to time without warning. 'Delegate, as much as you can, you're not fully recovered yet. But I'm relying on you to pull the department through. Phone me at any time if your work is obstructed.'

Paul thanked him, aware that he had at least one ally in high places.

Not long after Mr Bennett left, a plain-clothes detective knocked and entered without waiting to be asked. He flashed his badge. 'A few minutes of your time, may I?' His smile was ingratiating.

'Of course. I was expecting you to contact me at home.'

'We've been very busy here, looking for evidence. Then we had to interview those we suspected might be implicated in this appalling crime.'

'Was it a bomb?' Paul asked

'All I can say at this stage is that we've found some evidence that it was started deliberately. Now Mr Ashby, I understand that you attended a number of CND marches in the sixties?'

Paul sat for a moment in shocked silence. 'You've got records?'

'It's not so long ago. Have you ever been associated with the animal activists?'

'How could I? We depend on animals for our research.'

'I see. How well do you know your assistant?'

Paul hesitated. If they knew so much about him, the man might also know about his affair with Brenda. 'I've worked with her for over three years now.'

'Not very long.'

The interrogator was studying his nails. Paul raised his voice. 'Quite long enough to know she would never do something like this.' As he spoke a doubt flashed through his mind. He composed himself. 'She's as passionate about our work as I am. We're investigating a whole range of new anti-depressants, it's a terribly important project.'

His adversary raised his head. For the first time Paul caught an expression of interest on his face. 'My wife suffers from depression.'

'You know what it's like, then.' He caught and held the man's eye. 'I mean, you of all people must know how badly we need drugs with minimal side effects.'

The man nodded. 'She gets so constipated –'

The door opened and Brenda came in. She halted as she recognised his visitor. 'You again.'

He stood up. 'I'm just going, Miss. Glad they let you back to work.' He glanced across at Paul. 'Your bosses spoke highly of you.' Moving to the door, he added, 'Can I reach you both here, if you're needed again?'

'Of course,' they said, in unison.

The door closed behind him and they stood looking at each other as Paul battled with the agitation inside him. He longed to put his arms round her but it was not just the window, open to the courtyard, which held him back.

'You think I was involved?' Brenda made no move towards him.

'I tried to stand up for you.'

'That's not what I asked.'

Paul looked away, ashamed of the doubt that was making him flounder. 'You were concerned for the rats. You know people –'

Brenda cut in. 'Don't you understand anything about the animal rights movement?'

'Not really.'

'You must know the differences between the various factions. You can't be so ignorant.' She stood rigid, staring at him. Paul looked up and away again, longing to escape the accusation in her eyes. He couldn't deny his suspicions, though he wasn't sure what he feared. Perhaps she'd talked carelessly to some die-hard campaigners; encouraged them, without realising what she was doing.

After a moment she sat heavily in the chair nearest to her. Picking up a pencil, she started to doodle on the list of references he had been struggling to compile from memory. She took a deep breath. 'Let me quote from an official definition.' She spoke with exaggerated care, as if he were a four-year old child. '"The welfarists accept most current uses of animals, but seek to minimise their suffering and pain." That's me. "The pragmatists believe that certain species deserve greater consideration than others. They only agree to the use of animals if the benefits outweigh their suffering." ' She stopped. 'Perhaps I'm really one of those. Certainly my treatment by the police in the last few days will make me more radical.'

'And the others?' Paul asked.

'The fundamentalists. They believe people should never use animals for anything, regardless of the benefits. Most of them are Vegans. Among those a few will resort to violence.' She dropped the pencil and stood up. 'How could you think I was one of them?'

Paul thought she was going to hit him. He hated himself, feeling like an inquisitor, as bad as any policeman, but he couldn't stop the questions. 'Are any of your friends in that group?'

Brenda sat down again, putting her head in her hands. 'I don't think so.' There was a long pause before she spoke again. 'I can't blame you for doubting me. I do know some people in the movement but I'm sure they weren't the ones to do this.'

'How can you be so certain?'

She sighed. 'I thought I really knew them. Perhaps I made a mistake. It was difficult with the police, I didn't want to implicate my friends.'

'But this sort of thing has to be stopped. Someone must be brought to justice. If Martin dies, it will be murder.'

'I know. I gave them the names in the end. It may help them to track down the ones who did it. I just hope that, in their determination to find the culprits, innocent people aren't blamed.'

Turning to look up at him as he stood by her chair Brenda took his hand. 'You can't really think I wanted them to do that? Martin . . .' Her voice broke.

'I told them you were essential for the work to proceed, which you are.' Paul walked away to take his place behind his new desk. He leaned his forehead on his hands as he said, 'It's just that I'm so confused. My head hurts and I didn't know what to think . . .'

Brenda got up and moved to his side. 'Your poor hand.' She ran her fingers over the bandage that had been renewed at the hospital the previous day. The burn was taking longer to heal than expected. 'Your eyes are still bloodshot, and your hair . . .' She giggled as she ran her palm over his head. 'It's all frizzy at the ends. Did you know you have no eyebrows left?'

Perhaps it was the way he looked that had made everyone so concerned, not some fantasy that he was a hero. 'I was never in any real danger, the firemen saw to that.' He reached up and pulled her down so he could embrace her, feeling his body respond with all the excitement of a first kiss. At that moment he forgot they might be seen from the courtyard. His feelings for this woman could not be smothered, even by all the care Fran had lavished on him over the previous week.

She pulled away. 'Not now. We'll go back to my house as soon as we can escape. We'd better get on and try to rescue what we can from this mess.' She glanced at the list on which she had been doodling. 'I'll cope with the references. You have more important things to do.'

Paul sighed as she sat down opposite him. 'Thank God you're here.' He filled her in with the details of the arrangements he'd made so far. After they'd identified their priorities they toured the various places Mr Bennett had commandeered for their use.

Before Brenda arrived Paul had been on the point of despair. Without Martin, the task of redoing all their work had seemed impossible. As they tramped the corridors Brenda gave a word of encouragement to each member of the team and prompted Paul about the various bits of equipment they would need. With every minute they worked together he became more certain of her innocence.

Martin didn't return to work until six months after the fire. Paul met him at the entrance in order to shepherd him through the complicated new security measures that had been installed since the bomb. His features were almost unrecognisable. Areas of pale grafted skin were edged by bands of livid fibrous tissue that escaped from under the long hair, so incongruous on the head of such a spruce man. Although Paul knew that this was still his good friend and colleague, it took several weeks before he could look at him without a feeling of revulsion. When he did let his eyes linger on his face he was embarrassed, as if he had stumbled across his friend with no clothes on.

At their first departmental meeting Paul watched in horror as his boss tried to manipulate his papers. The scar tissue on his hands was hardening and allowed him very little movement of his fingers. He plucked at the stapled corner of the pages to manoeuvre them until they were balanced under his stiff thumb. Paul wanted to reach out to help but knew he couldn't patronise those hands that had, at one time, found their way sensitively from crack to crack up the face of a rock.

When the attack happened, it had featured prominently in both the local and national newspapers. Then, after several weeks, the journalists had moved on to other stories. The appearance of such a damaged man reawakened their ghoulish interest. A police spokesman gave defensive interviews, trying to explain why no one had been charged for the outrage. The detective visited Paul again but he could add nothing to his previous evidence. The upsurge of activity made the staff edgy.

Brenda arrived in his office looking distracted. 'They've had me down at the station again, for two whole hours. I had to go through all the names I gave them at the beginning of the investigation. They've made up a photo-fit picture of some suspect. Apparently two men were seen loitering outside the gate a few days before the bombing.'

'Did it match anyone you know?'

She shrugged. 'How can I tell? It didn't look like a real person.' She turned her head away as Paul tried to read her face. 'I suppose it's possible . . . anyway, he's emigrated to Canada.'

'Interpol could find him.'

'How can I say anything unless I'm certain? And I'm not.' Twisting back towards Paul, begging for him to understand, she added, 'Surely it would be worse to convict an innocent man than to let a guilty guy go free? Can't you see what I'm trying to say? People are desperate for a scapegoat, they won't be too careful . . .'

Paul couldn't bear to see her so distressed. 'Of course.' He put his arm round her shoulders. 'I'll back you, whatever you decide to do.'

'Will you? Do you really believe I had nothing to do with that bomb?'

Paul had been haunted by the memory of doubting her. He'd struggled to find a way to convince her that his misgivings had been momentary, more a product of shock than any real belief that she was guilty. 'You know I'll always be on your side. I've loved you since the day you walked into my life and I trust you implicitly. Nothing in the world can change that.'

She allowed herself to be consoled.

Over the following months they occasionally talked between themselves about who might have been responsible for the atrocity. But the police never found enough evidence to bring anyone to trial.

Paul settled back into a comfortable routine of work and domestic chores, spiced by his visits to Brenda. His flutters of guilt became less painful as the years passed and he could see no reason why the pleasure he took in both his women should ever change.

TEN

1990

As Sylvia led the line of science graduates up to the podium to receive her honours degree, her parents sat more erect in their seats. Paul felt Fran grasp his wrist. Their daughter held her gown in her left hand, determined not to trip. They watched as the back of her head dipped in a tiny motion of deference before she took her scroll. Only when she reached the top of the steps at the other side of the stage did she pause to look up. They waved and she smiled vaguely in their direction before being lost in the crowd.

She'd waited until she was twenty-three before deciding that she did, after all, want to take a biology degree so that she could work for the environment. Now, four years later, Paul turned to Fran and whispered, 'Isn't she great, our girl?'

'Yes. She's done us proud.'

Us. Paul let himself relax, leaning back on the small word. However much he'd betrayed his wife they were still together. He knew they were bound by more than the child they had reared. Tentatively, they were getting closer again, even occasionally able to make love in the bed that had, for so long, been the place where he'd felt furthest from her.

The end of the long line of figures wound down the steps. A chaplain gave a blessing, suitably vague so as not to offend any of the religious sensitivities in the liberal university. Then, from the back of the hall, trumpets sounded. Fran looked towards her husband with a broad grin and he bent to brush his lips against hers. *And the trumpets sounded on the other side.* He wondered if they'd crossed some sort of Rubicon.

Outside they blinked in the sunshine, waiting for their daughter.

A mass of people pressed round them as they stood lost in the strange surroundings, each comforted by the presence of the other. After several minutes they saw Sylvia coming towards them through the crowd. She led them to a grassy slope and spread out the rug Paul had fetched from the car, together with their picnic.

As usual Fran had prepared enough for at least double the number of people who were going to eat it. Other families sat around, the holiday atmosphere sustained by bursts of laughter. Sylvia called out to her friends and got up to offer a paper plate of sandwiches to a passing lecturer. Paul watched as a dog twisted itself round her legs and she stooped to pick up a stick. 'Come on then,' she called, 'if you want to play.' Running away to a space under the surrounding trees, she threw the stick again and again.

'I'd like a dog,' Fran said. She hadn't known she wanted one till the words were out of her mouth. Many years before, Paul had suggested they should get a puppy. At the time she'd felt unable to cope with the hairs on the carpet and paw marks on her beautiful new furniture.

'How would you manage, now you're working?' he asked.

'I have a free day each week and the weekends. I could train it to stay in the car when I'm on the road and give him a run at lunchtime.'

'How's the canteen food in Clifton these days?'

'Not much better than it was in your day.'

'Is that battle-axe, Mrs Jolly, still in the typing pool?'

'People complain about her but she's quite friendly to me.'

Paul knew he'd been one of her favourites and guessed that his wife was getting special treatment on his behalf. He wished he could talk about some of the things that mattered to him. 'Would you really like a dog? In the past –'

'It was different then.' Fran threw her head back. 'I'm not so fussy these days and the house seems a bit empty since Sylvia's been away.'

'What about your painting? Would you have time for that, as well as a dog?'

'I lost interest a long time ago. My pictures were hopeless, I just dabbled to fill in the time.'

Paul frowned. 'I thought it meant more to you than that.' Fran didn't answer. 'Wouldn't you like to take it up again? What about going to some classes?'

'My job takes me out of the house quite enough. What I want is something to keep me young, give me some exercise and not make too many demands.' She looked up at him with a teasing smile. 'You might even come home a bit earlier,' she said. 'Take it out before supper.'

Ignoring the implication that he neglected her, Paul mulled over the possibility. The idea of a stroll across the fields, with a dog at his heels, appealed to him. 'What sort d'you fancy?'

Fran had no time to answer as Sylvia flopped down beside them, breathless from her romp. Dividing the strawberries into small plastic dishes, Fran poured the cream over and handed them round.

As they were driving home with Sylvia squashed in the back of the car, her belongings of four years piled round her, Fran raised the subject again. 'We could ask the vet if he knows of any puppies in need of a good home.'

'I wouldn't want a small one. They yap so,' Paul said.

Fran laughed. 'I think you're hankering after the black Labrador you never had.'

Sylvia woke up in the back. 'Are you going to get a dog?'

'We're thinking of it. D'you like the idea?'

'I always longed for one when I was little, but better late than never.'

Fran felt the reproach. She hadn't provided all the things a child needed. No dog, and perhaps worse, no brothers or sisters, although Sylvia said loyally that she liked being an only child. Paul put a hand on his wife's knee and caught Sylvia's eye in the driving mirror.

'When you were small, your pony took all your time and your mother had everything else to do.'

Fran was grateful when he covered for her. Once they'd moved into the big house a dog would have gone with the lifestyle. She gave herself a small shake. She would not ruin their day with self-blame.

She turned round to look at Sylvia. 'You can take it for walks when you're at home. I know you'll be away, once you find a job, but until then you can help with the house training.'

By the time they reached home the dog was firmly established in their joint imagination. It wasn't long before a small mass of black fur was under their feet whenever they moved. Carrying his inappropriate name, Bruiser softened the tensions that sparked between them from time to time. From the moment he arrived, his unconditional love permeated the house.

August gave way to September in that first year of the new decade. Paul felt happier than he had done for a long time. He had no warning of the vice-like dilemma that was about to seize him, no premonition of trouble when Brenda came into his office and put a copy of the *New England Journal of Medicine* in front of him.

'Look at this,' she said, standing by his desk as he began to read. He could not immediately see how the new disease had any relevance to their work. They were not making food supplements. He looked more closely, wishing that Brenda would go away and leave him to read it by himself. He hated to be rushed when he was trying to understand something.

The American study compared the manufacturing process of several companies. Only one had produced the batch of Tryptophan that was associated with the new disease, eosinophilia-myalgia syndrome. 'The filtration process seems to have been at fault,' he said.

'Yes, but look,' said Brenda. 'They're using a new strain of bacteria for their fermentation. I bet it's been genetically modified in the same way that ours has.'

'That's not the point. They reduced the quantity of powdered carbon.'

'It doesn't prove that was the cause of the problem. It could have been the new strain that's making some by-product we don't know about. The same thing could happen to us. And we're just about to go to trials. We've got to stop.'

'Are you sure the strains are similar?'

'Of course I'm not sure, how can I be? But we have to play safe. We can't launch a new drug when it may have dangers that we haven't even considered. I'm getting worried about what we're doing when we play around with the genetic make-up of organisms. We don't know what we're creating.'

Paul felt irritated. She was making such a lot out of one very inconclusive article. 'It's worked so well. The production process has been speeded up out of all recognition. I'm sure it's going to be a really good anti-depressant, much less sedative than the ones we have at the moment.' He could feel Brenda stiffen beside him. Unfortunately she was often right when it came to assessing scanty evidence. The extra sense, which occasionally shot through her scientific thinking like an unexpected firework, was one of the things he loved about her. He sighed. 'Leave it with me. I need time to study it in more detail.'

Within an hour he had decided she was probably right. The paper provided no proof that the organism was at fault; but no proof, either, that it was blameless. They would have to destroy all of their last six months' work and start again with a new, pure strain of bacteria that had not been tampered with. It would mean going back to the original culture, losing all the ground they had gained and letting their competitors get ahead. The company wouldn't like that.

By lunchtime he had roughed out a report to Martin. During the afternoon Brenda helped him with the final draft. He thought wryly that her fluency with words put him in the shade.

Martin wasn't in his office, so he left it on the desk with one of the large red stickers saying URGENT. Then he phoned the psychiatrist who had agreed to run the first trial, to warn him there would be a bit of a delay.

'What's up?' he asked.

Paul tried to sound casual. 'Oh, just a bit of a hitch with production. I'll let you know as soon as I have any definite news.'

'Well, don't delay too long. I've got ethical permission and all the forms signed for the go-ahead. I'd like to work with you but Margosa are pushing me to try one of their drugs. My department needs the research money, you know.'

Next day Paul couldn't settle. He picked up a copy of his report and read it yet again. They had argued their case strongly and he wondered why Martin hadn't got back to him. By mid-morning, he could wait no longer. He walked down the corridor and knocked on his door.

'Oh, it's you, Paul.' Martin looked back at the sheets on the table in front of him. 'I'm surprised to see your name on this.'

Paul shifted his gaze. The room that had replaced the one burnt in the fire was even more sparse than its predecessor. A single photograph hung on the walls, one of Martin's glacial landscapes, blown up to the size of a poster.

His boss spoke again. 'There isn't a shred of evidence that this work is relevant to our research.'

Paul dragged his eyes back to look at the scarred face. The small muscular movements that used to provide a key to his inner thoughts had been obliterated by scar tissue. It was as if they were trying to contact each other with one of the lines of communication between them not just absent but skewed, giving off the wrong messages. Sometimes Paul found it easier to grasp the nuance of his words when they spoke on the phone.

'Brenda's worried about the genetic modification.'

'What about you?' Martin's voice was as smooth as an undisturbed snowfield.

Paul forced himself to answer. 'There's no evidence, but I don't think we can ignore the possibility.' Going over and over Brenda's arguments, he'd been convinced. Now he wondered if he had allowed her to influence him too much. 'I put the trial on hold. I thought it only fair to warn them there would be a delay.'

There was no obvious change in the figure sitting at the desk, only an increased immobility. 'You shouldn't have done that without consulting me. I see no reason to stop it. Our filtration process is perfectly safe.'

Paul was still standing. He had not been invited to sit. He was aware of the stillness in the room, as if the frozen wasteland in the photo on the wall had broken the bounds of its frame. 'But what about the new strain . . . ?'

'There's nothing here to implicate the bacteria.' He looked across the table. Paul felt a bleak distance growing between them. After a pause Martin spoke again, his words clipped and devoid of emotion. 'We can't afford to delay the work. There's too much riding on this drug for us to be deflected by some half-baked idea.' Paul drew in his breath as if to interrupt, but he was silenced by a tiny movement of Martin's right hand. 'These dangers are purely hypothetical. Without at least a preliminary trial we're only guessing. There are no grounds to stop at this stage.' He spoke with sharp authority and Paul knew it was useless to try and argue. 'You must phone and say there has been a mistake. The trial will go ahead as planned.'

Paul turned and left the room. His trust in Martin's judgement had never faltered before. He didn't want to lose faith in the man he admired so much. Walking back down the corridor he steeled himself to face Brenda and her intuitive certainties. As he turned the corner he saw her waiting outside to waylay him. He wasn't ready to talk to her yet; he had to think, to try and decide for himself what he believed.

She gave him no time. 'Well?'

'He isn't impressed. He says the trial must go ahead.'

'That's absurd.' She looked at him in disbelief. 'How can he be so blind?'

'There's no evidence to blame the bacteria. In his view.' Brenda stood looking at him, her hand flicking her glasses in the way that used to set his pulses racing. Now, the movement contained a fury that was about to break on his head. He raised his arm, as if to fend off a blow. 'Look, I have to think it out. Can I come to you tonight?' Surely they could sort it out when he took her in his arms.

'I'll go and see him. He must listen to me. You can't have explained the dangers properly.'

He hadn't said much so perhaps she was right. In Martin's presence his arguments had died in his mouth. He didn't have Brenda's conviction to fortify him; she'd make a better job of it.

* * *

He parked his car in the usual place and walked to her house by an even more circuitous route than usual, taking in a longer stretch of the river on the way. He thought back to that day, seventeen – or was it eighteen? – years before, when they had walked along this same path, taking care not to let their hands touch. How certain he had been then that the affair would go no further, that he would return to his wife with the wholehearted commitment that he so much wanted to give her. His moral sense had been blunted in the intervening years. He no longer felt that he was betraying her very badly, though deep inside he yearned for one woman who could reconcile him to himself: make him a whole man.

Alarm signals tapped in his chest as he approached the house. The battle was not now the pull between two women, but between two belief systems, between the demands of an advancing science and what those with a more holistic view called the precautionary principle.

It was worse than he had imagined. Brenda opened the door, her pale skin ash-grey. He bent to stroke Tibbles as he always did. With her lips drawn into a tight grimace, she led him into the front room where her computer was surrounded by papers strewn over the table.

'He wouldn't listen to me.'

'I was afraid of that.'

'Said I was too emotional, that my fears were due to my feminine imagination.' She picked up a pen and passed it from one hand to the other. 'He did say he'd read it again, though.'

They sat opposite each other at the table. It would have been easier in the kitchen, where they normally had a drink before climbing the stairs to her bed. 'Maybe you'll persuade him in the end,' Paul said. 'You do have an extra sense about things. It's one of your many charms.'

'Don't flatter me. It's got nothing to do with me. He's crazy. How can he put lives at risk?'

'He's not crazy. He's the best scientist I know. The rats showed no ill effects, not in any of the parameters we measured.'

'But there could be other effects. You only find what you look for.'

'The Japanese used a faulty filtration system. Martin says ours is impeccable.'

'We went over all that yesterday. It's not the filtration, it's the new strain of bacteria. I thought you agreed.'

'I don't know. OK, they modified the genes, and so did we, but we don't know the details.'

'That's the whole point. We don't know what we're dealing with. It's not an exact science. The new DNA may have gone in at a different site. And we have no idea what vector they used.'

'But the effect was the same. Their process was speeded up and so was ours.'

'Oh, for God's sake. I'm tired. We could go on all night and you'd still be sitting there, parroting one objection after another.'

She couldn't be half as tired as he was. He leant forward. 'I'm not a parrot and I don't want to argue with you. But I respect Martin's views. It's silly to reject all work on genetic replacement. I believe it'll provide enormous potential, once we have more evidence.'

'You hero-worship that man. Just because he's a cripple . . .'

'Don't call him that. His mind's as keen as ever.'

Her face creased with scepticism. 'I will not let it happen. I'll send a copy of our report to every member of the board.'

'You can't undermine his authority like that. Anyway, they won't take any notice without his signature on it.'

Her shoulders softened as she reached across the table to take his hand. 'They might with yours.' Now her eyes were pleading and her hand felt cool on his. She didn't know what she was asking. He'd worked with Martin for so long, it was like demanding he renege on a brother. With an effort he pulled away and said, 'I don't think I could do that.'

She stood up and walked to the window. As he looked at her back it seemed to take on a new rigidity. She spoke without turning round. 'Well, if he goes ahead with the trials, I'll resign. You'll have to as well.'

The idea had never entered Paul's head. He couldn't resign from the company that had employed him for nearly thirty years. Their work was at the cutting edge of a science that would bring enormous benefits to mankind. Another thought hit him as he clenched his hands where they lay on the table. If they resigned together there was sure to be talk. Rumours about their relationship would fly, their secret would escape.

Clutching at straws, he said, 'You're a scientist, you know we have to be logical.'

'What's logical about a man who comes into your house once or twice a month, strokes your cat, visits your bed and wafts out again?'

'Oh, come on. It's not like that.' She looked into the distance, not seeing the trees in their early autumn colours. He had no idea what it was like for her as she waited for his visits, armouring herself each time against the pain of parting. Although he was now sitting within a few feet of her, she had never felt so alone. Tibbles got up from his corner by the radiator and slunk from the room.

Paul couldn't look at her implacable back as he let his immediate thoughts surface. 'What would happen to Fran? She's also working for the company now. I couldn't risk her job too.'

'Oh, damn Fran.' Brenda turned then, put her hands on the table and leant towards him. 'It's been nothing but Fran, all these years. Can't you do something for me, just this once?'

'For God's sake. The company has been my life. It's just not possible to walk out on a whim.'

'Is that all it is? A whim?' Her face was only a few inches from his.

He raised his hand as if to smooth the hair from her forehead, but let it drop. 'Oh Bren, you know –'

'What I know is that I've always been the one to mould myself to fit into you. I've stuck by you, never asked for more or expected you to leave her or your precious Sylvia. Have you any idea what that's cost me? I have no family, no children to look after me in my old age. You've taken the best years of my life. Now you can't support me in this one thing that means so much.' She collapsed into her chair and burst into tears.

It was Paul's turn to sit rigid. 'You always said you didn't want children.'

'I don't. Didn't. But I might have got to like them if I had them. You stopped me having the chance to find out.'

'But that was the deal. I couldn't.'

'Wouldn't. That's your weakness. You're a weak man.'

'I hope not.'

'Well, you are. I think so anyway.' She sniffed. Paul reached automatically into his pocket for a handkerchief.

As he handed it over he remembered the previous evening in the garden at home. He'd held Fran's arm as they viewed the last of the runner beans and admired the Michaelmas daisies. Fran had got a midge in her eye and he had used the corner of the hanky to get it out. He had taken it for granted that his two lives would continue to run in secret, as they had done for so many years – railway lines that never met. He couldn't lose either of them now. The idea shocked him into action and he moved to crouch by Brenda's chair. His arm went round her shoulders. 'Oh my love . . .' He stroked her thigh and laid his head on her shoulder. 'Don't let's quarrel. We've been together for so many years –'

'Not together.' She had thought it was enough, that she could live like a man, not needing to possess her partner like other women. What a child he was when he needed her. Despite herself her hand came across on to his head.

He shifted under her touch, saying, 'Come to bed. Let me show you how much I love you.'

'You men. You think a bit of sex can heal everything.' She could feel herself softening but he'd hurt her, perhaps beyond repair this time. Paul looked up and moved his hand to pull her head down so that he could let his lips trace the outline of her mouth, nestling small kisses along the top and in the corners. 'I'll try to help in some way. Maybe our own director would have some influence with Martin. I wouldn't mind sending a copy to him. But the whole board . . .'

He led her upstairs, his fingers laced with hers. The bed looked so welcoming. He loved the matter of fact way they took off their clothes, so different from the shyness that had crept into the proceedings when he was with Fran. The bedsprings creaked with the familiar note as they climbed in. He buried his face in her hair.

'Um. You smell nice.'

'Do I?'

'Feel nice too.'

'Can't you support me? You said once, after the bomb, that you would always be on my side. They might listen if you added your voice to mine.'

'I'll try.' She felt his breath on her face, his hands on her breasts and knew with absolute certainly that he would not. He was murmuring to her now. 'My love, my love, come on. Let yourself go.' His body pressed against her and his hands moved lower.

'It doesn't feel the same,' she said. In a precipitous flurry he climbed on top and entered her. As he began to move he felt her go limp beneath him, her body a lifeless weight on the bed.

'It's no good. I feel dead,' she said. They lay still, sinking into the quagmire of their dying love. 'If I let myself feel, I'd hit you.'

'Hit me, then.' Anything would be better than this terrible nothing.

'I can't . . . it's no good.'

His excitement vanished and he slipped out of her but stayed with his weight heavy along her length, his head resting on her chest. He felt her ribs rise and fall as she spoke. 'It isn't all your fault. I know this is something I have to do, with or without you. It's more important than anything between us. It's easier for me. There are some advantages in having no family.'

'It's not just the family,' he muttered into her bosom, 'it's Martin too. I can't go against him after all he's been through.'

'I know. I thought we had something special. I can see now, there's no way you'll put me first, however much I need you. I was deluded. Get your bulk off me and go home.'

ELEVEN

2003

Fran walked slowly past the Nonsec gates with her head bent. When she got to the corner she turned to make her way back, willing Geoffrey to appear. With every minute that she loitered the chance of bumping into Jackson, or someone from the training department, made her feel more conspicuous. What a silly idea to try and meet him accidentally. Anyway, she was hungry now.

As she turned to walk past one last time she caught sight of three people emerging from the door of the building. Two smaller men flanked Geoffrey's large frame as they stood talking. He bent his head of luxuriant hair, first to one side and then to the other. She couldn't decide if his air of condescension sprang from an inner sense of superiority or just from the physical disparity. She walked slowly on towards the gate.

To her relief, Geoffrey dismissed the others with a wave of his hand and turned towards her. When he was close enough to recognise her, he smiled. 'Fran. What luck to meet you.' He took her arm with proprietorial pressure, his habitual ease making it impossible for her to judge what he was really feeling.

'I was passing.' Even to her own ears the excuse sounded unconvincing. 'Actually, I hoped I might see you.'

He propelled her along the road at such a rate that she caught her heel and would have fallen if he hadn't held her up.

'Steady,' he said.

'Steady yourself. Your legs are longer than mine.'

He laughed and took a firmer grip on her arm. 'It's just so great to see you.'

She hoped he didn't think she'd sought him out for more kisses.

That wasn't the reason – at least, she hadn't thought so. A shiver went through her, starting from the point on her arm where his fingers encircled it. Damn it, Paul had visited his mistress for so much of their married life; there was no need for her to keep faith now, nearly a year after his death. Give him a bit of his own medicine. She made a face as she had to accept ruefully that the dead couldn't be hurt in that way.

They went past the main door of the Hat and Feathers, where Geoffrey had courted Hazel so many years before, round the corner and down a small alleyway, to find a sandwich bar perched in a protruding wing of the building. In the past Paul had complained that Geoffrey would treat himself to a full pub meal, while the rest of them made do with the canteen. No chance of that now, worst luck.

'Ham and cheese all right for you? And some beer?'

'Tonic please.' He raised his eyebrows but she didn't explain. Stuffing his change into his pocket, he reclaimed her arm.

'I know a good place, out of the wind. With luck there'll be an empty bench. If not, we'll sit on the ground.'

They strode on for what seemed a long way. Fran's feet began to hurt. If she'd anticipated a cross-country hike she'd have worn her trainers instead of the court shoes that were cutting into the tops of her feet. They were tramping over grass now and with a gesture of impatience she pulled away from his grasp and kicked them off. Tossing her head, she ran the few steps to catch him up and take hold of his arm. The dampness quickly penetrated her tights but she didn't care.

When they reached the seats, spaced out on a wide stretch of grass between the road and the woods beyond, they were all occupied. Geoffrey led her into the trees, to a small clearing. He produced a black plastic refuse bag from his pocket and laid it, with a ceremonial gesture, over the fallen leaves and beech nuts at the base of a tall tree. Giving him a mock curtsey, she sank down. He settled himself beside her and took out the sandwiches.

'Well,' he said, as he handed her one of the packets.

Fran chewed in silence, looking through the trees to where the Avon gorge lay out of sight. She couldn't remember being in that particular spot before, although she thought she had explored every corner of the area when she was a girl.

As she ate, Geoffrey's free hand lay round her waist. She ignored it for a while, saying eventually, 'I know about Paul and Brenda.'

'You do?' Geoffrey sounded wary. 'What do you know about them?'

'I know they had an affair that went on a long time.' Did she imagine the small sigh of relief that escaped from his lips? 'You knew all along, I suppose.'

'I didn't know – I guessed. They were very discreet, Paul wouldn't have hurt you for the world.' He removed his arm for a moment to open his beer with a gadget on his penknife, then propped the bottle against the root of a tree. 'These things happen, you know.'

'Brenda said that. It doesn't help.'

'It was so long ago, isn't it water under the bridge now?'

Geoffrey was a man of clichés, a man who had gone through so many women himself. How easily he could let them slide into the past and out of sight. She couldn't allow her life with Paul to slip through her fingers like that. If her husband had been drawn away, enticed out of her grasp, she had to find out why. She took a breath and held it before letting out just enough to form her next words. 'There's something else isn't there? Some mystery to do with his work for the company. Not just that paper he wrote with Brenda . . .'

'You know about that, too?' Geoffrey's dark eyes, that could hold such apparent trust, flicked away from her face. 'That woman, she's become a menace, an activist of the worst sort. She used to be a good scientist. She and Paul did some useful things together but now she does nothing but stir up trouble. I should never have mentioned her. I regretted it the moment her name was out of my mouth.'

'I'm glad you did.'

'But it must have been so painful for you, to find out about them after so long.' His grip on her waist tightened and she felt him kiss the top of her head.

'Painful but necessary. I have to learn all I can about him.' She leant back into the crook of his encircling arm. 'Can't you understand? Until I know what he was doing, what sort of person he really was, I can't understand myself. Without that, I don't know who I am.' She stopped, afraid she sounded pompous. The few remaining leaves on the trees cast dappled shadows on the ground in front of them. Beyond, the wood was dense, allowing little light to penetrate. 'I think they're still trying to discredit him.'

'Who?'

'The company, or someone who worked with him.'

'Surely not.' Geoffrey shifted his arm and searched her face. 'What on earth makes you say that?'

Fran didn't know how much she wanted to tell him. 'Someone has been snooping round my house –'

' Don't be silly. You're imagining things.'

'A strange car has been seen in the village, several times.'

Geoffrey took a swig of beer. 'I can't think what the company could want, so long after his death. I imagine they'll have finished whatever experiments he had in the pipe line and moved on by now.'

Fran unscrewed the top of her tonic and gulped some down. 'What could he have been working on?'

Geoffrey reclaimed her waist. 'I don't really know much about the work he did in the last few years. The person who would know, if anyone does, is Martin. But I haven't seen him since he retired.'

Fran remembered how upset Paul had been after the fire. The worst thing was that Martin's fingers had been so badly burnt that he was never able to climb again. She wondered how he occupied his time, now he no longer had to make the journey to work each day. 'How long has he been retired?' she asked.

'He left eighteen months ago. I remember because I took my new partner to his farewell do. The company insisted on arranging a party, though I think he hated every moment. He and Paul had worked closely together after Brenda left. Then they appointed that bastard Jackson you were asking about.'

'Is his wife still alive?'

'Whose wife?'

'Martin's. I was wondering what he did with himself now.'

'She died some time ago.' He paused. 'His daughter had died too, you know. He always was a solitary sort of chap, would never come for a drink, even before the accident. After that he became a virtual hermit. Mind you, I don't know what else he could have done with a face like that.'

Fran had only seen him once, in the distance. Paul had told her of the awful scars and the way his face was pulled into a grimace by the grafted skin. An image of television monsters floated in front of her eyes. They were so clever these days, making human faces look like creatures from another planet. She felt herself blushing and wondered how she would manage if she met him. She always felt awkward in the presence of disability, ashamed of her own health. She had to admit that, despite the roll of fat round her middle, she knew she could look elegant and younger than her age.

They had finished their sandwiches and Geoffrey's arm was now round her shoulders. He leant towards her, his lips smiling, his eyebrows raised. She put her hands on his chest to push him away but the attempt was half-hearted. As she closed her eyes she felt her body soften. Then she pulled away. 'I didn't come for that. I mustn't let myself get distracted.' She got to her feet. 'Thanks for your help. I'll try and track Martin down.'

'Walk you to your car?'

'I think I'll go for a stroll. I haven't been to this part of the gorge for ages. But thanks again.'

'Keep in touch.' Geoffrey, ungainly now, kept hold of her hand, as if the bubble of his self-confidence had been pricked by her rejection.

Dear Geoffrey, such an extrovert. For the first time Fran caught a glimpse of an uncertain child under the veneer. He hadn't been quite as successful as he'd hoped; a seat on the board still eluded him. Tied to a new woman and child, he could look forward to no early retirement or a life spent on the golf course. With a spurt of feeling she threw her arms round his neck and drew his head down so she could kiss him again. Before he could respond too ardently she disentangled herself. 'Why don't you bring your family to a meal one weekend? I'd love to have a baby in the house for an hour or two. She might leave vibrations to jog Sylvia towards her maternal instincts.' She laughed as he reached out and regained possession of her hand.

'I'd like that. I'll give you a ring sometime.'

Fran walked away, turning once to give him a wave.

She decided to revisit the place near the bridge where she and Paul had slept on the day they met. As the path became rougher her shoes pinched unbearably. Stopping at the first spot with an uninterrupted view down the valley, she removing the pins from her head and kicked her shoes off again, as if trying to find her old freedoms through her wet feet and wind-blown hair.

A baby shrieked behind her. Turning, she saw a young woman kneeling beside a pushchair. The baby cried louder. Fran thought it was too small to be propped up like that. In her day it would have been in a large, comfortable pram, with big wheels, facing its mother so she could talk to it while she pushed.

'Oh, shut up,' the mother said, as she fiddled with the covers. 'I don't know what to do with you.' The angry desperation in her voice reminded Fran of her own feeling of helplessness when Sylvia wouldn't be comforted.

The woman, not much more that a girl really, took a bottle out of a bag and thrust it into the baby's mouth. She looked up at Fran. 'They say I shouldn't feed him when I'm out but shit, how else can I keep him quiet?'

Fran smiled. 'He's your baby. You do what seems right to you.' The bottle dropped to one side and the crying started again. 'Does he get very windy? Would you like me to hold him?' The mother looked frightened. 'It's OK, I'm used to babies.' Fran held out her arms and took the bundle, wondering why she'd lied. The girl shifted about, keeping a possessive hand pressed on to one of her baby's legs. They were both surprised when he gave a loud burp and stopped crying.

'That's better then,' said Fran, as she jigged automatically from side to side. 'How old is he?'

'If you're so good with babies, you guess.'

'About five months?'

'Six and a half.'

Fran blushed, feeling she had insulted both mother and baby.

'That's enough.' The girl seized him back and clasped him to her chest. She too jigged for a moment. Then he started to cry again. Thrusting him into the pushchair, she shouted 'Stop it,' and did up the straps so roughly that Fran had to clasp her hands together to stop herself intervening.

'Fucking babies! I must get on.' The girl rushed away, almost breaking into a run as she followed the curve of the path and disappeared. Fran watched them go before walking slowly away to her car.

As she drove back across the downs she found herself passing her childhood home. On an impulse she stopped, parked the car and clicked open the wrought iron gate. She had time to notice the flowerbeds were covered in a jumbled mess of builder's rubble before a workman appeared through the front door, carrying a stainless steel sink, the draining board spotted with white and blue paint.

'I wonder if I could see inside,' Fran asked. 'I used to live here.'

The builder looked her up and down, then walked past to dump his burden on a pile of broken bricks beside a lavatory bowl. Pipes lay along the inside of the front wall, where her mother had struggled to grow roses. They never did very well because the two sycamore trees, still standing in the road outside, took all the goodness from the soil.

'Lived here, did you? When you were a nipper?'

'That's right.'

'Well, I shouldn't let strangers in,' he said, at the same time waving his hand towards the door. She walked on up the path. When she saw the wooden letter box set in the wall, she stopped short. Running her hand down the sharp edge of the stone, she felt herself back at the times she had stood in her school blazer, waiting for someone to let her in. When she was eleven she was allowed to walk home alone from school but was not considered sensible enough to have a key. Her teeth clenched as she remembered.

Drawing a breath, she stepped inside. For a moment she didn't recognise anything. Then she realised a partition had been put across the hall so that the stairs at the end had disappeared. Through an open door on her right she could see into the sitting-room. She stepped in to find the shape of the room had changed although the fireplace was in the same place. The window at the end looked out on to what had been a spacious garden. Now, a bleak wooden fence constricted a small lawn. She recoiled from the view and looked down at the ladders and planks lying on the floor, together with a marble fire surround, broken in two pieces. Everything was covered in a thick layer of dust.

The builder had followed her in. 'We're stripping the flats and putting it back into one house again.' He looked round with professional detachment.

'We had a lovely brick grate, with a wooden mantelpiece.' Fran could see the polished wood and her mother's two Dresden figures that she must never touch. Muriel used to clean out the grate every morning. 'There was a gas poker,' she added, and stopped abruptly.

Picking her way towards the window, her eyes were drawn to the corner where her mother used to sit at her desk. Fran would lounge on the seat under the window, talking about her friends and the small doings of her day. Her mother's smile had been warm and encouraging. Only when Fran had started to go out with boys, in clothes her mother said were lower class – meaning they were too sexy – had their rows started.

As she turned back to look out at the pathetic remains of the garden, Fran could almost feel her mother's presence. After the end of the war her world had fossilised into a routine of bridge parties and efforts to upstage her friends with elegant sandwiches and tasteful furnishings. Not an easy task when there were few coupons and nothing but utility materials. Standing in the ruined room, Fran realised there had been a desperation about those women, as if they were striving for the pre-war years when ladies were Ladies. At the time it had driven her crazy.

The window seat had gone, eaten by woodworm, or perhaps ripped out to make more space when the house was divided. She turned to the man who stood watching her. 'What happened to that corner?'

'Come on, I'll show you.'

From the reduced hall he led her into what had been the boot room. Now, it was a passage. Her fingers could feel the stiff key in the door at the end that had led out into the garden. A bathroom had been created from a bit of the sitting room and the old toilet, where she'd fled to escape her mother's wedding plans on that terrible day, when Paul had been summoned and they had been dragooned into marriage.

'Do you want to see the rest?'

'Not now. Could I come back again?'

'Don't see why not.'

She held out her hand. The top of his head shone, the only hair a narrow fuzz above his ears. He had a kind face ornamented by a grey moustache. In her confused state she felt he must be old enough be her father. In reality he was probably several years younger than she was. 'Thank you so much. You've been very kind.'

'Houses are important, I know that.' He gave her hand a squeeze as she turned to go.

For the whole of the drive home she felt shaken by the vivid memories. If only her parents could have accepted Paul it might have been different. Even when they met him for the first time they'd been difficult. Her father had lectured him on the need for the country to have a nuclear deterrent, as if he'd forgotten they'd met on a CND march. When they heard he lived in Knowle there had been a shocked silence. Her mother believed that no one living on that side of the city was worth knowing. She had clung to her rigid conventions, ingrained no doubt by her own Victorian mother, as if they had been a lifejacket without which she would drown. At that moment, with a certainty that surprised her, Fran knew that her mother, too, had become frigid.

Now she wished she had gone upstairs and found the bedroom where she had seduced Paul that first time, one of the few occasions her parents had left them alone in the house. Their hands and bodies had been clumsy together, but she had carried him along with her and they had managed. Afterwards he had lain in her arms, his head between her breasts. He'd been her man.

She arrived home lost in her thoughts and didn't notice that Bruiser wasn't at the door to greet her. Only when she heard a whimper, a sound that sent prickles of fear up her spine, did she flick on the hall light. Her dog was sprawled on the carpet at the foot of the stairs. Blood trickled from his nose. With a cry she fell to her knees by his side. As she did so, she heard a noise behind her. Swivelling round, she saw a thickset man making for the door. She sprang after him, the furious movement driving her panic away. He turned, and she found herself looking at Jackson. 'What have you done to my dog?' she shouted, seizing the lapels of his jacket.

He shook himself free, then stood uncertain, looking from the prostrate bundle of fur on the floor to her furious eyes. 'It was an accident – he fell down the stairs – I didn't mean –'

Fran drew her hand back and slapped his face with all her strength. 'How dare you break into my house and attack a defenceless animal?'

He recoiled at the blow, his hand going to his cheek. 'I didn't break in. The back door was open.'

Damn it. Why hadn't she locked up more carefully? 'You're still trespassing. You've no business here. I'm going to call the police.'

She took a step towards the phone but he reached out and gripped her wrist, then leaned forwards as he slowly bent her arm behind her. 'I shouldn't do that if I were you.'

Fran glanced down at Bruiser who was trying to get to his feet, then up at her adversary. 'What do you want with me?'

Bringing his face even closer to hers, he growled, 'I know your husband was up to something. Making up some fancy results – to prove me wrong. He always had it in for me.'

Fran felt a cold weight in her stomach as her own uncertainties came rushing back. That file, the one he'd been working on right up until the day they took it back to his office . . . Defiantly, she spat, 'How little you knew him.' His grip loosened and she managed to jerk out of his grasp and turn away, winding her fingers together in order to stop her hands shaking. 'The one thing in the world he cared about was scientific truth. Ask anyone who ever worked with him. Martin would bear me out.'

'I wouldn't be too sure about that.'

'She looked back at him over her shoulder. 'Don't you believe me?'

He seemed to deflate as he spoke more gently. 'Look . . . I didn't mean to hurt your dog. But I'm really worried about your husband and Martin. I think they may have been involved in something improper . . . some illicit work . . . I need to be sure it doesn't come out and tarnish them both.'

'Well, you've searched my house haven't you? Rifled through all my belongings? Did you find anything incriminating?'

His lips twisted into a sort of smile. 'I've nothing concrete yet. But some records in his office . . . they don't make sense. We don't want the police butting in now, do we?'

His more reasonable tone confused her but she'd had enough. With a last burst of bravado she said, 'I've a good mind to ring the Managing Director. I bet he doesn't know what you're up to. I'll sue for harassment.' She stood up and he took a step backwards. Pressing her advantage, she continued, 'If my dog dies I'll get the company to stamp on you so hard that no one will ever employ you again. Now get out.'

He turned and slouched through the door, leaving it ajar behind him. As she moved to pull it shut she saw Mr Singh hurrying down the drive. 'Are you all right?' he called. 'I saw his car . . .'

Fran beckoned him in and sank into a chair, the remnants of her courage ebbing away. 'He's hurt my dog.'

'I'll phone the police.' Mr Singh picked up the receiver.

'No, it's all right. I'd left the back door open, he didn't break in.' She ran her hand over her forehead. She couldn't risk any sort of publicity until she'd discovered exactly what Paul had been working on. Her threat to involve the company had been a bluff. 'I don't think that man will trouble me again. He's had a good hunt through my things and didn't find whatever it was he wanted.' With an effort she pulled herself out of the chair and went over to Bruiser. 'I must get my dog to the vet. Could you help me lift him into the car?'

Between them they lifted him gently into the passenger seat. He lay quiet during the drive. After he'd been examined and X-rayed the vet said he had a hairline fracture of the skull. However, as he was conscious and all his limbs were working, he should be all right. She was to keep him quiet and get in touch again if she was worried.

That night she shared her bed with the injured dog, lifting him into a space by her feet and covering him with a blanket. She fell asleep almost at once. To her surprise, instead of her recurrent nightmare, she had a sexy dream, the first in years. She reached out for Paul, as she had done before. Surely, if she kept her eyes closed, he would be in the double bed with her still. His death, and his affair with Brenda, would be the dream from which she would wake. It was no good. No amount of wishing could bring him to life.

Drifting between sleep and wakefulness, she was in her old home, pausing on the stairs to kiss Paul again and again as she enticed him up to her bedroom, the one she had shied away from that afternoon.

Turning on to her back she found herself fully awake. She hadn't become cold on purpose. Some of her mother's frigidity had embedded itself inside her without her knowledge. Bunching the sheet between her hands, she rolled over again and pressed it into her face. She didn't want to know about the woman she had become. Or to accept the fact that it was not only Paul's fault that he had been unfaithful to her.

Sobs wracked her as she cried with an abandon she hadn't felt since his death. She soaked the piece of sheet in her hands, got out to fetch a handkerchief, then started again. A pause suggested the storm might be passing, but it was followed by another outburst that shook her body afresh. The need for a drink to numb her pain welled up inside her but she suppressed the urge by telling herself that she didn't deserve such relief.

After what could have been a lifetime she felt Bruiser's wet nose against her face. She struggled up to put on her dressing-gown and followed him down the stairs. Her eyes felt raw and every muscle in her body ached.

Standing at the door in the dawn light, she watched the dog make his established journey round the garden. Although he was a bit unsteady on his feet he navigated the lawn, stopping several times for a pee. If only he'd be all right she would never fuss about the pale patches on the grass again. He didn't bother to look for cats, as he would normally have done, but headed back into the house and curled up in his basket.

Fran pulled her big coat on over her night things and went outside again. It had been raining and drops of water hung on the branches of the bare trees. She found herself imagining that each one held a tiny germ of life, like an egg sac. Two birds flew purposefully past behind the trees, as a striking clock sounded in the still morning air.

TWELVE

2001

Paul had been huddled over his desk for more than an hour when Jackson pushed into his office like an inquisitive bulldog. He never knocked. 'I see you've got my copy of *Nature*.'

He had no more right to it than anyone else. Now he would monopolise it for the rest of the week. Making a quick note on his pad, Paul passed the journal over.

'Anything in it for us?' Jackson looked suspicious as he twisted his short neck to try and read what Paul had written.

'I don't think so but you'd better check for yourself.' The department had grown rapidly since they started to work on drugs against cancer. Jackson represented an extra layer of management. Paul wasn't sure if, in the process, he had been demoted or moved sideways. 'You may find something I've missed.'

Flipping to the contents page, Jackson said, 'You've noted something.'

'Only the address of that chap in California.'

'What do you want that for?'

'I'm wondering if he has any ideas about the starting dose of these new DNA reactive cytotoxics.'

Jackson gave a short laugh. 'Still worrying about that? If you expect him to share anything he hasn't yet published – with someone in a rival company, for God's sake – you must have been born yesterday.'

Paul sighed. Science shouldn't be like that: a matter of secrets. 'I expect you're right.' He was annoyed with himself for toadying to the man. If only he could talk directly to Martin, as he had done in the past. As the pressure on office space had increased, a coffee machine at the end of the corridor had replaced the common room. Sitting in comfortable chairs they'd been able to float ideas and discard them, bounce thoughts off one another before they were captured on paper and laid down in the minutes of some meeting. Martin no longer encouraged him to drop into his office unannounced. Instead, any suggestions had to be presented as a report in duplicate and sent via Jackson.

Once the man had left the room, Paul stood up and put his hands on each side of his spine, arching his back. The book Fran had found for him, on *How to Treat Your Own Back*, suggested this should be done several times each day. Ever since the sudden pain, when he was forking compost into the herbaceous border, he had tried to follow the instructions.

His domain still consisted of three laboratories. He set off on a tour of inspection. When Jackson had finish at the planning meeting he would be down again, looking for something amiss. If he found it he would be condescending for the rest of the day. Although Paul admired his concern for detail, he was irritated by his reluctance to talk about the principles that lay behind their work.

As he looked into the cage, where the mice with the tumours had now been given their third course of PN180 injections, Paul frowned. The animals were running around normally. The only difference he could see between them and the controls in the next cage was that the tumours on their necks looked smaller. Both sets must be measured today; the shrinkage had to be meticulously recorded before they repeated the blood tests the following week.

Jackson was impatient for success. He hankered for quick results, for a wonder drug that would cause no sickness or diarrhoea, no damage to healthy tissue, so he could dazzle the board of Nonsec and secure his future.

Although Paul shared the dream, he knew the ambition was unrealistic. Doxeril, the first drug he'd seen through all the stages of development, had not been much better than the one before. Later modifications were marginally better. The compound they'd been testing when Brenda resigned had not produced the unexpected effects she'd feared: her resignation had been a wasted gesture. All the same, traces of her anxiety were left in him, returning with each new drug, like the taste of raw onion that jolts the memory of the previous meal with every burp.

Paul sighed and took up the list of biochemical investigations. He read them through again and realised with a jolt that two tests for liver enzymes had been left off. The mistake was obvious. How could he have missed something so important? Jackson would say it didn't matter, the ones they had were enough, but that wasn't true. If he'd been working with Brenda she would have asked questions, stimulated him to think more carefully before they reached such a late stage in the trials. Once again he missed not just her responsive body but her acute mind.

He settled down to try and work out how they could repair the oversight most quickly. After a few minutes he put his pen down, wondering if it were worth the trouble. He knew that Jackson would convince Martin that they must forge ahead with the clinical trials. No paper, however well argued, would change their minds.

The trouble was that he needed a holiday. He must talk to Fran and see where she would like to go. She had a yen to go abroad, to Minorca perhaps, where Sylvia had spent a happy week. If they did that he would have to put Bruiser in kennels. Last time, one of the kennel maids told them that he howled for a whole day after they left. There was the garden too; the pots needed watering every day now it was getting warm and it would be a pity to be away when it was at its best.

That evening Fran cooked his favourite meal: lamb chops, the first picking of peas and their own new potatoes with lots of mint. As she put the plate in front of him she said, 'I've got some news.' Fetching her own plate, she sat down at the scrubbed oak table in the kitchen where they ate when they were alone. 'I've been promoted to the top job in the training department.'

'That's wonderful,' he said, looking at her more closely. A rare excitement hovered round her eyes; he hadn't seen her look like that for a long time. A sinking feeling started below his breastbone at the thought that her work could make her so happy. All he had ever wanted was to be the one to restore the sparkle that used to lift her face when they were first together. A touch or a word had been enough to make her glow. Now, her job was succeeding where he had failed.

'Are you really pleased?' she asked.

'Of course. I'm delighted for you. Provided it'll make you happy.'

She looked into his eyes and reached across to put her hand over his where it rested on the table. 'I can't tell you what it means to me. If drug reps are well trained they can play an important part in the education of doctors. I have lots of ideas about how to improve the course. Fewer lectures and more participation, for a start.' She took her hand away and he watched her eyes stray to a picture of her parents, standing self-consciously in the garden of their house. 'I've always felt a failure, ever since I had to give up my degree because Sylvia was on the way. I disappointed my father.' She looked back at Paul. 'I wish he could have lived to see me now.'

Paul wanted to say that wherever her father was, he would know of her success; but they had agreed, long ago, that neither of them believed in an afterlife. 'I'm proud of you,' was all he could manage.

Later they linked arms and made a slow tour of the garden. He pointed out that the first raspberries would be ready in a week or two. She picked some alchemilla mollis and three delphiniums. As he looked at the bunch, the soft yellow heads contrasting with the blue spires, he squeezed her hand. All his life he had yearned for beauty like that, a perfect union of opposites. Each flower wholly itself yet each complemented by the presence of the other. With his affection split between two women, he had settled for something less.

In bed that night he turned to give her the goodnight kiss that marked their friendship. Her arms came round him and for a moment he felt her pull him close. Did she want more? If only he was confident that he could manage it. Nowadays he seldom got an erection. If she flinched or uttered a word to suggest he was not welcome, he would lose it. Safer not to try.

Fran was often restless, but that night she slept peacefully and it was Paul who couldn't settle. Her regular breathing was a reproach. The time dragged on. Dozing, he woke again, the left side of his head throbbing with the premonition of a migraine. Although they attacked him less frequently now, their severity was still frightening. He opened his eyes wide in the darkness of their bedroom, then squeezed them shut. Yes, there were the zigzag lines. Fran let out a shuddering sigh, as if she might be going to wake. When her breathing resumed its rhythmic pattern he slipped carefully out of bed and tiptoed round the room to find his dressing gown and the pills that could stop the pain, if he took them soon enough. In the kitchen he poured himself some milk and carried the drink and tablets down the stairs to his study.

The top of his desk was empty. Nothing but a blotter and a pen in a holder disturbed the surface, as if the gleaming wood was waiting in readiness for some new project. Paul swallowed his tablets and sat looking into space. Brenda was lucky to have such passionate beliefs. All she had to do was follow what her conscience told her was right. He had far too many reservations about the extreme views of activists to be able to join her in that world. But he longed to find some way to live for the things he believed in, if only he could be sure what they were.

He got up and walked along his bookshelves. Darwin's *Origin of Species* had become separated from his biography, by a child's *Encyclopaedia of Dogs*. He reached out and returned the intruder to its right place in the corner, with the other books from his childhood. On the shelf below, an illustrated volume on saprophytic plants led to several about parasites and a tome on symbiosis. He remembered how fascinated he had been by the way organisms either competed with one another or learnt to live together with mutual benefit. He had been playing with the thought of extending that idea to different peoples, before his plans to visit Africa had been shattered so abruptly. Perhaps he should have been a sociologist, even though their methodology was often woolly.

Sitting back at his desk, he reached into a drawer for one of the coasters Sylvia had given him for his last birthday. He liked her knack of finding simple but unusual presents. He put his glass on the picture of a beetle rolling a ball of dung with its back legs. Fran was happy to use the ones in the set with the ladybirds on them, but she considered dung beetles unsuitable for her sitting room. Shades of her mother, Paul thought. If only he, or her father, had been able to help her break away and develop her own ideas. But no one had stood up to her forbidding mother.

What would his own father have said about it all if he had lived? Paul closed his eyes gently, so as not to risk the return of the intrusive lights. Could there even now be a chance to travel, to visit those places that had intrigued him as a boy? With Fran so happy in her work he could leave her for a while; go to Africa as he had planned, all those years before. Or even make a pilgrimage to Malaysia where his father had died. Opening his eyes, he knew he wouldn't want to go as a tourist. He had to be realistic. Young people with energy were needed for that life: he wouldn't be of any use now.

His fingers absent-mindedly explored the top of his head. The bald patch was growing bigger. He could no longer pretend that the strands of hair from the sides covered it.

His eyes scanned the books lining the walls of the room. What he did care about was the search for truth: a slow and painful business. One couldn't cut corners or try to do things in the wrong order. Damn that man, Jackson. In the morning he would bypass the bugger somehow, speak directly to Martin about the missing tests and the starting dose for the trial. His boss wasn't an unreasonable man.

Having taken a decision, Paul's head felt easier. He got up stiffly from the chair and climbed back to bed. As he started to doze he saw a cage with mice in it, but one was lying on its side at the back, not moving.

* * *

He pushed open the door of Martin's office and hesitated, the handle still pressing into his palm. Jackson sat at the side of the desk. An empty chair stood by itself in front of them. 'I've asked Jackson to be here,' Martin said.

The confrontation was just what Paul had hoped to avoid. He sat down and, ignoring Jackson's presence, he said, 'I want to talk to you. I'm anxious about the starting dose to be used for the pilot trial.'

Although he had spoken directly to Martin, it was Jackson who answered. 'I thought we agreed that we would work it out on the basis of relative weight? We seem to have found the right dose for the mice. The tumours are getting smaller.'

Martin looked into the space between them, his eyes guarded, whether by the scarred skin or a determination to remain neutral, Paul couldn't guess. Jackson shifted his position. In the process his chair edged towards Martin's side of the desk. Paul clenched his fingers, then deliberately let his hands relax. Again speaking to Martin, he said, 'I'm doubtful if the dose can be scaled up simply in relation to weight. We have to allow for the unexpected.'

'Of course,' said Martin.

Paul took a breath. 'The biochemical tests are incomplete. We've missed two vital ones. We can't be sure that it hasn't had an adverse effect on the liver.'

'How did that happen?'

'It was an oversight. I deeply regret it.'

Jackson gave a small smile. 'No problem. We can add it into the ones we're doing next week.'

'But we have no pre-treatment levels for comparison.'

Martin reached out for the file Paul was carrying. 'Let me see the tests you have done.'

His scars made it necessary for him to bend his head as his eyes travelled down the list. Jackson, who was reading over his shoulder, pointed and said, 'Look. We've included the two most important ones. Paul would want to start with a homeopathic dose that would tell us nothing.'

The first day, when he had been introduced, the man had insisted that everyone call him by his surname. It was only by accident, when Paul took a message from his mother, that he discovered the 'A' stood for Algernon. No wonder he preferred Jackson. Conceding to himself that he'd lost the argument about the tests, Paul changed tack. 'A small dose could at least tell us if the human DNA had any particular sensitivity to the drug,' he said.

Martin turned towards him. Paul could imagine that if he had not lost his facial mobility his eyes would have narrowed. 'I don't understand your anxiety. You've been happy enough with the way we've calculated the dose before. Can you explain?'

He was a fair man. If you could find your way through the tangle of company hierarchy he would still listen. Paul spoke with more confidence. 'This is the first time we've produced a specific DNA cytotoxic drug. It could have unexpected effects.'

Jackson leant forward. 'We're not the first company to go to trials. I wish to God we were. We're falling behind in the race.' He looked up and saw the shadow of disdain on Paul's face. 'We'll be using it on patients who are already very ill. What is there to lose?'

Paul looked down at Jackson's hand, pressed against the top of the desk. The skin over the knuckles was white where it covered the fatty ridges. For a muscular man his hands were decidedly podgy. Raising his eyes Paul looked directly at his face for the first time. 'We may hasten their deaths,' he said.

'We may prolong their lives. Possibly for a considerable time.' The two men glared at each other. Paul felt the full power of the man's ambition, but he didn't drop his gaze.

Martin broke the tension. 'We're back to the question of hypothetical risks. There's no evidence that the effects will be different from other cytotoxics just because it acts directly on the DNA.'

'That's the point. We don't know,' said Paul.

Martin turned his whole body towards him. 'Look Paul, the last time you made a fuss about DNA modification you were proved wrong. On the strength of the arguments you put forward with Brenda we did make further checks on our production processes, at considerable expense, and no faults were found.'

It was the first time Martin had criticised him about the incident. Paul realised that he would never be forgiven for wasting company money. He had been blind – with a thud he realised how naïve and stupid he'd been not to see the reason why he had never been promoted further up the chain. 'But this isn't the production process. It's the mode of action of the drug.'

'What do you suggest?' Martin asked.

'That we start with another batch of animals and do all the liver tests. If you must rush into clinical trials then start with a fraction of the dose you would use if it were calculated on a weight for weight basis.'

'That would be a waste of time. Time when people are dying,' Jackson said.

Unable to control the rancour in his voice, Paul replied, 'Time when the drug isn't earning its keep, you mean.'

Jackson opened his eyes, shaded now with innocence. 'That's not what I meant. You always imply that I'm influenced by finance. We do have to think about money, of course –'

'Yes. It's more important than risks –'

Martin raised a hand. 'This isn't the place for emotional argument. I'm surprised at both of you. In the absence of any other way of calculating a dose, one that has a chance to be effective, I can see no alternative but to use the well-established methods.'

A silence fell on the room. Jackson stared straight ahead. Paul knew that all further argument would be useless. He got to his feet. At the door he paused, hearing Martin's voice behind him. 'I'm sorry, Paul.'

He left, taking care not to slam the door.

When he arrived back in his office he carefully replaced the folder in its place on the shelf. The arguments he'd tried to build round the records had cut no ice with Martin. Indeed, it seemed he had decided to support Jackson's view from the beginning. The result had been a foregone conclusion.

As Paul tidied the remaining papers on his desk the walls of the room seemed to be squeezing his ribs, making it difficult to take enough breath into his lungs. He was aware of the endless corridors beyond his door, the offices and laboratories connected into a giant mechanical organism, in which he was just a single cell. He got up and made another turn around the room. Then he straightened his chair and went out, locking the door behind him. Security had been tight ever since the bomb. Although the doorman had known him for years, he still had to show his company badge as he passed.

He left his car in the park and headed for the river. It took half an hour to walk from the factory to the lock, from which the path led upstream to the pub where he had seen the otter with Fran. In his mind this lower reach had always belonged to Brenda. It was here that they had walked in the New Year after their affair started, and he'd covered some of the stretch on his journeys to and from her house. With his hands in his pockets he strode along, his head bent as he banished both women from his thoughts.

Leaning forward into the wind, his steps quickened. On his right side the current flowed downstream against his line of progress. He didn't look up to search the margins of the river for little grebe, or the overhanging branches for the blue of a kingfisher. He was oblivious to the changing voice of the water as it split to encircle a small island, the near channel a narrow hustling ribbon where the reflected light would, on any other day, have caught his attention. He would have paused in the hope of seeing a dipper. But now his feet carried him on, from one woman's territory to the other, over the stile and up into the woods where he had made love to Fran, watching the limbs of their unborn child moving beneath her skin.

He was breathless as he reached the top of the hill and walked to the gap in the trees. Looking up, he blinked as his eyes tried to adjust from the narrow vision of his shoes plodding over the ground to the expanse in front of him. In the distance to his left the city lay, hazed in the grey of industry. On the other side, and below him, the fields folded into each other, punctuated by clumps of dark trees. An occasional pearly glint showed him the course of the river. A thrush was singing. A sense of purpose began to take shape inside him, as if working from the periphery of his fingers and toes, via his backbone and up into his consciousness. He knew what he must do: the way in front of him ran as straight and uncompromising as a Roman road.

He looked down again at his shoes, covered with dust. They were his best, chosen along with his second-best suit, for the meeting with Martin. It didn't matter now what he wore. He had a job to do that didn't depend on making a good impression or winning the argument. All it needed was courage. For a moment he searched frantically for an escape route. Surely there must be another way. As his mind twisted in one direction and then another, he knew that no one and nothing, not even the memory of his father, could deliver him from the future that he'd chosen.

THIRTEEN

2003

The pervading smells of disinfectant and cabbage carried Fran back to the hours she'd spent waiting to waylay busy consultants or to press her data sheets into the hands of harassed junior doctors.

Some woman at Martin's house had told her he was seriously ill. His ward seemed to be miles from the entrance. As she made her way down the corridors she passed a porter pushing a trolley. His face was cheerful, despite the fact that his patient was gripping her stomach and moaning. Round a corner she glimpsed a group of students, status-symbol stethoscopes leaking from their pockets. Their laughter was cut off as a shriek of pain reminded them of the misery that lurked beneath the familiar hospital scene. A visitor, carrying a tied bunch of shop-bought flowers, made Fran look down at the three late-season roses in her hand, picked from the garden that morning. They were pathetic.

She had braced herself against the shock of the scars, but the sight of Martin's head perched, strangely puffy, above the emaciated arms and trunk, sapped her courage. 'You probably don't remember me. I'm Paul Ashby's widow. Geoffrey said he thought you wouldn't mind if I came.'

It was impossible to tell if he minded or not. A misshapen hand indicated the locker by the side of his bed. The jug of water and single card looked forlorn. She put the roses down. 'Thank you,' he said. 'Pull up a chair.'

The ward was crowded with visitors, some beds had three or more people huddled round. Fran could see no free chair and went out of the ward to find one. When she got back, her flowers had disappeared but as she settled herself, edging her chair in beside the drip attached to his arm, a nurse returned with them in a vase.

'I'm glad you've got a visitor today,' she said to Martin.

Fran thought she saw his eyes flash. 'I'm not a complete solitary. I do have some friends, you know.'

'Of course you do,' the nurse cooed, as she walked away.

Martin shifted in the bed. 'Why do they have to be so bloody reassuring?'

Fran blinked. From the things Paul had said she hadn't expected him to swear in front of someone he hadn't seen for years. Some life still flowed in a man who could kick against the patronising remark. He turned his head on the pillow so he could look at her without having to strain the eyes in his imprisoned face. 'What's brought you here?'

Goodness, he was direct. She couldn't match his blunt approach. 'I came to see how you were doing.'

'I doubt it. But thanks, anyway.'

'Is it serious?'

'I've got lung cancer. It's spread to my bones.'

Paul's last weeks had been a fight against breathlessness. At the time she could imagine nothing worse. Now, the picture of malignant cells, pressing and expanding inside the limited space of a bone, filled her with horror. She had to say something. 'That must be terribly painful.'

'I've got a morphine pump. They want to teach me how to work it, but my fingers are too clumsy to press the syringe accurately. The engineer chaps are tying to rig up a bigger one, so I can do it for myself at home.'

'Geoffrey told me your wife died. I'm sorry. Are you living alone now?'

'With various good ladies who pop in. I do OK.' He was silent for a moment, as he stared across the ward. 'Geoffrey is too full of himself by half. Don't trust him.'

Fran didn't want to talk about Geoffrey. 'Have you had any chemotherapy?'

'Some.'

' Were any of them the drugs Paul was working on before he died?'

'No.' The word seemed to explode from between the constricted lips. Fran tried to sink lower in her chair as Martin made a distracted movement of his hands. He wasn't going to help her; any further questions would be intrusive. But she'd come for a reason; she must try to make him understand. Leaning forward, she said, 'I have to find out what Paul was doing.' She looked away, not seeing the nurses and patients and visitors who milled about the ward. 'I don't seem able to accept his death.' Turning back to him she said, 'I expect you guessed he had an affair with Brenda. Everybody seems to have known. But that's not what's bugging me.' She paused. 'Not just that, anyway.' It was so difficult to explain. 'We grew apart in some ways. He didn't confide in me any more.' The figure on the bed made no response. What was the point of going on? In desperation she reached out and put her hand over the scarred fingers. 'Do you know what he was doing at the end of his life?'

For a long moment he didn't move. Then he nodded slowly. 'Yes, I know.'

'Please, tell me. You're my only hope.'

There was no reply from the bed.

'It's time you left.' Fran turned to find a nurse at her side. 'We're serving tea at any minute and my patient's tired.'

Fran looked around in alarm. A general movement started in the ward as visitors scraped their chairs back and collected their belongings. She couldn't leave now. Martin's hand winced under her grip. Contrite, she let go. 'Sorry.'

'It's all right.' He was silent. Then he appeared to pull the various bits of himself together, his head sitting better on his neck, his arms more securely attached to his body. 'I think you ought to know – but it isn't pretty. I'd rather write it . . .' He looked down at his useless hands, then seemed to find a reserve of energy as he sat forward. 'Nurse.' She hurried over, surprised by the strength in his voice. 'I've got some things to say to this lady. Can you find somewhere we can talk in private?'

'We're not supposed to move patients out of the ward.'

'This is important. I haven't got much time left. If you deny me this –'

'OK. I'll make an exception.' She winked.

Fran's heart went out to the man who couldn't wink back.

After a few minutes the nurse returned to help him into a wheelchair. They were taken to a lift and up three flights, nearly to the top of the building. 'All the side wards on your floor are full,' she said. 'This is the only one I could find in the whole hospital.' The empty bed looked grotesque with its pile of pillows at one end and the bed cradle at the other, like a two-headed animal with no body in the middle. She put the chair by the window and tucked the drip stand into the corner. Fran sat opposite in the one armchair. The nurse showed her how to depress the lever of his morphine pump if he wanted a top-up, and then pushed the contraption down beside his thigh. As she did so his dressing-gown slipped and his urine bottle was exposed.

They looked out over the city. Cabot Tower showed behind the University, with the spire of St Mary Redcliffe, the sailor's church, over to the left. Fran remembered the day she had gone inside, after she had learnt of Paul's affair. She glanced across at Martin. The privacy he had demanded didn't seem to have made it any easier for him to talk. A picture of his tongue, burnt and swollen in his mouth, came into her mind. That was silly, he had the physical ability to speak perfectly well. Some other paralysis kept him silent.

He shifted, trying to get comfortable. 'She was always trouble, that one.'

'Brenda?' He nodded. 'I'm getting used to the idea that she and Paul ...' Fran still hated to couple their names together. 'If she made him happy –'

'That's not what I'm talking about.' He dragged his eyes away from the view and looked across at her. 'I'm sorry, it must have been awful for you, but there were bigger things at stake.'

'Something to do with the work?'

'She was a nuisance then and she's much worse now. She's a fanatic who has worked her way into a position of considerable influence, lecturing all over the world and doing so much harm.'

'I heard her recently, in Bristol.' Fran twisted her hands together. If she wanted honest answers she had to be truthful herself. 'I couldn't help being moved. She spoke well.' She hoped he didn't despise her, thinking she'd been swept along with the gullible crowd.

Martin transferred his attention to the window again. In the silence his head shifted from side to side in small jolts, as if his mind were visiting the different parts of the city: the industry and traffic, the tall cranes and hooting ships, the shops and houses, each holding its human burden. When he spoke it seemed to be more to himself than to his visitor. 'It's such a scary world, we clutch at straws. The dangers are so big, global warming and terrorism, things like that. Few people nowadays have any sort of faith to help them. No wonder they listen to bigots like Brenda – single-minded passions appear to offer simple solutions.' He looked down at his hands, then up to Fran, as he went on, 'But what does that lead to, eh? Animal activists, who have no thought for people as they fight for their precious mice.' The rigidity of his face loosened to allow her a glimpse of irony.

She put out her hand. 'Your fingers –'

Irritated, he shifted in his chair. 'That's not what I'm trying to say. What matters is the damage her tactics are doing to the advance of science. Do you have any idea of the potential in our genetic work? We will be able to fit our drugs to individual people. The whole of therapeutics will be transformed. With this prize within our reach, we have a duty to go on. Every delay means more suffering.'

'Was that what Paul was trying to do?' He had allowed her hand to lie on his, but now he pulled it away and rubbed his leg.

'Could you work this thing? Give me a bit more?' She reached for the pump and pressed the syringe to the mark as the nurse had shown her. She had to be patient and let him tell her in his own time. He closed his eyes. They must have sat in silence for several minutes before he shuddered and opened them.

'It's not just our work. Her meddling is holding up so many other advances. There's the chance to wipe out genetic diseases altogether – just think what that would mean. We may be able to find out who is susceptible to which diseases so that we can take evasive action, learn how to avoid those ills that each of us, individually, is most likely to suffer. If I had known . . . maybe I would have stopped smoking sooner. It's a matter of interaction between genes and the environment. We have to find out all we can about genes if we're to harvest the full benefits.'

Fran felt as if she was in a lecture theatre, listening to a master of the art giving his well-prepared paper, illustrated with a personal detail to give it punch. 'And Paul . . . ?'

Martin's fluency deserted him as quickly as it had come. There was another long silence before he said, 'I was wrong. I thought he was under her spell, even after she left. I never really trusted his judgement once they had written that paper. But he was right and I was wrong. We were going too fast.' He closed his eyes again.

'Too fast for what?'

'Too fast with the clinical trials. I should have listened to him, not to that upstart Jackson.'

'He kicked my dog downstairs,' Fran said. 'He's a horrible man.'

Martin continued as if she hadn't spoken. 'If I'd listened to Paul things would have been different. He wouldn't . . .'

'He wouldn't what?'

For a moment Martin looked at her with penetrating clarity. He might be under the influence of morphine but he knew exactly what he was trying to say. As her eyes held his they seemed to retreat further into their sockets and she felt him slipping away from her. The door opened to admit a woman with a tray.

'Staff nurse said you were in here. We mustn't let you miss your supper.' She balanced the tray on the empty bed while she moved the table and arranged it over Martin's lap. All the time she chattered, as if the silence she had interrupted was a contamination that she had to wipe away. 'That's such a lovely view. Look over there, my house is just behind the hill and I can see the hospital from my top window. Just let me lift your feet so the frame can go underneath. You must eat and keep up your strength.' She didn't seem to notice that he had closed his eyes again. Nor had she any idea that Fran was fighting the temptation to tell her to get the hell out of the room.

When she brought the tray and started to tuck the napkin into the neck of his pyjamas Fran could bear it no longer. 'It's all right. I'll help him.'

'You do that, dear. It's so good to have friends. I'll be back later with the teapot, and I'll bring an extra cup so you can have one with him.'

'That would be lovely,' said Fran, willing her to go away and never come back.

As the door closed she looked at the crumpled figure propped in the chair. She despaired of ever recapturing the lost moment. His breathing was more regular as if he was slipping into sleep or unconsciousness. If she could get him to eat something, perhaps he'd revive. 'Martin?' He opened his eyes and stared through her. 'They've brought your tea. It's mince and mashed potatoes and carrots. Would you like me to help you?' He nodded. She fetched an upright chair from beside the bed and squeezed it in next to the window. Then she reached across to take the plate on to her lap and manipulated a bit of mince and potato on to the spoon. 'Open,' she said, as she held it to his mouth. He did as he was told and swallowed without too much difficulty. Another instalment and then another went down. He'd eaten almost half of the food before he closed his eyes again. 'That's enough.'

Putting the plate back on the tray she wondered if she should risk some of the yellow blancmange, or another question. 'You were saying about Paul . . . ?'

'Was I?'

'You said he did something . . . ?'

'He made records. Detailed records.' Martin opened his eyes. 'I couldn't destroy such vital evidence. So I hid them away. I convinced myself they proved nothing.'

'Fran sat forward. 'You hid them? Where? Where are they?'

He didn't seem to hear the urgency in her voice. 'I hadn't got the guts to admit I was wrong. Only when the patients . . . it was too late then. I was a coward.'

Fran had to lean forward to catch what he said. The last word hung in the air like a twist of smoke from a distant bonfire. His eyes closed again and she saw there were tears in the corners. One overflowed and was caught on a ridge of scar tissue where it sparkled in a ray of sunlight that had edged in through the window. Distressed, she took a tissue from her bag and gently wiped his face and eyes. He lifted his hand to touch hers.

'I'm so tired. I'd like to go back to bed now.'

Fran sensed that the admission had cost him much. But she couldn't leave it like that. 'Paul worked on his notes every day till he died. What was he writing? I have to know.'

Martin's eyes were closed and his breath came in short gasps that deepened into a long shuddering sob. Then he was still for so long Fran thought he'd died.

'Martin?' she whispered.

His eyelids flickered. She hurried out to fetch the nurse. By the time they returned, Martin seemed even more out of it. The nurse put a finger on his pulse.

'He's exhausted. I shouldn't have let him talk for so long.'

'He had things he wanted to tell me.'

'I know.' She took him back to the ward and called for help to lift him into his bed. Fran hovered by the door. 'You'd better go now, ' the nurse said.

'Can I just say goodbye?'

'Only if you're very quick.'

By the bedside Fran looked down at him. She didn't know if he was aware of her standing there but as she watched, his lips moved. She bent down to try and catch what he was saying. 'Ask Mr Bennett,' were the only words she heard. The name meant nothing to her. Straightening up, she looked down at the remnants of the scarred man. Then, leaning over him again, she laid her lips on his face where the tear had lodged. 'I think you're a brave man, whatever you say. Thank you.' He made no sign of having heard her. As she walked down the stairs and out of the building, she ignored the tears that ran down her own cheeks.

'Oh good. Scrabble. I wondered when we were going to start again.' Hazel took the glass of gin and tonic, not noticing that Fran added none of the spirit to her own glass. The board was open on the table with the green baize bag of letters waiting by the side. During the previous winter they'd played once or twice each week. Although Hazel liked to think her visits were a help to her friend, she also enjoyed the game: and the fact that she always won. As the November days had dragged on, the darkness arriving noticeably earlier each evening, she'd missed her trips out to the comfortable country house. Fran had been unusually brusque when she had tried to wangle an earlier invitation.

Hazel took her seat across the table, noticing that her friend's face looked different. The lines under her eyes were darker, but balanced by a more determined tilt of her chin. She wasn't to know that Fran had been practising, playing one hand against the other, while she wrestled with the problem of the unknown Mr Bennett.

'I've ordered a pizza delivery. One of those deep ones, from a new place. That all right by you?'

'Of course.' Hazel tried to keep the disappointment out of her voice. She was tired of the pre-cooked food she lived on in the city and had been looking forward to one of Fran's home-baked dishes. In the past her friend had taken such trouble to tempt her with new vegetarian recipes.

It was a difficult game, with one side of the board blocked quickly. If it hadn't been for a lucky chance to use her Z in the word zenith, on a triple word score, she might even have lost. Fran was playing so well, Hazel's growing curiosity made her determined to find out what was going on. Once the food had arrived and the glasses had been re-filled she began to probe. 'How are you doing?'

Fran didn't answer at once. Hazel was a dear, and she might be useful, but she could be insensitive. She hadn't mentioned Martin's death, though perhaps she hadn't seen the notice in the paper. The day after her visit Fran had rung the hospital but they'd told her he was too ill to see anyone. Within a few days he was dead.

'I bumped into Geoffrey a few weeks ago,' she said, trying to sound casual.

'How was he?'

'Friendly as ever. Quite flirtatious, in fact.'

'Oh Fran, when I said you should get out and meet people I didn't mean Geoffrey. He's the last person you want to get tangled up with. He's so unreliable with women. He has a baby now, you know.' Fran heard the old hurt in her voice.

'He told me. He seems a doting father.'

'You really must steer clear of him. He's bad news.'

There was something about Hazel, with her flowing scarves and new-age convictions, that provoked Fran to rebel, as if it were her mother who was lecturing her. She would take her own decisions, see whomever she wanted to see. 'Geoffrey reminded me that Paul worked closely with Brenda Starling. I suppose you always knew about their affair.'

Hazel's fork paused, its helping of pizza suspended in mid-air. She lowered it deliberately on to the plate before she spoke. 'I hoped you'd never find out.'

Fran felt foolish. She hated the idea of the whispers in corners, of nudges as she walked past. She felt hot as she realised that the trainees she had taught with such confidence had probably been sniggering behind their hands. But she was damned if she was going to allow herself to become a recipient of Hazel's pity. 'I called to see her, and then I went to one of her lectures. She holds her audience wonderfully. I quite like her, we might even become friends.'

'How could you, when she betrayed you for so many years?'

'I might ask her to a meal.'

'You're crazy. I don't want to see Geoffrey or his beastly baby. He never let me have one.'

For a moment the depth of Hazel's pain was exposed. Fran felt a surge of gratitude for the daughter Paul had given her. She put her hand out in a gesture of comfort, but her friend pulled away to concentrate on her food. After a few moments she said, 'I should have warned you, but I didn't know for sure. It was just rumours, and I'm no rumour-monger.'

'I'm glad you didn't tell me. Paul and I were happy. Whatever he had with Brenda, it didn't threaten us.' As she spoke, Fran was surprised to find that she believed what she'd said. Hazel could wallow in her hatred of Geoffrey's other women. Her fears for Paul were different now. 'Does the name Mr Bennett mean anything to you?'

'Bennett? I don't think so. Why do you ask?'

'I think he worked with Paul and Brenda.'

Hazel shrugged. 'I've no idea.'

Fran tried a different approach. 'They worked on a lot of classified material. Did you ever type any of it?'

'I didn't do much for them. I only went to Keynsham occasionally when they were really stuck. I was a good typist, you know, fast and accurate. I never saw anything suspicious between them. They were very skilful in public.'

What a one-track mind she had. 'I was thinking about the work,' Fran said. 'I expect the secrecy drew them together. I wonder how the company keeps all those things safe from inquisitive eyes?'

'What a funny idea. I don't know. '

'I'm sure other biotech companies would try to search out their confidential files. I expect they have spies working there.'

Hazel frowned. 'That's a bit melodramatic.' She paused. 'Some files do have blue stickers on them. We were never allowed to open those.'

Fran was driven by an urgent curiosity. 'Did they keep them anywhere special?'

'I've no idea. Why should you care?'

'Oh, I don't really. I suppose it was just seeing Brenda and listening to her campaigning.'

'Gosh, you don't think she was a spy for another company, do you?'

'I shouldn't think so, but you never can tell.' Let her believe she was interested in Brenda. Fran already regretted having said so much, and certainly wouldn't mention her visit to Martin. 'Ready for a return game?' Her voice was light. When she lost again, despite all her practice, she wasn't too disappointed. At the door she tolerated the extra hug, the implied sisterhood, now she too was a deceived woman.

Back in the sitting room she stared at the board and empty glasses. Since her visit to Martin she'd been in a state of suspension, unable to retreat to her previous deadness or to go forward. She didn't know what she was looking for or if she wanted to find it. Although she had considered asking Brenda to a meal, before she knew about the affair, the suggestion to Hazel had been an act of bravado. Now she saw it was the only way she could get the help she needed. They'd both loved him. If they were to uncover the truth, they must work together.

FOURTEEN

2003

Three days before Christmas the phone rang. Fran tensed. On each occasion she had tried to call Brenda the answer phone was on. She'd left a message but as the days wore on her resolve had wavered. Picking up the receiver, she held it carefully away from her head, as if a snake might hiss in her ear. It was a man's voice.

'Oh, it's you,' she said. Geoffrey's languid vowels were unmistakable.

'Hi. You sound odd.'

'I was expecting someone else.'

'I was just ringing to ask how you are. Did you get to see Martin before he died?'

'I did. But he was very ill.'

'I'd like to hear about your visit. I wonder, could I pop round to wish you greetings of the season?'

Fran could hear Hazel's voice warning her against him. 'I don't know. How's the baby?'

'She's doing fine. I'll bring some photos to show you.' It sounded innocent. 'Can I come tomorrow evening?'

'OK,' she said, with an inner shrug at Hazel.

'I'll bring a little something to toast the season.'

'Look –'

'Maybe you could rustle up the odd crust?'

The cheek of the man, inviting himself to supper. 'You mustn't stay. You'll want to get back to see that child of yours, before she goes to bed.'

'You let me worry about that. I only want to see that you're OK.

Christmas is a funny time, especially when you're on your own. You are alone, aren't you, no family arrived yet?'

Perhaps he was just being kind. 'They're coming later.'

'I'll see you, then.' She made no more excuses but turned her mind to the days ahead. Sylvia was going to Richard's family. Then they were coming to her on Boxing Day. Fran hoped it might be a sign of impending commitment. Paul's sister Lizzie and her husband Charles were also arriving that day, bringing their slides of Tanzania. They had been running a hospital in Arusha while the resident doctor was away on sabbatical leave. The last time Fran had seen them was at Paul's funeral.

She hadn't decided yet how she would spend Christmas Day itself. Hazel had invited her to go to a hotel in the Cotswolds that advertised, "Traditional Festivities and all the Trimmings." The idea of paper hats and synthetic jollity, families pretending to be happy when they were not, filled Fran with gloom. She would rather spend the day alone, take Bruiser for a walk if the weather allowed. If not, she could curl up with a box of chocolates and watch the Queen's speech. Paul and Sylvia had both been scornful of royalty and for years she'd hidden her own sentimental interest. Now she was free to indulge herself.

Standing in front of her full-length mirror, she removed the last of her clothes. The bath water was running. She pressed her hands over her hips, then cradled her breasts. Although she'd managed to feed Sylvia for several months they were still well-rounded, different from the sagging bags she'd seen occasionally through her mother's bedroom door. Turning sideways, she pulled in her stomach. Despite the roll of fat her outline wasn't too bad. Was it possible that a man could still enjoy her body?

She blushed as she hurried to turn off the taps, where the water was luxuriously deep and the bubbles threatened to spill over the rim of the bath.

After a long soak she fished a pair of black satin pants and matching petticoat from the back of a drawer. She had no idea how many years they had been there or why she had bought them.

Perhaps for one of the rare occasions when she had tried to rekindle Paul's interest. Her black dress slipped easily over her curves. She wound a red scarf under the collar and fixed it with the metal scarf-ring Paul had given her. The stork, embossed on the flat front, no longer reminded her of unplanned babies.

While waiting for Geoffrey to arrive she lit the sitting-room fire and tried different lighting effects. The central bulb accentuated the lines in her face, but just two wall lights made the room feel cosy.

He bounced in and kissed her lightly on the cheek. There was no sign of the randy man she had been expecting with a mixture of excitement and dread. He was dressed casually in a check jacket and open-necked shirt, more suited to June than December. In the kitchen he produced a bottle from a supermarket carrier bag. 'I hope it hasn't warmed up too much in the car. I've had it on ice so it should be OK.'

Fran wondered how he had got out of the house with a bottle of champagne. Did his woman know where he was? She let the thought float away from her as she reached for the glasses. She'd been so good, not a single drink since that week of cold turkey. She would damn-well enjoy the evening; the future could take care of itself. As he opened the bottle she ran her tongue over her lips. It was Christmas, after all.

She led him into the sitting room, carrying the cashew nuts and Bombay mix. Although she hadn't cooked anything special a packet of smoked salmon was defrosting, just in case he insisted on staying for some food. Geoffrey raised his glass to her. 'What are you doing over the festive season?'

'The family are coming on Boxing Day.' Fran went on to explain that she was looking forward to being alone on the day itself.

Geoffrey frowned. 'You could have come to us but we'll be with her parents.'

'Really, I don't mind. When you've lived alone for a year the idea of solitude isn't frightening. In fact, one craves a certain amount.' She paused. 'Provided friends call from time to time.'

He smiled, his brown eyes lingering a fraction too long on hers before he helped himself to some more nuts. 'How's Hazel?' he asked.

Fran told him about her visit to the Cotswolds. He smiled. 'She always was a bit of a hedonist. Why didn't you go with her? You could afford it, couldn't you?'

'She asked me, but it's not my thing.'

'No.' he looked into the fire and back to her face. 'I wonder what your thing is?'

'I've asked myself that often enough.' Fran smiled. 'I don't really know. Before I was married I loved to roam the countryside. I turned down invitations so that I could have the weekends to myself. I took a sketchpad with me.'

'You draw?'

'I used to, a bit. And paint. But the pictures never satisfied me. When I started work again I gave up trying.'

'Didn't your parents worry about you, out there on your own?'

'They didn't know. I couldn't come to much harm. All I had to do was find my way back to a village and wait for a bus. The service was good in those days.'

'You were an independent girl, weren't you?'

'I suppose so. Then I met Paul . . . on a CND march.'

'He was always one for causes.'

Fran struggled to remind herself that Paul had distrusted this man. He re-filled her glass and left the room. She heard the front door open and shut, then his footsteps going into the kitchen.

'I've put another bottle in the fridge in case we want it. If not, you can use it for your family party.'

'Shouldn't you be getting home?'

'All in good time.'

Champagne was wonderful stuff; it lifted her spirits better than any other drink. As she turned the glass in her hand, watching the bubbles, she thought of her bottles locked away in the cupboard. A locksmith could open it for her. She felt sure she had the self-control to drink in moderation now.

Geoffrey moved on to the sofa beside her and she made no attempt to push him away, feeling comfortable as she turned her face up for his kisses. His hand moved to her breast and she felt his fingers caress the nipple. She shifted her position and, giving a small laugh, he reached across to the other side, then smoothed his hand down her body. She experienced none of the revulsion she had thought was ingrained at the core of her being. After a few minutes he released her and she sank back on to the cushions, heavy with disappointment.

He leant over and ran his finger down the side of her face. Smiling, he said, 'I'm awfully hungry. We've got all evening together. Have you any food?'

'What about your partner?'

'Oh ... she's gone ahead to her parents with the baby. I'm joining her tomorrow.'

So that was it. He had arranged this, planned to seduce her in her own house when his woman was away. 'Can't you live one night without a woman?'

'My darling Fran, it isn't like that. You must know, I've fancied you for years. I promise you we won't do anything that upsets you. We'll have some food and enjoy it. Let the evening take care of itself.'

'I've only got smoked salmon and fruit.'

'It sounds scrumptious.'

What a kid he was. No grown man would use a word like that; it reminded her of scrumping apples, small boys climbing over walls, giving the farmer the slip to pinch goodies that didn't belong to them.

She lit two candles and put them with the food on a small table at the side of the room. For a while Geoffrey talked about himself. He seemed to accept that he wouldn't go any higher in the company, but he hoped he could hold his present job long enough to get a good pension. 'It's a tough world out there now. Nobody's job is safe, with all the mergers and take-overs. I think I've made myself indispensable but you can never be sure, with young upstarts appearing behind me all the time.' As if remembering their last conversation he added, 'That Jackson is using every trick he can think of to get on to the board.'

Mention of the man cooled the excitement within her. Looking at Bruiser, stretched out in front of the fire as if it had been lit especially for him, she frowned. Her dog had aged rapidly in the last few weeks. Although the vet could find nothing specifically wrong, he seemed to think that the injury must have caused some brain damage. Fran was tempted to confide in Geoffrey – he was so gorgeous – but she stopped herself. It was clear he was falling behind in the rat race. If some exposé of Paul would help his own chances, he wouldn't hesitate to use it. Instead, she asked, 'Did Martin really think so much of Jackson?'

Geoffrey shrugged. 'I'm not sure.' He cut himself another slice of bread and asked if she wanted any more salmon. When she shook her head he took the remains on to his plate. 'Sad about his death. How was your visit?'

She answered with care. 'He was very ill, but he talked a bit. He implied that much of the work that Paul and Brenda did together was confidential.' Keeping her voice as disinterested as possible, she added, 'I suppose you have to be careful about records?'

'Goodness yes, both in pharmaceuticals and the new foods. There's enormous commercial competition these days, you can't be too careful.'

'How on earth do you do it?' she asked, her eyes wide as she turned towards him.

'You know how the security system was tightened after the bomb. It's even worse now. Guards on the doors, everyone wears badges, that sort of thing. Then there's a special room, in the basement at Keynsham, where the hottest files from both places are stored when they're not in use.'

Fran got up to fetch the second bottle from the fridge, not daring to let him see her face. Blue marked files, kept in the basement at Keynsham ... But Martin had said he'd hidden Paul's work. Would he have chosen such an obvious spot or marked it with a sticker? 'I wish I'd known him better when he was working with Paul,' she said.

'He wasn't much help to you, then?'

'Not really. What sort of man was he? Would he have taken files home with him so he could work on them in the evenings?'

Geoffrey laughed. 'He and Paul were two of a kind. They both preferred to work overtime, leaving everything in its right place before they went home at night. I'm afraid I sometimes break the rules and carry a record out of the building. Especially if I've got behind with some urgent task.'

'You sound human,' she said with a laugh, determined not to reveal her thoughts. If Martin were that methodical the chances were he had filed Paul's record somewhere in that room. A wild picture of climbing in through a window flitted across her mind. She poured the fizz slowly into Geoffrey's glass so the bubbles didn't overflow, then stood by his chair, her body pressed against his shoulder. His arm came round her and he nuzzled his head into her stomach. 'You're really something,' he said. She kissed the top of his head before pulling away to fill her own glass and sit down again.

They drank: his hand crept across the table as his eyes sought hers. He was never going to remain faithful to one woman and she was no threat to his family. She had no wish to take him away from the mother of his child. She stood up again to fetch the fruit bowl. He was behind her now, his arms around her middle, pulling himself against her while his hand worked up under her dress. 'Can we go upstairs?'

The straightforward request made it easy. He was so relaxed about the things that had become such a minefield of embarrassment with Paul. She nodded and led him by the hand, making sure that she closed the door behind her.

Upstairs she pointed to the room she'd reoccupied with Bruiser. Luckily the dog had made no move to leave the fire. Without warning she felt paralysed by shyness. Escaping to the bathroom she removed her pants and cleaned her teeth. How awful if she had bad breath.

Returning to the bedroom, she found Geoffrey standing in a shirt, the lower edge lifted by his arousal. He moved towards her to draw the black dress up over her head. Instinctively she turned her back, shielding her body with her arms. With one hand he drew back the bed covers, guiding her between the sheets with the other.

'Could you turn out the light?' she asked.

'Darling Fran. Can't I look at you?'

'I'm all wrinkly and fat.'

'I don't believe that. Anyway I like curvaceous women.' With a small sigh he got out to flick the switch, leaving the door ajar so that a shaft of light from the corridor softened the darkness. On his way back to the bed he took off his shirt. Without thinking she opened her arms to welcome him: then abandoned herself to his experienced caresses. As he tried to enter her a stab of pain made her cry out.

'Sorry. Am I hurting you?'

'Don't worry. It's been a long time.'

Geoffrey eased himself to her side. 'I think you weren't quite ready. We've got all the time in the world.'

Fran was reassured when she felt his erection against her side, as firm as ever. With Paul, she'd been afraid to move or say anything in case he went soft. Geoffrey was prepared to let her enjoy the slow climb up the slope of her arousal until she felt so moist that she knew she was as soft and warm as the inside of a new baked loaf. This time, when he eased himself inside her, the sound that forced its way from her lungs, up past her larynx and lips to echo round the room, was a cry of pleasure. She felt her body dissolve beneath him.

Afterwards, as they lay side by side, she was surprised to find she felt no guilt, merely a deep contentment.

'God, I'd die for a cigarette,' said Geoffrey.

'Would a cup of coffee do instead? We were too occupied after the meal – I forgot to make any.'

He turned and put his lips softly on hers. 'Better than nothing,' he said.

She slipped out of bed and put on her bathrobe. When she returned with a tray he was snoring. Sitting in the chair in front of her dressing table she watched the bedclothes move with each breath. She couldn't pretend to love the sexy bastard, but she would always be grateful to him for helping her discover that she was still a woman: still alive. And she felt happy that she'd not overdone the drinking. Or had she?

* * *

Church bells rang out as she made her way along the riverbank with Bruiser walking quietly at her heels, no longer with the energy to snuffle in the reeds for water rats. The car was behind her in a lay-by beyond the pub. The bar would be crowded later and she didn't want to get hemmed in. The day stretched out in front like an artist's board, prepared but empty, ready for the unknown picture that hovered between the tubes of paints and the imagination of the artist. The freedom she had felt in her youth was in her bones now.

Her small backpack held egg sandwiches, an apple and a Mars bar together with a bin liner – she'd pinched that idea from Geoffrey. Spreading it on a log, she sat and watched the river while she ate half the sandwiches. The church bells fell silent. It must be eleven-o-clock, far too early for lunch. She stretched out her legs, filled with the joy of making her own decisions, big or small. She could choose what to eat and when, who to invite into her bed . . . she smiled, wondering what other paths were waiting to be explored by her liberated feet.

After she'd thrown her crusts for two mallard that were circling hopefully in the water, she went on up the path through the wood. Her walk hadn't been planned, but as her breath started to come in gasps she knew where she was going.

When she reached the place where big trees guarded the dell, as they had done all those years ago, she spread out her plastic bag and rested her back against a trunk. The exposed roots that gripped the ground like fingers were still covered in moss, brown now in the colder air. Her breathing settled and she sat forward hugging her knees. Slowly she let herself think back to the time in bed with Geoffrey. Since then she had been aware of a deep feeling of peace inside her. She turned to look at the place where she had lain with Paul. What a waste. The feelings, which had come so easily then, had returned too late, produced in her by the wrong man. Now she really had given her mother grounds to disapprove. She smiled. The clouds still drifted over the valley below; the river followed its same sinuous course.

Bruiser came and pushed his nose into her lap. She reached into her pack for dog biscuits and the bottle of water. After taking a swig she poured a little into her hand, holding it out for him to lick before it escaped between her fingers. After three or four scanty handfuls he raised his head, water dripping from his chin. Ambling away from her, he rubbed himself against a figure that stood on the lip of the hill.

She'd heard no sound of the man's arrival; he could have been forced up from the ground beneath his feet. His hair curled down to his collar and his jeans were tight over a trim bottom. She grinned to find herself noticing such a detail. As he bent down to stroke Bruiser's head she heard him say in a lilting voice, 'You're a nice chap, where have you come from? Are you all alone, then?'

He turned and saw her, raising a tentative hand. She waved back, to put him at his ease. Men were so careful nowadays when they met a woman alone. With Bruiser she was never frightened, even though he showed a friendly interest in all newcomers. She winced, remembering how he'd been attacked in his own home.

The man took a few steps and hesitated. She got to her feet and walked towards him, but as she got nearer she realised he looked familiar. 'I think I know you?'

'I'm not sure . . .'

Now she remembered. 'You had a microphone. At the meeting.'

His lips spread into a wide smile. 'You're the tidy lady I found a seat for under the window.'

'That's right.' She blushed at the thought that he'd remembered her by the unsuitable clothes.

'This your dog?'

'Yes. He's called Bruiser.'

'Seems friendly.'

'Too friendly to be much of a guard dog.' They stood in silence, both looking out over the plain.

'Great spot, isn't it?' he said, determined to be polite. 'I often come up here when I want a bit of peace.'

His voice had a trace of some foreign accent Fran hadn't noticed at the meeting. She felt she was trespassing on his ground and shouldn't be there.

Realising the remark was a bit tactless, he added, 'You all alone, on Christmas Day?'

'I've got my family coming tomorrow but I enjoy my own company sometimes.' She stopped, then found herself saying, 'I came up here with my husband, when we were both young.' He turned and raised an eyebrow. Perhaps he'd heard her nostalgic tone. 'He died a year ago.'

'Bad luck, that.' He asked no questions but the sympathy in his voice was warming.

'What about you? Are you spending the day by yourself?'

'I'm meeting friends for a bit of a bash this evening.' He made no move to leave.

Fran found his presence comforting. Taking a quick peep at his face she decided he was older than she'd thought. Mid-fifties? As he gazed out over the valley his regular features seemed to hide a hint of melancholy.

After a moment, he said, 'She was good, that speaker.'

'Who, Brenda?' He nodded. 'She's very persuasive.'

'You need to be if you're going to get anything done. I can't hold forth like that. More of a doer than a speaker.'

'Really?'

'Last year, I was nabbed destroying a rape crop. Got six months.'

'In prison?' Fran was startled – she hadn't realised she was talking to an ex-convict. 'How did you cope?'

'I managed. Made some good friends, even though they'd got themselves on the wrong side of the law.' He paused. 'When the case finally went to court they gave me a year. Remission helped, of course. I only had to serve six months. But everyone was shocked. It was steep for a first offence. I'd expected probation.'

She tried to imagine what it must be like to be arrested for one's beliefs. Brenda would probably know. Even if it hadn't happened to her, she must have friends who had suffered. 'Did she visit you in gaol?'

'Who?'

'Brenda Starling. The speaker at that meeting.'

'She doesn't really know me. She's a big shot. I'm just cannon fodder.' He paused. 'I'd love to meet her properly.'

'What's your name?' Fran asked.

'I'm known as Jez. Short for John Edward Zbieranowski. My parents were Polish but I was born in this country. No one can pronounce my surname, so Jez is easier.'

'I'm Fran. Would you like a sandwich, Jez? There aren't many left, but you're welcome to share what I have.'

'Thanks.'

She fetched her plastic bag and spread it out again on the brow of the hill, offering him a corner. He laughed as he sat on the grass beside her, saying that his trousers were pretty waterproof and anyway he didn't mind a bit of damp. Fran found that, after all, she was glad to have some company. To be with someone who had no claims on her was restful. She broke the Mars Bar in half. He produced a penknife from his pocket to cut the apple. Refusing any water for himself he cupped his hands for Bruiser while she poured it in. When she had put the bottle back in her pack he said, 'This is cool. I was feeling lousy . . . my girlfriend left last week.'

'I'm sorry to hear that. You must be lonely.'

He shrugged. 'The relationship wasn't really working.'

How easily people gave up these days. There seemed to be none of the commitment that she had taken for granted. She didn't know if she would have left Paul if she had found out about his affair.

Anyway, it was too late to fuss about that now.

Jez continued to explain. 'She couldn't take my time in prison. They presumed I was the ringleader so I got longer than the others.' He shrugged. 'Being older, I suppose they wanted to make an example of me.'

'Were you?'

'What?'

'The ringleader.'

"Oh, I don't think so. It's a very collective thing.'

She looked at him more openly, trying to see him working in a field of yellow rape. 'You remind me of that gardener – the one on the telly – with curly hair.'

His laugh was easy, the echo mixing with the noise of the rising wind in the trees behind them. Running his hand over his head he said, 'I don't know the difference between an eelworm and a maggot. Do you?'

'Not really. I think eelworms attack potatoes.' The sun, which had emerged briefly to send a ray of winter light across the valley, disappeared again. 'It's tough being alone,' she said.

He turned towards her, his eyes soft with concern. 'Do you miss your husband much?'

'Yes and no. He was having an affair that went on for years and years.'

He put his fingers over hers as they lay on the plastic bag. 'That must have been awful for you.'

She nodded. 'I didn't know about it until recently. The marriage seemed good enough at the time. And we were together at the end.'

Jez rubbed his thumb over the back of her hand. 'You must be very strong.'

'I thought it was love,' Fran gulped. What on earth had driven her to confide in this complete stranger? Jumping up, she said, 'We'd better get going. I need to move and get my blood circulating.'

As they walked down the hill together it was natural for him to take her hand and slip it into his large pocket for warmth. When they reached the river he made to turn left, towards Bath. She frowned. She had been wondering whether to ask him to join her for a drink in the pub; not that she really wanted to go in. Or even if he would like to come home with her for a cup of tea. She hesitated, not wanting to let him go. 'When are you holding your next meeting?' she asked.

'There's one in South Wales in mid-January. The ravages of globalisation again. Are you coming?'

'I don't know. I feel a bit mixed about the subject. Who's speaking?' He mentioned a name she'd never heard, assuming it would fill her with admiration. 'I'm not a proper activist,' she said. 'I'm only half convinced.'

He smiled at her. 'Then you're halfway there. Like the best religious people, you can have doubts.'

'The trouble is, I always see both sides of the question. I suppose genetic engineering is as dangerous as Brenda says.' Thinking of Martin, she added 'But when I hear all the promises for medicine, then I don't know.'

'I'm not against all research but it must be controlled. When new organisms get into the environment we haven't a clue what they're doing. Those arseholes' – he softened the 'r' in his mouth, taking the sting out of the word that would normally have made Fran wince – 'they play havoc with traditions in the third world . . . they just make me mad.'

'Brenda feels the same.' Suddenly there was so much to talk about. Fran shivered again, it really was getting cold. 'Look, I live out in Somerset, but if you'd like to come back with me we could light a fire and warm up.' As she spoke she felt embarrassed, as if she was trying to pick him up; so desperate for company that she would snatch at any man.

To her relief he considered the suggestion carefully, then looked at his watch. 'I'd love to but I have some posters to finish and my friends are expecting me –'

Hurriedly she interrupted. 'Of course, it was a silly suggestion and anyway, I have to prepare for my visitors tomorrow.'

Jez took her hand and squinted into her face. 'If you're interested, I could drive you to the Welsh meeting, then we can talk some more. Shall I give you a bell?'

'I'd like that.'

He produced a pencil from his pocket and she wrote her number on the inside of the Mars Bar wrapper she'd scrunched in her pocket. He tore a piece off, wrote his own and handed it back.

'Cheers,' he said, turning to go.

'Cheers, thanks for the company.' She began to walk in the opposite direction. 'Merry Christmas,' she called after him, as she remembered what day it was.

FIFTEEN

2003–2004

At the end of the celebratory meal next day Sylvia and her Aunt Lizzie were doing most of the talking. Richard sipped his port as he watched Sylvia's eyes sparkle, despite the fact that she had drunk nothing but orange juice. Charles was picking small bits of shell from his nuts with neat fingers that had, until recently, been repairing the bodies of his African patients.

Presiding at the end of the table, Fran noticed that the two men were shy of each other. She hoped that, once they had space from the chattering women, they would find some common interest. She let her eyes drift towards the decanter. No one else seemed ready for a second glass of port. She had only allowed herself one glass of wine with the turkey but she knew that the second bottle in the kitchen was still half full.

She got up with a quick movement and went to make the coffee. Draining the remains of the wine into a tumbler, she downed it in one gulp and let her breath out with a sigh. The meal had gone well, despite her anxiety that she wouldn't be able to cope on her own. She hadn't cooked a traditional spread, with all the trimmings, since Paul's death. For a moment she tried to imagine what it would have been like to have Geoffrey sitting opposite her, charming her family with his easy smiles. God no, she didn't want him anywhere near the people she loved. Jez now . . . She blushed. How ridiculous, she'd only just met the man.

Richard pushed the door open with his back and dumped a pile of dirty plates on the draining board. 'Shall I load the dishwasher?'

'That would be great.' He worked quickly so that the machine was full before the kettle boiled. 'I'd like to try and move them into the sitting room,' Fran said. 'Would you check the fire for me?' She was beginning to treat him like a son-in–law. She must be careful. Twice before she had allowed herself to get fond of Sylvia's boyfriends, only to miss them badly when her daughter sent them packing.

The phone rang and she heard Sylvia ask who was calling – then pause. 'I'm fine . . . I'll see if she's in.'

She put the receiver down and went into the kitchen. 'It's Brenda. You don't want to speak to her do you, Mum?'

'Of course I do. I asked her to ring.' Sylvia followed her mother back into the hall and hovered by her side. Fran tried to wave her away. 'Go and look after the others.' Sylvia still hesitated.

'Hello? Can you hang on a moment?' Holding her hand over the mouthpiece, Fran whispered, 'It's OK. Really it is. She can't hurt me, I promise. But I must talk to her about something.'

Sylvia raised an eyebrow and went back into the dining room, shutting the door behind her.

Fran held the receiver in both hands as she perched on the chair. 'I'm sorry to keep you, I've got the family here. How are you?'

'I've been abroad and only got back yesterday. To find your message.'

'Is there any chance you could come here for a meal? I need to sort out Paul's books and I wondered if you'd like one or two to keep.'

'D'you mean that?'

Fran tried to keep her voice steady. 'I'm getting used to the idea that you and he . . .' She took a breath. 'You said you were worried about him. I'm beginning to think something was going on before he died.'

'What makes you say that?'

'Things have happened . . . I can't talk now.'

'I'll get my diary.'

Fran ran her teeth over her knuckles while she waited. Brenda suggested a day in the third week in January. After agreeing the time Fran was about to ring off, when she remembered the main reason she'd wanted to see Brenda again. 'Just a minute . . . do you know someone called Mr Bennett? He probably worked at Nonsec.'

'Bennett? The only person I can think of is one of the directors. Why d'you ask?'

'He might be able to help us.'

The silence at the other end of the line went on so long that Fran thought she might have rung off. Eventually Brenda said, 'He was very supportive of Paul after the fire. But that was years ago. He may have retired by now.'

'Could you find out for me?'

'I'll ask around.'

'Fran explained the way to the house and replaced the receiver. As she sat staring across the hall she found she was shaking. Sylvia came out of the sitting room and put an arm round her shoulders. 'It's OK, really it is,' Fran said again.

'Oh, Mum. Why can't you leave things alone?'

Fran looked up. She'd have to tell her daughter, try to make her understand. The voices behind the closed door had gone quiet. 'I can't explain now, we'll talk about it later.'

After settling her visitors for the night, Fran lay awake. Restless, she kicked off the covers. The thought of destroying her daughter's trust in her father was more than she could bear. She shivered and got out of bed to spread her duvet again. There was Lizzie too. If Paul had done something dishonourable it could shatter her belief in the man who had been both brother and father to her.

She gave up trying to sleep and tiptoed down the stairs. In the cupboard three sleeping tablets were left from the twelve prescribed after Paul died. She took them out, then put them back. Her hand wavered over the port bottle but with an effort she decided to try milk instead. Paul had vowed it was just as good as any drug. After warming it in the microwave she sat and took slow sips, imagining the blood being drawn to her stomach, leaving less to power her brain.

Back in bed, Fran continued to worry. She'd assumed that Brenda was concerned with Paul's reputation. Now, in the dead hours of the night, she could feel a ruthless streak behind the blue eyes of the woman, who seemed just as likely to use him for her own ends.

As she drifted into a troubled sleep she decided to play safe. Stick to the books, she told herself, no need to let on about anything else.

They woke to a hoar-frost and a world transformed. Every branch and blade of grass was heavy with strands of frozen dew. When they'd gone to bed the night before there had been no suggestion of a change in the weather. Fran blamed the sudden drop in temperature for her disturbed night.

Lizzie and Charles were like children, pacing across the grass and exclaiming at the crisp footprints behind them. 'Now we know we're back in England,' Charles said, as they sat down to breakfast. 'Africa was never like this. I'd forgotten how beautiful it could be.'

Everyone agreed it was just the day for a walk. The round trip, down the lane, across the fields and back by the river, was so familiar that Bruiser could have found the way blindfolded. Sylvia strode out in front with Richard. On the way back they stopped at the spot where Fran had almost fallen in, before she stopped drinking. What with Geoffrey's champagne and the wine the previous day she knew it would be difficult to break the habit all over again. She must persuade Sylvia to take the remains of the port away with her.

The men stared into the water as they talked about fish farming. As Sylvia climbed out on to a familiar branch of the willow tree, Fran quickened her step, with Lizzie by her side.

'We might stop at the pub on the way home,' Sylvia called after them.

'That's fine,' Fran replied over her shoulder. 'I want to put some potatoes to bake and make a salad. See you.'

In the house Lizzie flopped into the wicker chair and watched as Fran bustled about in the kitchen. 'Can I help?' she asked, without moving.

'No, stay there and talk to me. It's been ages since we had a good natter.'

'How are you?'

It was the question Fran had been expecting and dreading. Lizzie had been such a good friend in the years when Sylvia was growing up. Her listening skills were those of a good nurse, but now that Fran had the chance to talk she wasn't sure what she wanted to say. 'I think I'm recovering. I don't feel as dead as I did. The books warn you that the second year is often worse.' She shivered. 'I do hope not.'

'Books. Don't take any notice of them. Everyone's different. I've known people who haven't really started to grieve for six or seven years, while others are back to normal within months.'

'I'm not unhappy all the time. Sometimes I can go for hours, even days, without thinking of him. Then something hits me, like a mention of CND on the radio, or a stray caterpillar.' She reached down into the bottom of the fridge to get some celery and cabbage for the coleslaw she was making.

Lizzie smiled. 'His wretched insects – they were so important to him.' She looked out at a flock of starlings that had discovered the crumbs Fran had thrown on to the lawn. 'I wish he were here so I could tell him about Africa. He was always so keen to go there . . .' She stopped, embarrassed as she remembered why he had not gone.

'I feel so responsible. I ruined his life.'

'Don't be ridiculous – you must never think that. It takes two to make a baby and he adored you. He was lucky to have such a good marriage.'

If only you knew, thought Fran.

'He was a romantic,' Lizzie continued. 'A dreamer of dreams when he was a young man. Always trying to make up for not being . . .' she stopped. ' I don't remember our father, you know. But he did, all the time.'

'He didn't often speak about him.'

'No, but I could feel the shadow in his mind.' Lizzie paused to try and find the words to express what she had always known but never spoken about. Her brother had been special. Until that moment she hadn't felt able to share her memories with anyone, not even Fran. 'Paul wanted to understand what made his father go back to Malaya, after all he'd been through. He agonised about whether his death was some grand gesture, or an act of desertion.'

Fran took two apples from the bowl on the windowsill and started to chop them for her salad. So many things jostled in her mind: Paul's affair with Brenda – the miserable Jackson, the evening with Geoffrey ... If once she started the words would pour out, an unstoppable river in full flood. Lizzie knew about grief and loss but she would find it hard to forgive infidelity or to understand Fran's mixed feelings about Paul's mistress. She certainly wouldn't approve of her own little fling. The rest of the party burst in, making further confidences impossible.

When the time came for them to leave, Lizzie gave her a big hug. Fran felt like a fraud, undeserving of such love and sympathy. When Richard immersed himself in the engine of his car, saying that it wasn't firing properly and he had to clean the spark plugs, Sylvia took the opportunity to take her mother's arm and lead her into the sitting room. 'What is this with Brenda?' she asked, as she guided her mother on to the sofa and sat down beside her.

Fran didn't know how to soften the blow. 'She had an affair with Dad, for many years. I only found out recently.' Of all her concerns this was the only one based on solid fact. She looked up and was surprised by the stricken look on Sylvia's face. It must have been her own paranoia that had made her think everyone else knew about it.

Sylvia stared at her mother. She had never wanted to believe her father had been unfaithful. It was only when Brenda had been so solicitous and friendly in the rape field that she had begun to wonder. How could her mother take it so calmly? Angrily she said, 'Why did you have to find out?'

Fran took her daughter's hand. 'Try to understand. I have to discover all I can about the things he kept hidden. Otherwise, I can make no sense of our life together. Until I do that, I'm stuck in the past.' She stopped and bent down to look into Sylvia's face. ' I have to know, about his work also.'

'What is there to discover about his work?'

'Probably nothing.' Sylvia had suffered enough shocks for one day. Fran put her arm round her daughter's hunched shoulders. 'I was devastated when I first found out about Brenda. But I've come to realise it isn't that important. He loved us, I know he did. Whatever happened between them, we came first.' Looking away, she added, 'I couldn't tell Lizzie, though I love her dearly. Her morals are very old-fashioned.'

'Of course you couldn't tell her. But I wish you'd trusted me sooner. You must have felt so alone.' Fran squeezed her hand. 'Can I tell Richard?' Sylvia asked, getting up.

'Of course. If you're close to someone, it's better not to have unnecessary secrets.'

At that moment he came into the room. 'All fixed. Ready to go?'

Sylvia moved to the door. 'Take care, Mum.' On the step she hesitated, as if about to say more. Richard raised his eyebrows at her but she gave a tiny shake of her head, kissed her mother and walked down towards the car.

'You too. I love you so much.' Fran raised her hand to wave, then let it drop. 'Hey, wait . . .' She turned and ran to the pantry to fetch the bottle of port. 'Please take this with you.'

Sylvia climbed back up the steps. 'Are you sure?'

'I don't want it in the house.'

'Good for you.' Sylvia gave her mother a big hug. 'Richard will really enjoy it.' Then she was gone.

Fran waved till they turned the corner, feeling, as she did each time they drove away, that her life was disappearing with the car. Then she straightened up and went inside.

The day of the Welsh meeting arrived. Fran drove to a Park and Ride on the outskirts of Bristol. With the memory of Jackson's uninvited visits to her house still vivid in her mind, she had decided not to tell Jez exactly where she lived. After all, she hardly knew the man. As he opened the door for her to climb into his van, a nostalgic whiff of turpentine stopped her.

'Sorry about the smell,' he said. 'D'you mind if we make a short stop on the way? A chap has agreed to exhibit a couple of my pictures.'

'I didn't know you were an artist.'

'They won't sell, never do.'

'Is it just a hobby?'

He shrugged. 'I don't make any money.'

'What do you do?'

'Oh, this and that. I get some design work and teach twice a week at the college. I used to work in schools. Then the system got to me.' He shot her a quick glance. 'The truth is, they sacked me when I went to prison.'

'That's hard.'

'Said I was a bad example. Didn't give a shit about the reasons.'

'I would have thought you were a good role model. You cared enough to do something.'

'That wasn't how they saw it.'

They drove on in silence. The van was an old one, the engine so noisy that it didn't encourage conversation. Instead, Fran gazed out of the window and mulled over her recent telephone conversation with Brenda. She'd rung to say that Mr Bennett had retired from the company and was living in Portugal. Apparently he seldom accompanied his wife on her trips to England, preferring to stay abroad in the warmer climate. Brenda was going to try and discover his address so she could bring it with her when she came to lunch.

As Fran looked down at the water flowing under the new Severn Bridge, she had the wild idea that she might travel to Portugal to see him. Only then could she discover what help, if any, his insider knowledge could be. Would she really have to go so far, on what would probably turn out to be a wasted journey? Maybe she could extend the trip a little and think of it as a holiday.

They rattled on, not stopping till they got to the outskirts of Cardiff. 'I need some petrol,' Jez said as he drew off the road in front of some pumps.

Fran leapt out and paid. He didn't try to stop her. When they reached the gallery he carried in three large canvases. While he unwrapped them she wandered round but could find nothing she liked. When she turned to look at his work, she saw two portraits, one of a young man and one of a child about ten years old. The third picture was a beach scene with three children at the water's edge. Fran caught her breath. She'd always loved figures painted from behind. Her mind went back to the time Paul and Sylvia had spent at the seaside while she organised the new house. When she'd joined them she'd felt an intruder. Sylvia had been in a constant sulk, Paul silent and withdrawn. She wondered now if that had been the beginning of the rift between them. It must have been about the time Brenda had joined the staff.

They arrived early for the meeting and went to a pub for a snack. Fran reluctantly took out her purse again but Jez stopped her with a gesture. 'It's my shout this time.'

Although she could afford to pay, she put her money away with relief. When he'd let her pay for the petrol she'd been afraid he was just a scrounger.

They sat at a table near the fire and Jez started talking about globalisation.

Fran pressed back into her seat, battered by his passionate arguments. 'You should meet my daughter, she's the one who knows about these things,' she said.

'Aren't you interested?' he asked.

'I've been trying to read a bit, since deciding to come to this meeting. I'm not sure you can rubbish all trade like that. As far as I can understand it, economic growth leads to less poverty.'

'That's true, but the growth has to come from the people themselves. From within.'

'Without the capital to get things started that's not going to happen. And where foreign capital can get in easily, the most growth takes place.'

'Where d'you get that from?'

'I read a report of the UN Development programme.'

Jez shot her a look. 'You must show it to me sometime.' He

paused, then said, 'You're OK. A thinking woman. I like that, even if I don't agree with you.'

Fran sat up straighter. 'I can't help being suspicious of fanatical people. Brenda –'

A gust of laughter made them look up. Three smartly dressed men were leaning on the bar. They must have been in their late twenties, early thirties perhaps. Picking up their glasses, they turned and walked past in matching suits, a picture of correctness, each wearing a sober but marginally different tie. They took over a table in the middle of the room, their voices loud, chairs pushed back and limbs loose. The one opposite Jez and Fran regarded them with a mixture of disdain and disinterest. Snatches of conversation reached them. 'My graph shows ... Andy's really please with my sales ... What I do is ...'

'They're so confident,' Jez said under his breath. 'They think they own the world, when really they're slaves to the company.'

Fran was reminded of Geoffrey. He'd looked like that when he was younger. Against her will she saw Martin again, lying in his hospital bed. He hadn't been owned by the system, not completely. Neither had Paul, surely not ...

Jez turned to her. 'What are you thinking?' His voice was sympathetic now, more like the man she had met on the hill. His face changed so quickly; a minute before he had looked bitter.

'I was remembering my husband. He worked for a drug company – the same one that employed me as a rep.'

'They're some of the worst. Selling their drugs for crazy prices. Using their patents to block the use of cheaper stuff. Look at the problem of AIDS in Africa.'

'My sister-in-law has been working there for the last year. She told me how, in Tanzania, one in five women die in childbirth. When it's time for the baby to be born the woman says to her existing children, "I am going to the sea to fetch a baby. The way is long and hard and I may not return."' Fran looked up to catch an expression of such desolation on his face that she wished she hadn't said anything.

Jez shook himself, as if determined to snap out of his mood. 'It's so complicated. Difficult to know how any one person can help at all.' Changing the subject, he said, 'My girlfriend is going to New Zealand. Ex-girlfriend. She won't find such misery there, I hope.'

'Do you miss her a lot?'

He shrugged. 'I dunno. I'm trying to paint her, but I can't really remember her face.' He looked up. 'I'd like to paint you.'

Fran felt herself being examined by half-closed eyes. 'What do you see?'

'I'm not sure. Something trapped, perhaps.'

'I loved my husband. We were together for almost forty years.'

'That's a hell of a time.'

'I don't think I knew him very well, even at the end. I don't know what he was doing . . .' She stopped, uncertain how to go on.

'Do you ever know anyone? It's a lonely business, this living. You get together for a bit, then part. In the end you're alone.' He paused. 'You do all the important things alone. You're born alone and you bloody well die alone.'

'But your mother is there when you are born, and there's usually someone by your bed when you die. I held my mother's hand.' She didn't add that she hoped Sylvia would be there for her.

'I mean, spiritually alone.' He sounded distant and misunderstood.

His view was so bleak. If you touched something real, Fran thought, even if it was only for a moment, you weren't alone. And you had the memory.

Jez looked at his watch. 'Can I get you another tonic?'

She'd found it so difficult to resist a drink when they entered the pub. Now she said, 'I'd love a . . .' no, damn it '. . . a coffee, if they have it.'

A little later, as she stirred sugar into her cup, she watched the light from the fire play across the face of her companion. His moods changed so quickly. 'Something happened to my husband. He had a secret . . .'

Jez's eyes, darker now under his brown curls, pierced her with an intensity that made her feel the clothes were being stripped off her body. She dropped her gaze. 'I don't know what it was. I can't let go of him till I understand.'

Jez reached across the table and took her hand. 'Can I do anything?'

'I don't suppose so.' It was no good. She couldn't protect herself from his sympathetic gaze. What the hell, if she made a fool of herself it was just too bad. 'I may have to go to Portugal to find a man . . .'

'Why Portugal?'

'He's retired there.'

'Whereabouts?'

'I don't know exactly.'

Fran studied the beer mat in front of her. It advertised German ale and the picture of a street scene looked foreign. 'I don't know how I'd get there. Fly, I suppose. Hire a car if it's out in the sticks. I've never driven on the right side of the road.'

'Well, if you want a driver, I'm your man.'

She looked up, startled. What an extraordinary idea: but rather comforting. Her thoughts raced, not sure what he was suggesting. Perhaps he wanted to wangle a free holiday. Women of a certain age had to be careful with younger men. She jumped up and seized her black anorak. 'We must go, we'll be late.'

He followed her to the van and drove in silence to the hall where the audience could have been cloned from the one that had listened to Brenda. Fran had chosen more suitable clothes this time, and wasn't conspicuous in the crowd, even though she felt naked to the man sitting beside her.

During the lecture she found it impossible to concentrate. If Paul's secret could damage the company, Jez would be only too happy to use it for his own ends. He would try to winkle it out of her with those penetrating eyes. She had never been good at keeping secrets, but she was practising. She'd told Hazel that she hadn't seen Geoffrey again; that she'd been alone all Christmas Day. Jez wouldn't be taken in so easily.

At last the speaker got to the end. After a few questions, the doors of the hall were thrown open and the people streamed out. The light was fading rapidly outside and a raw wind swirled in. Fran couldn't wait to regain the safety of her own home. Jez, who seemed to know everybody, had gone to talk with a crowd of people by the platform. As she stood shivering by the wall she thought that it was like a club, you were either in or out. If you weren't for them, you were against them. By the time Jez was ready to leave she was frozen to the core.

'What did you think of it?' he asked, when they got back in the van.

Fran tried to find something intelligent to say. 'I'm afraid I didn't follow it closely. He seemed very passionate ... I suppose he's right.' She made an effort. 'But I still think poor countries need investment, or how can they begin to raise their standard of living?'

'That's true. But when those wretched multinationals go in they use up all the reserves, then do a runner. The people are left much poorer and their land is all fucked up.'

She sat forward. 'Surely we must share the benefits of medical science, at least? Our technology must be of use to them.'

'We don't fit our help to their needs. We sell them machines that break down, fertilisers that weaken the soil, genetically modified seed that produces a good crop for one year, but then the seed turns out to be sterile. The farmers ruin themselves buying new seed instead of using what they've saved. It's a damn clever trick.'

'I don't believe the company did that on purpose. They made a mistake.'

'I doubt it.'

Fran sighed. 'People can be stupid, but most of them want to do the right thing. I don't believe in original sin.'

Jez laughed, an infectious sound that made her smile. 'Actually, I don't either. It's great that you make me argue my case like this. But the companies are such big and greedy buggers – totally out of control.'

Jez began to give more examples of exploitation. She wondered if his passion was born of having been on the receiving end of prejudice himself. His immigrant parents, probably Jews fleeing from persecution, had survived in a foreign land. As she bumped on the hard seat of the van she feared that her belief in the goodness of man was only possible because her own life had been so easy. She shifted to expose different parts of her anatomy to the lumpy cushion. God, she was tired. Brenda was coming to lunch the next day and she'd done no cooking.

Jez glanced across at her. 'You must be exhausted.' His voice had changed in the abrupt way she was beginning to recognise. 'It's been a long day,' he said.

She closed her eyes and listened to the rattles coming from the back of the van. 'It seems noisier without the pictures.'

'Sorry about that, my dear. I think some cans of paint have got loose. D'you want me to stop and fix them?'

'I don't mind. I just noticed.'

'Why don't you try and get some shuteye?'

The next thing she knew was the sudden quiet as he switched the motor off and the contents of the van came to rest. 'We're here,' he said. She blinked, gathered her wits and opened her door. It was bitterly cold again after the fug in the van. 'I'll wait to make sure your engine starts,' Jez said. 'Are you fit to drive?'

'I'm OK. The cold's woken me.'

She got into her own car. Turning the ignition, she wound down the window. 'How can I thank you? It's been such an interesting day.'

He smiled. 'Introduce me to Brenda some time. That would be a grand way to repay me. And you did stump up for the petrol,' he added with a grin.

'She's coming for a meal tomorrow.'

'Really?'

'We have to talk about some stuff, but if you want to join us after lunch you're welcome.'

'Yeah, I'd like that a lot. I'll give you a ring in the morning and you can tell me how to find your house.'

The eagerness in his voice made her wish she hadn't asked him. 'You must be freezing, you'd better go.'

He reached in through the open window, took her hand and bent forward to raise it to his lips. 'Drive carefully.'

As he walked away to his van she absentmindedly ran her mouth over the place where his lips had touched her skin.

SIXTEEN

2004

Dust rose from the books as Brenda worked her way along the shelves in the basement study. She reached for a volume, flipped the pages, snapped it shut and replaced it with a neat movement that left no room for doubt.

'I'll go and see to the lunch. Take your time,' Fran said. She laid the table in the kitchen with care, trying to make her movements as neat and decisive as those of the woman downstairs. Only once had she seen her hesitate over anything, that moment in the café when she had asked for help. Opening a bottle of white wine (she'd only bought the one), Fran wondered if her guest would rather have beer. Or she might not drink at lunch at all, preferring to keep a cool head for the afternoon. Fran couldn't understand what had attracted Paul to a woman who seemed so mannish. How had she kept him interested all that time?

When she went back down the stairs she found Brenda sitting on the floor frowning at a book on her lap. It was the one with the pencil marks in the margins and sentences underlined. 'I don't know where he got that. He never marked his books,' Fran said.

'Was he always interested in parasites?'

'I think it was just his fascination with how organisms reacted together. He really wanted to be a field biologist, preferably working in some distant land.'

Brenda put the book on top of two others beside her on the floor and shuffled back to scan the bottom shelf.

'Would you like a glass of wine?' Fran asked.

Her visitor looked up. 'That would be lovely.'

'White all right?'

Brenda nodded. One hurdle crossed, thought Fran. At least the alcohol might ease the atmosphere, and she'd only have one glass herself.

Over lunch Brenda asked about Sylvia. Fran found herself confiding her worries. 'I really liked Richard when he was here the other day. I wish they'd just get on and have a baby – they'd manage somehow.'

Brenda seemed genuinely interested. 'You know, we met on demonstrations a couple of times. Sylvia seemed very keen on her environmental work. Do you think she might want to work abroad, as you say her father did?'

The idea was one that Fran preferred not to consider. This woman would probably encourage Sylvia to think her work was more important than having a family; that the world had too many people in it anyway. Not content with stealing her husband, she would now take her daughter away. All chance of filling her house with the laughter of grandchildren would disappear. 'I suppose you think children are a waste of time.'

'Not at all.'

As if she hadn't spoken Fran continued. 'Well, I don't agree. Until you've had a child you don't begin to grow up yourself. You can have no idea the demands it makes on you. It changes you, stretches you into altogether different shapes. You can't possibly understand.'

'I suppose I can't.'

Fran looked across the table and was startled to see Brenda twisting her glass with a look of misery on her face. She tried to say something kind, but her voice came out bitter. 'I don't suppose you ever wanted any.'

Brenda went on staring into her glass. 'I didn't, not until it was too late.' She looked up. 'But I would never try to influence anyone else, one way or the other.'

Fran was not convinced. 'You couldn't have worked in the way you have if you were a mother. You care so much about your causes, you must want others to follow in your footsteps.'

'Not necessarily my way.' Brenda lifted her glass and drained it in one gulp. 'We activists are very single-minded, perhaps warped. I don't know.' There was a silence. Then, 'Can I have some more wine?'

Fran, shaken by the exchange, fetched the bottle from the fridge and filled Brenda's glass. Then she opened a tonic for herself.

'Aren't you having another? You're not driving.'

'I'm being a bit careful just now.' Changing the subject she asked, 'What do you think Sylvia should do?'

'I hope she'll follow whatever her heart tells her to do. I suspect she wants a family –'

'She does,' Fran broke in. 'She's said so often enough, but she's worried that Richard won't stay with her.'

'These days that's always a possibility.' The blue eyes looked across the table at Fran. 'At least you didn't have to worry about that.'

'Did you want him to leave me?'

'Of course. But I didn't admit it to myself for years. I thought what we had was enough. Only . . . it wasn't.'

Fran tried to adjust to the real woman in front of her. Since she had known about the affair she'd imagined her as a sort of demon, a one-track automaton. It was easier that way; she didn't want Brenda's pain as well as her own. A stark image of Paul rose in her mind, two faces looking in opposite directions. She didn't know what had happened to the middle of him. She was reminded of the bed in the side ward, with two heads and no middle, where she had talked to Martin. 'Did you find out where that director, Mr Bennett, is living?' she asked.

Brenda reached down and took a piece of paper from her briefcase. 'He's bought a house in the Algarve. Somewhere out towards Cape St Vincent at the extreme western tip. Can I ask why you wanted it?'

'I went to see Martin just before he died.'

'Our old boss?'

Fran nodded. 'Geoffrey said I ought to talk to him. You know Geoffrey? Yes, of course you do.' She remembered the party all those years ago, where the woman in front of her wore a red dress and danced with her husband.

'I know Geoffrey. Very presentable, but I wouldn't trust him very far.'

'That's what Paul used to say, but I'm quite fond of him.' Fran smiled as warm feelings flowed through her again.

'Why did you want to see Martin?'

Fran got up to put the plates in the sink and fetch the cheese board. She was confused now, uncertain if she wanted to say anything more. As she sat down at the table again the doubts that had kept her awake during the night flooded back. 'In the café you said you wanted my help.'

Now, it was Brenda's turn to hesitate. 'It's probably nothing. I just have a feeling that there's a part of Paul's work that's left unfinished.'

'Why do you care?' Fran hadn't meant the question to come out in such an aggressive way. 'I mean. . . is it for him or for your fight against the company and what they're doing?'

'I'm not sure. Probably both. Did Martin say anything?'

'Only hints. He was very tired. He went into a coma and didn't regain consciousness. What a brave man he was.'

'Brave? Yes – probably. But he wore blinkers.'

'Have some cheese? They're all English, except for the blue, that's Irish. I got them for Lizzie. You know, Paul's sister. They're back from Africa. They were here when you rang.'

'He was very close to her, wasn't he?'

'Very, but she has quite conventional beliefs. I doubt if he let on about you.'

Brenda chuckled. 'I'm sure he didn't.' An unexpected feeling of conspiracy passed between them, but Fran still couldn't decide how far she could trust her.

There was only one way to find out. 'There's something I want to tell you, but I have to know that you won't use it against Paul for your own ends. I mean, go public with anything we discover. Too many people who loved him, Lizzie, Sylvia . . . I couldn't bear it if their faith in him was destroyed.'

'Why should it be?'

'Well it might – if he was working on something that went

against his beliefs, or if he was trying to put right some previous mistake.'

'What mistake could he have made? He was always so meticulous.'

'I'm not the only one interested in what he was doing before he died.' Fran told her briefly about Jackson.

Brenda frowned. 'He said he thought Paul was trying to discredit him? I left the company ages before he arrived but from what you tell me that wouldn't have been a bad thing.'

'Whatever we find out I need your reassurance that you won't use it for your own purposes.'

They sat and stared at each other until Brenda looked away and sank back in her chair. 'I can't believe he was doing anything underhand. But if it's any help I promise not to say a word to anyone, without your agreement.'

'That sounds fair, but can I trust you?'

Brenda shrugged. 'That's for you to decide.'

She was right, Fran thought. What a wimp she was to waver like this. Martin had found the courage to admit he'd been wrong. If the secret was important enough for him to humble himself in that way, surely she could take a chance. 'When he was dying, Paul worked on some papers, every single day until he went into hospital for the last time. I think he was trying to set some record straight.'

'Paul never showed you what he was doing?'

'He took the greatest care never to let me see anything.'

'What did Martin say – exactly?'

Fran closed her eyes as she tried to remember. They were in that room, looking out over the city. Something about Paul being right. 'He said Paul was right and he had been wrong. They were going too fast. He'd been a coward.' She opened her eyes. 'It cost him an awful lot to say that.'

'Anything else?'

'I can't remember. It was detailed work ... oh yes ...' She hesitated. 'He said he never trusted Paul's opinion after he wrote that memo with you. You had too much influence on him. You were holding back the progress of science.'

'He would say that. I told you he lived in blinkers. But those papers . . . no other clues?'

'None.'

They sat in silence. Then Brenda got up, walked to the window and back, to stop by the side of Fran's chair. 'We've got to get a sight of them. You know that, don't you?'

Fran also stood up and reached for the kettle. She wished now that she'd lit the fire in the sitting room, but she'd been determined not to make her visitor too comfortable. Hospitality had its limits. 'I don't think Geoffrey would help,' she said. 'He's too much of a company man.'

'As I said, I wouldn't trust him anyway.'

'I did find out from him that they keep all the secret files for both establishments in the basement in Keynsham. They're marked with a blue sticker, Hazel told me that.'

Brenda gave her a searching look. 'So you've been thinking the same –'

'I don't know what you mean.'

'You think we're going to have to steal them.'

'I've thought about it, but it wouldn't be possible. We'd have to get past the security guards and if anything went wrong I couldn't face going to prison.' She thought of Jez.

Brenda stared into the fire. 'We need some inside contact.' Her head jerked up. 'Is that where Mr Bennett comes in?'

'The last words Martin uttered to me were, "Ask Mr Bennett." He didn't speak again.'

Brenda rubbed her forehead and flicked her glasses up her nose.

Fran was picturing the documents on the last occasion she had seen them. A plain brown file with a pocket, the sheets of paper inside held in small bundles by paper clips. She had glimpsed columns of figures interspersed with writing. 'Have you any idea what he could have been doing? I'm so afraid it was something –'

'I don't know. Honestly I don't. I have some ideas, but it's too early to say.' She got out of her chair and fetched the three books she'd brought up from the study. 'May I take these with me? I'll let you have them back but I'd really like to study them when I have more time.'

'Of course. But you must keep them. I wanted you to have something of his.'

'You're very generous.' Brenda looked at her watch. 'I ought to be going.'

'Could you stay for a coffee? I've got someone calling who would very much like to meet you.'

'Who's that?'

'A chap called Jez. He was an usher at your meeting. He took me to a meeting in Wales yesterday. Did you know he got six months for destroying a modified rape crop?'

'Um, I think so. I heard some of them got unexpectedly harsh sentences.'

'You didn't visit him?'

Brenda gave a small shrug. Fran noticed a pink tinge creep up the skin of her neck. 'I'm no good at that personal support stuff. I'm better on the platform. That's why people like your Sylvia are so useful – to add the human touches.' She sat down again. 'Have you decided what to do about Mr Bennett? Will you write to him?'

'I'm not sure. I'd rather speak to him face to face. If I wrote first he could turn me down out of hand. Although I have no idea what he could do to help, I feel I'd have a better chance if I just turned up.' The doorbell rang. 'That'll be Jez.'

Fran introduced them and busied herself with the coffee as she listened to their conversation. Jez asked questions, flattered to be so close to one of his heroines. Brenda tried to show a polite interest about his time in prison. 'Was it as awful as they say?' she asked. 'It's only luck that has kept me out so far.'

'It wasn't easy.' Fran could hear the bleak note in his voice. 'I'm not a natural martyr, but I probably coped better than some of the younger men would have done.'

Fran remembered that he had not only lost his job but his girlfriend as well. Brenda ought to be more appreciative. Instead, she began to tell him about her latest projects, a visit to Barcelona, followed by California in April.

'What will you do there?'

Irritated, Fran put the coffee on the table. Jez was looking at Brenda as if she were some sort of prophet.

'I want to see the effect of all that logging for myself. I might even spend some time in the branches of a redwood tree.' Her voice had a competitive note. She too could suffer; she wasn't just a talking head on a platform.

'I'd give anything to come with you,' Jez said.

Fran sat down opposite them. Grand plans were all very well but individuals got caught up in the mechanics of protest. Breaking into their duologue, she turned to Jez and said, 'I've been telling Brenda about Paul, my husband. Were you serious when you said you might come with me to Portugal?'

Brenda looked from one to the other. 'You're taking him with you?'

All at once things were moving too fast. 'I don't even know if I'm going yet. But he did offer.' Turning to Jez she said, 'If we do go, you must get one thing straight. Brenda has promised me that whatever happens she will not divulge anything we discover without my permission. If you want to take this any further I need to have the same promise from you. Otherwise, we stop talking about it right now.'

They sat silent, looking at her. Brenda fiddled with her coffee cup. 'I still don't really understand what you're so frightened about.'

Fran tried again to find the words she wanted. Speaking to Jez she said, 'Paul was an honourable man. He believed in scientific method. You formulate a hypothesis, and then you create controlled trials to prove or disprove it.' She stopped, feeling silly to be repeating his words with Brenda in the room. 'He believed that the results should be freely available to everyone.' This was not what she was trying to say; she hadn't explained her real anxiety. She lifted her head. 'I'm afraid that at the end he did something . . . he wasn't a well man.' She stopped and looked at Brenda, and felt herself fill up with hatred as quickly as a tumbler held under a gushing tap. 'You influenced him with your extreme ideas. You twisted him and he lost his integrity in the process. You corrupted my husband and made him fake his results, not to discredit Jackson but to support one of your crazy causes.' There, it was out.

Brenda sat motionless in her chair, her eyes fixed on Fran's agitated face. 'D'you really believe that?'

'It's what I suspect.'

Jez looked at the two women, confused by the emotion that had erupted in the room. Brenda got up from the table again and stood gazing out of the window. There was a long silence before she turned. Fran expected a verbal onslaught to match her own.

When the reply came it was measured. 'You may be right, but I don't think so,' Brenda said. 'I believe he did some proper, detailed work that should have been made public long ago. That creep Jackson is trying to find it and destroy the evidence of some blunder, made by him or by the company. If Paul gave the file to Martin he must have covered it up too, though it's hard to credit such action in the man I admired.' She had been staring at the floor as she spoke, but now she lifted her head and looked at Fran. 'When he talked to you in the hospital he was asking you to put right some wrong he'd done. Why else would he have admitted he was a coward? You told me how painful it was for him to say he had made a mistake.'

She moved back to the table and sat down again to look across at Jez. 'You don't understand. Fran has reason to mistrust me, which is why I gave her that promise. If you're to help us you should give her the same pledge.'

Jez felt something touch his knee and looked down into Bruiser's eyes. He fondled the soft ears and the animal lay down, letting his head fall on the tidy shoes that he'd chosen to wear in place of his trainers. He brought his eyes back to Brenda's face.' I don't understand your part in all this. I can't see what you have to gain if the company is not to be discredited.'

'We might learn something that would help the cause of more responsible science. I don't think we'll discover a man who compromised his beliefs. My guess is that Fran will be happy for us to use what we find. If I'm wrong, and we discover a flaw in the man who shared her life, I'll forget the whole thing.'

Jez felt the power that exuded from her small frame. He looked across at Fran. What was it about these women that made him feel so excited and protective? 'I don't see what the problem is. It's none of my affair. I could just do with some southern light. I'd pay my own way. Take myself off to paint when you're busy. You wouldn't have to tell me what you found out.'

'Wouldn't I?' Fran searched his face. 'I have a feeling you might get it out of me, if you thought it would help your fight against big business.' Jez said nothing. 'How would you have felt if your girlfriend had done something for good reasons, but then the records were used for some public cause and she was humiliated?' Even as Fran was speaking she felt it wasn't fair to ask him to muzzle himself to protect the reputation of a man he'd never met. Bruiser was still lying on his feet; at least the dog trusted him.

'It's difficult,' he said, looking down at his hands resting on the table. 'When does the individual have to be sacrificed for the greater good? It's a philosophical question.' He looked up into Fran's anxious face and felt something shift inside him. He didn't owe this woman anything. After all, she was a virtual stranger. Yet she had occupied his thoughts with a strange persistence since they had met on Christmas day.

Brenda got up. 'Look, I must go. This is between the two of you.' Turning to Fran, she said, 'I wish I could come with you, but as I told Jez, I've got all sorts of commitments for the next few months.'

Fran showed her to the door, her smile strained. She could not have borne much longer in her company, certainly not shut up with her in a car, travelling across a foreign country. 'I'll keep in touch. You won't forget your promise?'

'No. That's something I can do for Paul.'

Damn the woman. Fran didn't stay to watch her car turn out of the drive. As she shut the front door she found Jez behind her. 'I've got my paints in the van. Would you sit for me? Just for a short time. I'd love to do a full-length picture, with Bruiser at your feet. If I got started now I could work on it at home.'

Fran ran a hand over her forehead. Her head ached but she didn't want to put him off. 'OK. I'll light the fire in the sitting room.' After she had put a match to the pre-laid grate she went upstairs for dustsheets to cover the carpet.

He fetched his easel and positioned her on the sofa. She would have liked to be able to watch him as he worked, to study his expressions and try and decide how much she could trust him. He frustrated that idea by turning her towards the window so that the light fell on her face.

He worked quickly, making some sketches before beginning to mix his paints. It was strange to have the smell of turpentine in the house again. She tried to sit still in the welcome silence but before long she sneezed. 'Sorry, I think I must be getting a cold.'

Jez put his brush down, moved to her side and put his arm round her shoulders. 'I expect you got thoroughly chilled yesterday. And it can't have been easy having Brenda here.' He paused. 'You said your husband had an affair . . .'

Fran sighed. 'You've guessed right. Brenda was his mistress. Was it so obvious?'

'Not really. As I watched you both . . . have you met her before today?'

'Several times. But this is the first time she's been in my house. It was a bit of a strain.'

Jez squeezed her shoulders. 'Can I get you something? A whisky and lemon perhaps? I find it wonderful for the sniffles.'

How little they knew about each other. 'Thanks, but I'm on the wagon.'

'Oh . . .'

Now he'd despise her. She felt too awful to try and dissemble. 'You'd better go or you'll catch my germs.'

'I'll give you a buzz in a day or two.' He folded his things away and stowed them back in the van. 'Would you like me to take Bruiser out for a run before I go? You're not up to it.'

The kindness was nearly her undoing. She spun round to take the lead off its peg. 'Thanks so much. Just open the door and push him in when you get back. I think I'll go straight up to bed.'

'You do that.'

She fell into a restless sleep until, some time later, she heard footsteps on the stairs. For a moment she lay frozen, imagining it was Jackson back again. Then she heard the soft, foreign cadences. 'It's only me. I've brought you a cup of tea.'

Jez put it by her bed and felt her forehead. 'You're boiling. Would you like me to call the doctor?'

'I'll be fine. It's only a cold.'

'I'll leave you then. Take care of yourself.'

Despite a course of antibiotics, Fran lay in bed for more than a week. Only when Sylvia rang to say she was coming for lunch did she drag herself up.

When she saw how drawn her mother had become she felt a moment of panic. 'You look awful. You should have told me you'd been ill.'

'I'm getting better now. Come in and get warm.' As Fran noticed the bloom that lit her daughter's face, and the swelling beneath her parka, she felt a surge of excitement that made her sit down with a bump in the hall chair, feeling strong and weak at the same time.

Sylvia laughed. 'You've got it in one. I'm pregnant.'

'That's wonderful. Oh, I'm so pleased.' Fran paused to savour the news. 'I hope you're pleased, too. And Richard.'

'Yes, we planned the baby. We're going to get married.' Sylvia took off her coat and hung it on a peg.

Fran leapt up, but sank back feeling dizzy.

Sylvia put her hand on her shoulder. 'Come and sit in a comfy chair while I tell you all about it.'

Fran was glad to have the support of her daughter's arm as she moved on to the sofa. 'When is it due?'

'The beginning of June, they say. I knew at Christmas, but it seemed too early to tell anyone then and you had your own problems.' Sylvia searched her mother's face, then looked her up and down.

Fran was reminded of her own mother, looking to find fault. 'I'm all right really, I've just had a bad go of bronchitis.'

'But you're never ill. Something must have lowered your resistance. I bet it was that wretched Brenda. Have you seen any more of her?'

'She came for a meal. She isn't wretched, she's rather nice. I can see how Dad could have fancied her.'

'How can you be so forgiving?'

'It's hard for you to understand. Your Richard is entirely yours, and I hope he will be, always. But love isn't a finite thing – you don't necessarily take love away from one person if you give it to another.' Sylvia's face was mutinous. 'Look, I can't expect you to understand. Can you just accept that she doesn't upset me too much?'

'I suppose so. But I can't think I'll ever like her again.'

'You don't have to. Just let me be friends with her, if I want to be.' Fran felt exhausted by the effort of explaining. 'Tell me about you. I want to hear everything. How are you, have you had scans and things?'

'I've just got the results of the latest test. They say the baby's heart is fine.'

'You're not still worrying about Dad's illness?'

'It's such a funny thing: cardiomyopathy.' She moved the word in her mouth as if it had a bitter taste.

'But you had a check up at the time and they said it wasn't inherited.'

'I know, but . . .'

Fran couldn't let anything spoil her delight. 'What about the wedding, d'you want to have it here?'

'We've made some plans . . .' Sylvia put her hand on her mother's arm. 'I do hope you won't be upset. We want to get married in London and have a party at our own home. Just a small one.'

'That's fine. All I care about is that you do what you want. I had enough of conforming to my mother to last two lifetimes. I don't mind if you get married in the desert on a couple of camels, or in the air swinging from parachutes. Have you decided on a date?'

'We've booked a provisional time in two weeks, but we can postpone it if that's too soon for you. You might not be well enough.' Sylvia gave her another searching look.

'Of course I'll be well enough. You'll want to get on with it before you're too big.' Oh, shit. Her mother's voice was speaking through her again.

'Something must have happened for you to get bronchitis. You've never had it before, have you?'

'I got very chilled. I went to a meeting about globalisation in Wales. I was so keen to blend in with the crowd that I didn't put on enough clothes.'

'That was Brenda's doing, I bet.'

Fran laughed. 'No, actually it was a man I met on Christmas Day.'

'A new man, Mum?'

'A friend. He's younger than I am, so don't start getting ideas.'

'How much younger?'

'Oh, five or six years. Maybe more.'

'That's nothing.'

'As I said, he's just a friend.'

'Pity. Never mind, there'll be others.'

'Perhaps.' Fran got up to put another log on the fire. 'After your wedding I might go away for a few days and get a bit of sun. Have a sort of convalescence.'

'That's a brilliant idea. Where would you go?'

'I'm not sure, possibly the Algarve. It would be warm and it's not too far.' Fran was relieved that her daughter was too occupied by her own plans to want to know any details.

After Sylvia had left she made herself walk up and down the stairs three times before she flopped back on to her bed. If she was to get to London in two weeks she must build up her strength. It would have been so nice if they could have had a reception in the house. She could have filled it with flowers and the big table from the garden would be fine for a buffet meal. She forced the flow of thoughts to a stop, holding her lower lip between her teeth. She would not follow in her mother's footsteps and hijack her daughter's wedding.

SEVENTEEN

2004

As they followed the signs away from Faro airport Fran concentrated on the map. 'D'you want to go by the motorway as far as possible or use the 125? It runs closer to the sea.'

'Anything's better than a motorway. They're soulless,' Jez said.

His phone call, to repeat his offer to drive her in Portugal, had nudged Fran out of her lethargy. The journey to Sylvia's wedding had been exhausting and she'd accepted his offer to book the flights and car with relief.

Once they'd negotiated the roundabouts and flyovers to reach the road that would take them almost the whole way to Sagres, Jez turned to her and grinned. 'That wasn't too difficult.'

Fran wasn't sure if he was reassuring her or himself. 'You've had your hair cut short. Why have you done that?' The question was out of her mouth before she could stop it. With no curls at the sides his long face looked more serious. She noticed a few grey hairs among the brown. 'I'm sorry, that's personal, I shouldn't have asked.'

He laughed. 'Your Mr Bennett isn't likely to be impressed by a boyish cut. We don't want him thinking I'm one of those leftie activists.'

'He's not "my" Mr Bennett, and there's no reason for you to meet him. You can drop me out of sight of the house, once we find it.'

'I've looked out some tidy trousers and a tie, just in case.'

Fran glanced at his jeans, the clean ones he donned for meetings, not the paint-spattered ones he'd worn when they'd met briefly to finalise their plans.

Looking beyond him, out of the driver's window, she saw a gentle landscape, punctuated by low hills. It would be fun to drive up there if there was time. Still uncertain how they would get on together, she'd only planned to stay for three nights. It would probably take her all that time to find Mr Bennett and extract what she needed from him.

They drove on, making desultory conversation about the scenery and the villages they passed through. Beyond the window on her side of the car she glimpsed the high-rise buildings of tourist-laden towns. Signposts pointed to Quarteira, Albufeira, Portimao. She consulted the map again and said, 'We're making great progress. Shall we try to find some quiet place for lunch?'

'I'm in no hurry. I'd like to get on a bit.'

Paul had grown to expect his meals on time, becoming morose when he was hungry. Fran had assumed the lissom man by her side would need to be fed regularly in the same way. She knew so little about him. 'Can I ask how old you are?'

He smiled without taking his eyes from the road. 'I'm fifty-five. Halfway to the big Six O. What makes you ask just now?'

'When your hair was longer you looked younger.' It seemed the easiest answer, but as soon as she'd spoken she was dissatisfied. 'It isn't that. I was wondering how you've managed to remain so flexible as you've grown older. Able to drop everything and come here at short notice.' She thought of the ways she'd ossified with Paul. Her role, as the dependent partner, had started after Sylvia was born and had remained to some extent for the rest of their marriage. Only briefly after the fire, and at the end when he had been so ill, had she discovered a hidden strength. Never in all that time had she argued with Paul, as she had done with Jez on that trip to Cardiff. She relaxed into her seat as she listened to his answer.

'I struggle to push my life into a shape and then have to deal with the boxed-in feeling. It drives me mad. I'm fierce when I've got a picture on the go, putting a set time aside every day. Even if I don't pick up the brush, I force myself to stand in front of the easel. But I loathe the thought that the next day, the next week, I'll just be doing the same goddamn thing.'

Fran sat forward. 'At home, I'm always making lists of things to do. But when everything's planned, there's no room for the unexpected.'

Jez reached out and put his hand on her thigh. 'That's it, exactly.'

A shiver of excitement began under his fingers. Glancing up at his profile she saw the prominent cheekbone balanced by the well-defined line of his jaw. From this angle he was so good looking. A longing to run her thumb over the depression under his eye made her turn to watch the road in front of them, pretending she was unaware of his touch. She was an old woman, a plaything for someone like Geoffrey perhaps, but of no interest to this man, someone she could admire for his passions, even if she didn't agree with everything he said. A slight pressure of his hand confused her.

Unable to avoid the centre of Lagos they entered the town, passing two chimneys with a ragged stork's nest on each. They parked the car by the sea front and walked up a cobbled street between older buildings, a relief after the ubiquitous apartment blocks, to sit at a table on the pavement and share a piece of sticky almond cake. Afterwards, standing by the sea wall, they inspected the boats in the marina where yachts and cruisers were moored, two or three deep. One had raised its sail and was heading for the sea.

'God, look at those lines,' Jez said. 'Built to use every puff of wind.' He paused. 'Human beings are crazy. We make things that work brilliantly with nature yet we find it impossible to live with each other.'

Fran wasn't listening. She was watching the white hull and buff sail on the aquamarine surface under the azure sky. Half closing her eyes, the colours became shapes in their own right. The headland on the other side was shaded with brown, a still projection against which the passing boat moved. For the first time in many years she felt her fingers twitch. She clenched her teeth and turned away, walking quickly back towards the car.

'I'd like to come here and make some sketches,' Jez said, as he caught her up.

'You do that.'

He spun round, surprised at the change in her voice. Her lips were compressed, her face pale in the clear light. He thrust his hands into his pocket, rebuffed by the defiant tilt of her head.

Back in the car he picked up the map. 'What about that lunch, then?'

Fran leant over, ashamed of her tart reply. It wasn't his fault she'd lost the will to paint. 'This road looks interesting.' Her finger traced a white line close to the sea. 'Shall we try this place, Salema? Can you wait till then?'

He nodded, and started the engine.

As they turned off the main highway they could have been entering a different world. The surface of the road was rough. Jez slowed the car, not just to protect his passenger from too many bumps, but to enjoy the vistas of sea that opened out on their left side. Shrubby heath dotted with wild flowers led to the top of steep, rocky cliffs. After a couple of miles the road descended sharply to a valley where a stream ran through thick, green rushes.

'Look, terrapins,' Fran cried, as she pointed to a bank of mud. Jez pulled into the side of the road and they watched the animals glide, one by one, into the water. Then he allowed the car to move on down the hill without starting the engine. When they got to the bottom they stopped again and listened to the silence. Frogs croaked and a buzzard called overhead. They heard the tinkle of approaching bells as a herd of russet-coloured cows meandered down a sidetrack to mill around the car. Fran laughed as a muzzle poked in at her window, a piece of grass dangling from the soft lips. Jez leant across to encourage the beast away with a gentle push of his hand. His arm stayed along the back of her seat. It felt natural for his lips to brush her cheek before his head slipped on to her shoulder. She sat immobile, unwilling to be the one to break the peace.

A truck appeared, the first vehicle they'd seen since they took the small road. Jez pulled himself up and they both returned the waves of the children perched on the back. The cows began to make their way towards the bridge across the stream. Jez started the engine and followed, keeping a safe distance.

Salema was a charming place, with fishing boats pulled up on the slipway. Tables stood outside the restaurants. They had no hesitation in choosing the one with a balcony next to the beach. Bread and an oily dip appeared, together with rounds of creamy cheese. Jez ordered a glass of red wine. 'Do you mind if I drink? I don't want to put temptation in your way.'

Fran let her eyes travel out over the water. The sun glittered on the small waves. 'I'm trying to learn how to drink in moderation. If I have just one glass, will you help me not to have another?'

Jez nodded. It took a long time for the food to arrive and while they waited he pointedly ordered one more glass and a bottle of water. For a moment Fran wanted to hit him. She was a grown woman, for god's sake. Clenching her teeth, she studied the guidebook on her lap. Once she had eaten the five surprisingly large sardines with boiled potatoes that had been put in front of her she felt better, even grateful to him. Sitting in the sun, she began to drift. Her search could wait. For the moment it was enough to be in such a different place, looking at the sparkle on the sea, eating and drinking with a man who seemed to enjoy her company.

The hotel was perched on a cliff above a bay, where a breakwater created a small harbour. Jez stood on his balcony and gulped the clean air. He had bought his own ticket, but Fran had insisted on paying for his room in return for his services as a chauffeur. He'd never stayed anywhere so luxurious and the comfort nagged his socialist conscience.

As he looked down, Fran appeared and walked to the edge of the garden. She shielded her eyes and gazed across at the houses on the other side of the water. Jez still couldn't understand his impetuous decision to come away with her. She was attractive, no doubt about that, but something else had pulled him towards her. Standing there by the sea, she was too far away for him to pick out the lines of her face. He wanted to have her close, exposed in front of him so he could explore her shadows and curves – not just those of her face, or even her body, but of her whole self. Only with his paint-brush, or during sex, could he find solace for the nagging isolation inside him.

Fran turned and saw him looking down. She waved but didn't signal for him to join her. Instead she turned away from the sea and disappeared behind a wing of the building. A few minutes later he saw her walking towards the village, bouncing slightly as she stepped out with the purposeful gait of a younger woman.

At supper they found a table in an alcove where they watched occasional fishing smacks pull round the corner into the calm water. Sitting high above the scene, insulated by the glass in the window, Jez imagined the sound that must punctuate the bustle as each boat moored and unloaded its catch.

Fran's voice broke the silence between them. 'I think I've found out where he lives.'

'That's quick.' Jez looked down at the table and broke off a piece of his roll. He had imagined them searching for the house together, sharing the hunt. He'd wanted to be the one to help her discover whatever she was looking for with such barely concealed desperation.

'It's not in the village at all but out towards the fort.'

'What makes you think that?'

'I asked in the supermarket. When I mentioned the name of the road, the girl pointed and held up three fingers. I think she meant kilometres.'

'Why didn't you enquire at the desk here? Their English is good.'

Fran looked out of the window, craning her neck to see the hotel's very own stork's nest. The man at the desk had said it brought good luck. She couldn't see any sign of the sitting bird; it must have snuggled down for the night. Dusk was falling and small points of light had appeared on the quay below them. 'I suppose I want to cover my tracks, in case it all goes wrong. The girl in the shop has no idea who I am or where I'm staying.' She couldn't explain, even to herself. 'I don't want to compromise him.'

'Who?'

'Mr Bennett.'

'Why didn't you phone him first, to find out exactly where he lives? For God's sake, you don't even know if he's at home.'

Fran shrugged, irritated by the criticism. She didn't know herself. She'd told Brenda she was afraid he would refuse to see her, or take fright and run away. But maybe, ever since Jez had first offered to drive her, she'd set her heart on making this journey with him. A part of her, stifled for so long by Paul's solicitude, wanted to take risks: to travel in a new country with a new man, to show up on the doorstep of a man she'd never met – and damn the consequences.

Jez watched her troubled face. 'I'm sorry, not my business.'

'It's all right. I've not been very logical about it.'

Perhaps he hadn't been very logical himself. Had he, after all, made the journey in the hope of finding something to discredit the company? For several minutes he concentrated on his food. Eventually he said, 'If you don't mind me asking, what is it you want to find out?'

'If I knew that I could have written to him. The trouble is, I don't know. Paul kept some records . . . they were very secret. I suppose I want to ask Bennett if he knows what they contained, even to tell me where they are and how I could get hold of them.'

'Would they discredit the company?'

Fran dropped her fork so that it clattered against her plate. 'That's all you're interested in. It's not about the company – I wish I'd never let you come with me. I just want to know what happened to Paul. Why he retreated from me as our marriage went on. How much it was my fault . . .' The people at the next table were staring at them. Embarrassed, she dropped her voice. 'You can't possibly understand, you've never been married.'

'I was once. It didn't work out.'

Fran was surprised. She'd imagined him moving from girl to girl, never able to commit himself – running away when things got difficult, like Geoffrey. 'I'm sorry. I didn't know that.'

Jez shrugged. 'It was hard. I loved her. She had a miscarriage.' Speaking to some spot behind her shoulder he went on, 'things were wonderful until, one morning, she complained of not feeling well. I took no notice and went away for the day on a demonstration. By the time I got home she'd been taken to hospital.' He looked into Fran's face, his eyes bleak. 'She never forgave me for not being there when it mattered. She seemed to think that if I'd been with her they might have been able to save the baby. The marriage went downhill after that.'

Fran blushed as she realised how glibly she had judged the man. Reaching across the table, she took his hand. 'I really am sorry. It's hard to imagine what it might be like to have loved and lost completely.' She found herself entwining her fingers with his, as if to take a firmer grip on their friendship. 'Although Paul went away from me in so many ways, we had a chance to be close again, at the end.'

'My wife remarried. She's got three children now. I never go near her – it's the least I can do.'

They sat in silence. Then, as if by mutual consent, their hands unclasped and they went on with the meal.

By ten o-clock the following morning, Fran was walking towards a rather plain house. She'd expected a retired company director to have bought some rambling farmhouse and done it up in exquisite taste with no concern for the expense. Instead, the place in front of her had an air of modern suburbia. The white walls and ochre roof tiles were the only concessions to the climate

Jez remained sitting in the car, parked just beyond the entrance. She'd wanted him to drive away, visit the fort perhaps or go back to the hotel, but he had insisted on staying to see if anyone responded to her knock. Before she reached the door it was flung open by a broad-shouldered man wearing a tweed cap.

'Mr Bennett?'

'Who wants him?' His bushy eyebrows rose, pushing the lines on his forehead closer together.

'May I talk to you for a moment?'

He reached behind him to pick up a bag of golf clubs. 'I'm on my way out and I'm late already. We've got a tournament all this week.'

'Please, I'd like a few words.'

'Can't you see I'm in a hurry? Who are you, anyway?'

Fran hadn't imagined she would have to explain while she stood on the doorstep. His large frame moved towards her, blocking out the light from the far end of the small entrance hall. She was forced to step back as he pushed out, turning to close the door behind him.

'I'm Paul Ashby's widow. He worked for Nonsec. Do you remember him?'

The fingers in his pocket stopped fumbling as he hesitated. Then he drew out his keys and locked the door. 'Yes, I remember Paul. Never got the recognition he deserved.'

Fran stepped forward and put a hand on his arm. 'Martin said I should speak to you.'

'Martin Emery?'

'Yes. I need some information. Can you help me?'

He hitched his bag of clubs further on to his shoulder with a movement that threw her hand off his sleeve. 'I'm retired now, I have nothing to do with the company.' He moved away from her towards the car parked in his drive. Opening the boot, he thrust the bag inside and went round to the driver's door.

'Please wait.' She ran after him. 'It's not about the company. I want to find out about my husband.'

'I'm tied up all this week.'

'But I'm only here for two days. I came specially all this way to see you.'

He walked over to open the gate and saw Jez sitting in the car. 'Did he bring you?'

'He's a friend.'

Mr Bennett grunted and walked back to his car. 'Shut the gate behind me, will you?' Issuing commands evidently came naturally to him. As he climbed into the seat he put his head out of the window. 'If it's that important you'd better come back tomorrow evening. About six.' He nodded towards Jez. 'Bring him too, if you like.'

Fran watched until his car was out of sight.

'Was that the man?' Jez asked, coming to meet her.

Fran told him of the assignation. 'He invited you to come with me.'

'So how does that grab you?'

She looked out over the scrubby bush of the headland. Exposed to the Atlantic winds, few trees interrupted the flat expanse that extended to the cliffs and the sea beyond. 'I don't know.'

Jez opened the car door for her and folded his long frame in behind the wheel. 'You don't have to decide now. What would you like to do? We've got the rest of today and all tomorrow.'

Fran put her hand up to his face. 'Thank you.'

'What for?'

'For not harrying me. For being here.' She kicked off her shoes and leaned back. 'I'd like to see a bit of the country, while we can. Not anywhere on the coast,' she added. 'Somewhere inland, away from the tourists.'

Jez studied the map. 'We could go up into the hills. There's a place called Monchique. It's marked as a thermal spa.'

'Sounds good,' said Fran. 'I'm in your hands.'

She must have dozed for much of the journey, only opening her eyes when she heard the tone of the engine change and felt the car swinging round sharp bends.

'I'm taking you up to the viewpoint at Foia. Nine hundred and two metres above sea level. Says so on the map.'

Fran sat forward, scanning the vistas that opened out at the side of the winding road. At the summit they got out and stood watching as the wind blew the last remnants of cloud away, revealing a huge panorama stretching out all around them. A sharp intake of breath made Fran turn. A look of wonder on her companion's face forced her to snatch her eyes away, afraid she'd trespassed in some private place. As she absorbed the expanse of hills, the interplay of light fields and darker woods, the small white houses tucked into the crevices, she felt a lift of excitement that filled her chest and made her long to throw her arms wide and cry out. Not wanting to break the spell, she merely squeezed her fingers into fists and lifted her chin.

She felt Jez turn to gaze in the other direction, where the sunlight lit the distant ocean. 'Great, isn't it?' he said, taking her hand. She could only nod her agreement.

Walking back to the car, he asked if she would like to drive.

'I'll take my turn if you want, but I love being driven by you.'

'Just as well. I'm not a good passenger.'

They sat for a time studying the guidebook. 'What about this place, Silves? It seems to have a cork museum with a good restaurant. If you can bear fish again.'

Fran could hardly believe she was travelling with a man who enjoyed driving around to discover new places. If only Paul could have taken her out of herself like this . . . but what was the use of wishing.

They drove down from the summit, drawn closer by the experience they had shared, all the more telling because they hadn't talked about it. A few kilometres lower they stopped at the spa. A stream cascaded over man-made weirs and they scrambled some way up beside the water. The buildings in the village seemed curiously deserted and they did no more than peep into a couple of windows, catching sight of women in uniform and a steaming pool.

Continuing down the mountain they reached the lower slopes, where cork forests provided dense shade at the side of the road. They stopped to examine several trees whose bark had been stripped from the ground to head height or above. The texture of the underlying wood varied from smooth to rough, depending on the time since they had been denuded; time for the bark to reform. Letters and symbols marked the trunks in different coloured paints, only significant to those who could read the language. In a clearing, piles of rolled bark were stacked like carpets in a warehouse.

It took them several enquiries before they found the museum. After a brief tour, looking at the various ways cork could be used, the machines for making bottle corks and photographs of the men at work when the industry was in its heyday, they made for the restaurant. On the way Fran visited the shop and bought some table-mats for Sylvia as an extra wedding present.

Lingering over their meal of clams fried with pork chunks, they began to talk with less restraint. 'Tell me some more about your husband,' Jez asked.

Where could she start? The memory of him lying in bed, his briefcase clutched to his chest, erased all earlier images. 'He worked so hard in the last few weeks of his life. Then there was a day he insisted I take him into his office, ill as he was. We drove through the gate in the high security fence. I left the car by the front door so he had less far to walk. We took the lift to the second floor.' She stopped. 'I haven't told you about Jackson, have I?'

'Not yet,' Jez said. 'Go on.'

She filled him in briefly about the way she had been harassed, before continuing the story. 'We met the man on the corridor and he asked what on earth Paul thought he was doing. When Paul said, untruthfully, that he had come to fetch some books, Jackson became unbearably attentive, pulling a chair forward and offering to go himself to fetch anything he needed. Paul told him sharply that I was helping him and we managed to make our escape.' Even now, the thought made her shiver. As she spoke she was hearing again the words Paul had muttered. *Interfering bastard. He could ruin everything.*

' So . . . when you got to the office?' Jez asked.

Fran shook herself. 'He collapsed into his chair, struggling for breath. I thought he was going to pass out right then and there, but he pulled himself together and unlocked a drawer at the side of his desk. He added some papers to those in the file he'd been working on. I was watching his every move but he looked up and shouted at me to go away. I waited by the window until he was ready to leave. As I turned I saw him put the key of the drawer in his pocket. He also took the key from the door of his office.'

Fran stopped, surprised at the details that had only surfaced as told them to Jez. She'd forgotten about the keys, and the way he'd struggled out to the post box when they got home. If only he'd let her go she would have read the address. 'He probably sent them to Martin,' she said. 'But he's dead now.'

'What happened then?'

'He was near the end. Two days later he went into hospital and never came out. The doctor said the trip had made no difference, his heart muscle was just too damaged to recover. But I've always blamed myself for hastening his death.'

'That's natural but not logical. If he needed to do this thing, you had to help him.'

She looked into the sympathetic face in front of her and glimpsed the possibility that she might be able to forgive herself one day. Her guilt had been eating away at her for months and she'd told no one, not Lizzie or even Sylvia. Now she had stripped away her defences and left herself vulnerable. 'Do you really believe that?'

'I'm certain of it. You have to let people lead their own lives, however ill they are.'

The silence, which lasted for some time, soothed her.

Then Jez said, 'And you have no idea what happened to the papers?'

'I think Martin hid them somewhere.'

'Brenda said you'd talked to him?'

Fran told him about her visit to the hospital, glad to escape from the circular thoughts that plagued her when she tried to understand Paul's behaviour. Coming to the end of her tale, she said, 'There, now you know as much about it as I do.'

Jez took her hand. 'I wanted to know. I want to know all about you.'

Fran looked down, confused by the hope that this complicated but attractive man might be genuinely interested in her. When she looked up he was still gazing into her face. 'I don't know so much about you,' she said.

'But you do. No one else knows the reason my marriage failed. Somehow I was able to trust you not to judge me too harshly.' He got up to pay the bill.

In the car she snuggled into his side. 'I wish we could stay longer.'

'Why don't we? We could try and change our flights.'

Her body sagged. 'Let's see what happens tomorrow. For a moment, I'd forgotten.'

EIGHTEEN

2004

'Sherry?' Mr Bennett looked at Fran, the decanter in his hand. She shook her head. He raised his eyebrows. ' A glass of white wine, then?'

'That would be lovely.'

Jez accepted the sherry and passed the dish of nuts their host indicated with an extended forefinger.

Settling himself in what was obviously his accustomed chair, Mr Bennett asked how they liked Portugal. Fran told him of their excursion the previous day and their trip to the fort that morning.

'That stone compass-dial is amazing,' Jez said. 'Do you really think Henry the Navigator used it in the fifteenth century?'

'No reason why not. He was a great man. Explorers and map-makers gathered here from all over the place.'

The conversation shifted to the cork trees. Again it was Jez who kept the talk going. 'Do you have any idea why the industry is in decline?'

'Synthetic materials are often considered better these days,' Mr Bennett replied. 'Plastic stoppers in wine bottles, for instance. It's ruining parts of the economy here. The ecology too. A unique habitat is being destroyed.'

'Paul would have been interested.' Fran took a sip of wine. 'He used to be passionate about wildlife when we were first married.' She began to feel impatient. She hadn't come all this way to talk about cork.

For several more minutes Mr Bennett continued to ask polite questions about their hotel and discussed the food of the region with enthusiasm. Frustrated, Fran remained silent, restless in her chair.

Turning towards her at last he said, 'I don't know how I can help, Mrs Ashby. Your husband and I only crossed paths occasionally.'

'Please call me Fran.' She had been determined to keep her cool. Now the moment had arrived she couldn't think of a subtle way to approach the man who was watching her, his eyes bland. 'Did you come across his assistant, Brenda Starling? They had a long-standing affair.'

He looked away. 'I met her at the time of the fire, before she left the company. I didn't know there was anything between them. Sorry to hear that.' A small twitch started in his left cheek. Fran felt bewildered. He'd been so brusque the day before and meticulously polite when they arrived. Now his face had softened.

'It's not so much the affair, I've come to accept that . . . but I know so little about his work.' She took a deep breath. 'At the end, when he was so ill, he continued to work every day. It was as if his notes had become more important than anything else in his life. I don't know what he was doing but he often looked so anguished that I started to think his different loyalties were fighting each other.'

'How do you mean?'

Fran tried to explain how she had come to believe he had been torn by his duty to the company, his ideals and Brenda's causes.

Mr Bennett frowned as he drained his sherry. 'He could have been upset by the commercial greed that had come to dominate the board.' He got up and lifted the wine bottle. Fran shook her head, putting her hand over her half-filled glass. 'That was why I resigned,' he continued. 'In the end they only seemed to be interested in short-term gains. No idea about forward planning.' The decanter was empty and he reached for an unopened bottle of sherry. Pouring directly into the two small glasses, he slopped some on to the polished table and didn't seem to notice when Fran mopped it up with a tissue from her pocket. 'It's heartbreaking, because the work is really important. We need better food crops if the starving are to be fed.' He looked up. 'I was mainly interested in that side of the work.'

'And all that G-M modification Brenda is so rabid about?'

'It has to be the answer in the end.'

'But what about the dangers?'

'There are also dangers in traditional breeding. That lettuce . . .'
He stopped. 'I mustn't bore you.'

Fran shook her head. 'We want to understand.' It would be good
for Jez to hear some of the arguments on the other side.

'They used ordinary methods to breed a lettuce that was
resistant to white fly. Crossed a wild, naturally resistant lettuce
with a cultivated one. Worked well. Only thing was, the result
turned out to be poisonous to humans.'

'Would G-M have been any better?'

'It would have been more controlled. In the conventional cross,
each parent lettuce contributes – maybe 20,000 genes. Any one of
those could have been carrying the resistance. We don't know if it
was the same one that contributed to the toxic effect. If a G-M
technique had been used only one gene would have been replaced.
It might still have been toxic but the research needed to prove its
safety would have been manageable.'

Fran had stopped listening. 'I'm sorry, it's a bit too technical for
me.'

Jez sat forward in his seat. 'This is so interesting.'

Mr Bennett was about to resume but Fran intervened. 'I was just
wondering what Paul really thought about it.'

'I can only guess that he would have looked at each problem as
it arose, with a cool mind. Designed careful experiments. If he'd
been part of the team we could have gone forward sensibly, step
by step.'

'Martin said they were going too fast.'

'You say he told you to speak to me? I wonder what he wanted
me to do for you.'

'I need to find those records. And soon. I'm not the only one
looking for them. A man from the company, Jackson –'

'That smartass?'

'He's been searching my house. He kicked my dog –'

Mr Bennett was startled. 'Whatever for? Was it attacking him?'

Fran couldn't help laughing. 'Bruiser is the gentlest creature in the world. Jez will bear me out. He used to chase cats but the largest things he ever caught were flies. He would drive us mad snapping at them in the garden.' Remembering how clumsy he had become since his fall, she added, 'I doubt he'll even catch those now. The kick threw him down the stairs and he fractured his skull.'

'That's serious. Did you inform the police?'

'They might ask awkward questions. You see, I still don't know what Paul . . .'

Mr Bennett got out of his chair and paced to the window. 'I never liked Jackson. He's been trying to wangle his way on to the board for a long time. He'd stop at nothing.'

'Even blackmail?' Jez spoke quietly but the word seemed to reach into every corner of the room.

'What sort of evidence could this file contain?' With his back to them Mr Bennett seemed to be talking to himself. 'If Paul had discovered something to discredit one of the directors, or some company policy, Jackson could use it to lever himself on to the board. He's still desperate to get there.'

He turned from the window, propping his ample backside against the sill. 'But I have no guarantee that it would be any less dangerous in your hands.' He looked directly at Jez. 'Apart from being a friend of Fran's, what's your interest in this? I know nothing about you. What do you do for a living?'

'I'm an artist, or try to be.'

Fran's voice was sharp as she cut in. 'He doesn't have to be involved. Go out for a bit, Jez. I want to talk to Mr Bennett alone.'

'No need for that. I was just about to say that I have been an activist. I've demonstrated against globalisation and the planting of G-M crops. Got into trouble for it too. I can't promise I won't do that again. Big business often has terrible consequences. But as far as Nonsec is concerned, I'm here because of Fran.' He turned away from Mr Bennett to look directly at her. 'I haven't really committed myself before but now I'll give you my word. I'll do nothing without your agreement.' After holding her gaze for a moment he transferred his attention back their host. 'Brenda has given her the same assurances.'

Mr Bennett moved his eyes from one to the other. 'I admired Martin. When he came on the board a few years before he retired, he talked more sense than most of the others. He must have had good reason to send you to me.'

Fran got up and went to join him at the window. They gazed out across his back garden, a large, unkempt patch with wind-blown shrubs she didn't recognise. 'Geoffrey told me all the records were kept in the secure room at Keynsham.'

'You have been busy – picking his brains and Martin's, then coming all this way, on the off chance that I might be here. Who else have you seen?'

'That's about it. My friend Hazel used to work there as a secretary but she doesn't know much. So, how do I get in?' She watched him tip his head back and throw some nuts into his mouth, then wash them down with a third glass of sherry.

'You need a pass. But I doubt if any member of the present board would give you one. Few of them are in sympathy with Paul's view of things. Or mine.' He scratched his bald patch. 'I used to know one of the security men who carried a set of keys. Did him a favour once. Don't know if he's still in the same job, though.'

'Could he get me in?'

'You can't go.' Jez jumped up to stand behind them. 'You might bump into Jackson or someone else you know. I'm the one who has to do it.'

Mr Bennett looked keenly at Fran. 'Do you work for the company?'

'I was a rep. I retired last year.'

'So, even if Jackson's not hanging around, your face would still be familiar to some of the staff?'

Fran shrugged. 'Probably, I ran training courses ... couldn't I say I was visiting a friend? Or collecting some belongings? Or –'

Jez broke in. 'But then, when they discover the file has gone, they'll connect your appearance with the loss. I've never been inside the building. As far as I know I haven't met anyone who works there, apart from Fran and Brenda. I'm the obvious one to go.'

'But you might get caught . . .' she stopped. How could she let him risk a second conviction?

'It's a risk for me too,' said Mr Bennett, as if he had guessed what she was thinking. 'If I was rumbled they could sue me for industrial espionage. How can I be sure one or both of you are not out to damage the company? I may not like the way they do things, but basically the work is important. I've still got some shares and I wouldn't want a scandal.'

Jez moved towards the door. 'I'll stretch my legs, take a turn in the garden. Just remember, if anyone is going into that building, it's me.' Without giving either of them time to reply he left the room. They heard the front door slam behind him.

Left alone, Fran and Mr Bennett looked at each other. After a moment he said, 'This friend – I assume he's important to you.' It was more of a statement than a question.

There was no doubting his meaning. Fran dropped her eyes. She couldn't lie to the man standing beside her; she liked him and he'd supported Paul. 'I don't know how much . . . ' She giggled. 'He was determined to come with me this evening. He wasn't sure I'd be safe with you.'

Mr Bennett smiled. 'Do you trust him?'

Again, she didn't know how to answer. 'I didn't fully, till just now. He's been wonderful to travel with.' To her surprise she found herself saying, 'I trust him more than Brenda.'

'They both seem a bit fanatical.'

'I admire her, though I don't have her beliefs – in a way I wish I had. She's very persuasive when she lectures. But I do realise how desperately we need new drugs.'

Outside, Jez appeared round the side of the house and started to walk towards a gate at the end of the patch that led out on to the shrubby land beyond. When he reached it he leant on the top, gazing towards the cliffs. 'Paul died of heart failure due to cardiomyopathy,' Fran went on. 'There aren't any drugs for that yet.'

'He was a good man, your husband.' Mr Bennett put a hand on her shoulder. 'Pulled the whole show together in a remarkable way after the fire. He should have come on the board. He and Martin together would have had some influence. I couldn't do much by myself.'

Fran's eyes travelled round the room. It contained few clues to the man by her side. She could see no family photographs or pictures of anything other than a few boring landscapes on the walls. Only an executive toy on the desk, a silver golfer with a moveable arm, provided a key to his obsession.

'Do you live here alone?' she asked.

'My wife joins me from time to time.' Wistfully he added, 'But she's no golfer. Likes to go home during the tournament. It lasts for several months,' he added, as if he wanted her to understand his position. He glanced at his watch. 'The lady who cooks for me has left a fish stew. She makes them brilliantly. And one of their marvellous chocolate cakes. Would you join me? I expect there's enough for three.'

'Thank you, but we're due back at the hotel for supper.'

He let out a small sigh and turned away. 'I'll write a letter of authority, on company paper. I've still got some upstairs. What's the full name of your friend?'

'It's Polish – I don't know how to spell it.'

Mr Bennett opened the window and called for Jez to write it out in full. Then he went upstairs and Jez rejoined Fran in the sitting room. They sat in silence. Before long their host returned with a sealed envelope in his hand. They got to their feet.

'I've addressed it to Parsons, the security man who will remember me, and asked him to let you into the record room. However, I doubt if you'll find what you're looking for on the shelves. Jackson is now head of his department and will have access to the room. He's sure to have searched it thoroughly before coming after you.' He wrinkled his nose as if the mere thought of the man had a bad smell. 'He's a nasty bit of work. If there were something in the safe he wouldn't hesitate to use it.'

Jez, who had been reading the name on the envelope, looked up. 'A safe inside the room?'

'Only a few of the board members know of its existence. I think Martin will have stowed the file away in there.'

For a moment all three of them stood motionless. Fran heard a seagull call through the open window. Then, looking at Jez, Mr Bennett said, 'I'm still not sure if I should tell you the combination. Fran says it's only now she feels she can trust you and I've known you for less than an hour. What if you change your mind and decide your cause is more important than your promise to her?'

Jez moved to the door as if to retreat from the discussion again. When he turned, Fran saw deep hollows under his cheekbones, as if his face had fallen in. Speaking to Mr Bennett in a firm voice he said, 'OK – here it is. Once before I lost my chance of happiness. I put a cause before the woman I loved. I've always regretted it. I can never make it up to her, she's gone out of my life. But if I'm true to my word, this time, it may go some way to repay the debt. I'm asking you to believe I have a good reason to prove my integrity, to myself as much as to anyone else.'

Mr Bennett studied him for a moment, then shrugged and leant forward to whisper in his ear. Taking Fran's arm he led her towards the door. 'If Parsons has left the company I'll have to think again. Maybe I'll come myself . . .'

'I don't think you should do that. It sounds too risky.'

'I seldom go back now. The climate is so awful and the food here can be really good, if you choose carefully.'

When they reached the front door Fran said goodbye and found herself kissing his cheek. He reddened like a schoolboy.

'I can't begin to thank you,' she said.

Jez shook his hand. At the gate Fran looked back and saw him standing on the steps. 'Let me know if I can do anything else,' he called after them, raising his hand and wiggling the fingers.

Jez circled the envelope above his head before climbing back into the hired car.

For the rest of their stay in Portugal the letter that Jez held in his pocket formed a barrier between them. Fran sat in silence much of the time, raging against herself. If Jez tried to start a conversation she answered with clipped monosyllables, so he gave up trying. The easy companionship and flirtatious mood of the first two days had vanished. Neither of them returned to the idea of extending their visit.

By letting Jez hold the combination to the safe, Fran felt she had betrayed Paul in the worst possible way. She couldn't understand how it had happened. The two men seemed to have ganged up on her, colluding with her own fears of recognition or of having to confront Jackson yet again. From time to time she made half-hearted attempts to get him to divulge the combination. He refused to give it to her. How could she have been such a coward? All her new-found independence had deserted her at the crucial moment. It would have been better to let the documents moulder away in the safe forever. But then, if Jackson did get on the board, he would discover the combination and that would be even worse.

She'd planned to go home from the airport by train, but Jez fetched his van from the long-stay car park and insisted on driving her. 'I'll bring your things in,' he said as they drew up outside her house.

'I'll make us some tea. Then you must be off.'

'I'm in no hurry. Where would you like your case?'

'First door on the left at the top of the stairs.'

On his way down Jez took time to look at the pictures. They were a motley selection of prints, reproductions that Fran had collected in her youth and brought with her when they were married.

'I see you like the impressionists,' he said, as he moved from a Monet with brightly coloured boats to a Sisley landscape.

Fran poured out the tea and found some stale biscuits in a tin. 'I never trusted my artistic judgement. Those were safe and undemanding.' She was glad to talk about something other than the file.

Jez seemed to sense something of her misery. 'Look, I know you'd rather I didn't even touch those papers. If it makes you any happier, you could come as far as the entrance – disguised in some way – so that I can hand the file over to you immediately. I'm not going to stand about in the corridor reading it, waiting to be caught, am I?'

Trying to smile Fran said, 'You mean dark glasses and a floppy hat?'

'Something like that.' He paused. 'I've never seen the place. What's the security like? You'd have to stay out of range of any CCTV cameras.'

'They're on the walls of the building. A main gate and porter's lodge is the only break in the high security fence that surrounds the inside car park. Senior staff are allowed to park in there but they have to present a special pass.'

'We need a driver, so that you can hide if we pass anyone familiar on the road. Do any of your friends know about your trouble?'

'Only Brenda.' The name hung in the air between them.

'I'll ask her then,' Jez said. 'I want to speak to her anyway about this trip to California.'

A thump in Fran's chest was followed by a hollow feeling. 'Are you hoping to go with her?'

'It's on the cards, if some funding can be found from one of her organisations. She's keen to have me along.'

Fran wanted to scream. Not content with stealing her husband and worming her way into Sylvia's affections over so many years, Brenda now had designs on Jez. She'd never even noticed him until they'd met in her house. What a fool she'd been to let herself get fond of him.

'When will you sit for me again?' he asked. 'I'd like to get on with the painting before I go.'

'I'd find it difficult to settle to anything until we get the file.' She stood up. 'The first thing is to find out if this security guard still works there. I'll ring and see if I can speak to him.'

She went out into the hall and got through to the company switchboard. While she was talking, Jez wandered round the room, looking at the photos. When Fran returned he was holding the one of the three of them at Sylvia's graduation.

'Your daughter is beautiful. I'd like to meet her.'

Fran snatched it out of his hand and replaced it on the top of the desk. Why did he feign an interest in her, when he was going off with Brenda? She must finish the task she'd started and then put him out of her mind. 'Parsons does still work there, but he's on holiday. I had to pretend I was a distant relative.' She gave a nervous laugh. 'They say he's on main shift next week, eight till six, so that should suit us quite well. I wonder what time would be best?' Sinking back on to the sofa, she felt defeated. 'I suppose I'll have to ring Brenda and tell her how far we've got.'

Jez sat down beside her. 'You're exhausted. Why don't you leave that to me? I'll arrange something with her and let you know.'

Fran rubbed her eyes. 'Provided you promise not to go and do anything without me.' She put her hand on his arm. 'I must be there, just outside the gate at the very least.'

'Of course.' He stood up. 'I'd better be going.' He turned towards the door. Fran followed. Now he was leaving she searched desperately for some way to delay him. "I didn't tell you ... I used to paint a bit, too. Years ago.'

Jez looked up sharply. 'You never said. There I was, babbling on about this view and that, and all the time you were looking at things with a painter's eyes too.' He sounded hurt. 'I'd like to see some of your work.'

Fran regretted sharing her secret as soon as she had spoken. 'I've only saved a couple of paintings. They're somewhere in the loft. I probably couldn't find them.' Even the thought of looking at them again made her blush. 'Anyway, I don't let anyone see them – I was never any good.'

Jez put his hands on her arms and looked at her with enquiring eyes. 'You should let me be the judge of that. I'm a good tutor, you know, even though I'm only a very moderate painter.'

'Perhaps I will – sometime.'

With great care he bent down and kissed her on the lips. 'Is that a promise? I'll hold you to it.'

Fran flushed. 'You'll be in California, sitting in a tree with Brenda.'

'Only for a short time.'

Fran could hardly bear the excitement that churned inside her, tempered by the fear that he was playing with her. 'Get on now, I must have some rest.'

'Of course.' He reached out and took her face in his hands. 'You are beautiful, you know.'

'For goodness sake. I'm old.'

He gave her shoulders a gentle shake. 'Don't say that, Fran, it's not true. You have years of active life ahead of you. Once this matter is sorted out, you'll learn to live again, you'll see.'

Fran pulled away and opened the front door. 'Drive carefully.'

He waved and blew her a kiss before turning the van and rattling down the drive and out of sight.

NINETEEN

2004

Fran passed through the next few days in a fog of suspense, sleeping badly and waking to find her body aroused by dreams she couldn't remember. Each time she relived the kiss that Jez had given with such deliberation she was thrown into turmoil, not knowing if he was just being kind to a woman in distress or if he had meant something more.

With Geoffrey the message had been so clear. He had wanted sex; love was not an issue. If only she could separate love from sex, enjoy whatever Jez had to offer and go on her way unmoved. As she wandered round her house she imagined her hands running over his buttocks. The longing to look and touch and smell his body, to let her being mix with his, made her legs feel weak.

When the phone rang, her hands shook in expectation. Hearing Brenda's voice, she blushed to realise that daydreaming about Jez had driven Paul to the back of her mind.

Brenda told her that she and Jez had decided mid-morning would be the best time to try for the file and they'd arranged it for the next day. She would collect him first in her car and then come on. 'Is eleven-o-clock alright for you?'

As Fran listened the muscles of her throat tightened. She could see their heads close together as they made plans, her dead husband the excuse for their intimacy. 'Why can't we go in my car?'

'I've got to drive so you can hide if necessary. You know you're a liability around the place. And the van Jez uses is far too conspicuous.'

She was right, of course.

When they arrived to collect her, Jez jumped out and folded the passenger seat forward so she could climb into the back seat. As they drove through the countryside he asked Fran to describe the folder once again. After that they didn't speak. She stared miserably out of the window as the trees and fields gave way to suburban houses. This was the way she had driven with Paul on that last journey. He had sat beside her, his precious burden disguised in a plastic carrier bag at his feet. On the way home he'd replaced the folder by a couple of books and asked her to carry them. He'd obviously felt it necessary to continue the deception, that he was collecting goods rather than delivering them, until he was safely back in the car.

They reached the car park across the road from the porter's lodge by eleven thirty. Jez clambered out, smoothing his hand down an elegant long coat that he wore over a dark suit. Fran wondered if he had hired the outfit for the occasion. As she began to climb out after him he put his hand on her arm.

'I'll be better alone. You stay in the back so I can leap in fast if we need to get away quickly.' His voice held an authority Fran hadn't heard before.

She looked up at him, ready to argue. It was not what she had planned. She realised he must have been humouring her when he'd agreed she could go as far as the gate. But if she wasn't going to get the folder herself it was obviously silly to expose herself – just because she was afraid he would read the contents.

'Do as he says,' Brenda chipped in. 'It makes sense.'

As Fran hesitated, Jez was striding away towards the entrance, carrying a briefcase and looking every inch the salesman, his coat buttoned neatly across his chest. The two women watched him go up to the porter, who was standing by the door of his lodge.

'Oh goodness, I know that man,' Fran said, sinking down in the back seat of the car. 'He used to be in the other building when I first went back to work. He's an old grouch and a stickler for protocol. Thank God I didn't go.'

After some conversation, that they couldn't hear, the man picked up his mobile. Jez looked relaxed as he waited until a man in a different uniform, with brighter buttons, appeared. Then he produced the letter from his pocket and followed him across the compound and in through the side door. All they could do was sit and wait. Fran bit her nails, something she hadn't done since she battled with her mother. Brenda drummed her fingers on the steering wheel, looking at her watch every few minutes.

After a quarter of an hour she started the engine. Fran sat forward. 'You can't leave him.'

'Don't be silly, I'm just turning the car round. I'll put it in that gap by the exit, so we can make a quick getaway.'

Facing the gate now Fran was in a good position to notice the green car, the wing still buckled, when it turned into the car park. 'My God, it's Jackson,' she whispered to Brenda, as she folded her body sideways out of view. 'Why wasn't he in at the beginning of the day like everyone else? What rotten luck!'

Brenda sat immobile for a few moments. Then under her breath she said, without looking round, 'He's coming over.'

He reached the car. Speaking to Brenda through the open window of the driver's door he said, 'This is a private car park, you'll have to move on.'

Fran, knowing she couldn't stay hidden, straightened up and handed Brenda a map that had been on the floor. 'I've found it,' she said. 'It had slipped down under the front seat.'

'Why, Mrs Ashby, I didn't see you.' His voice took on a touch of excitement – or was it nervousness? 'What are you doing here?'

'I'm with my friend,' Fran said.

His eyes flicked to the empty seat beside the wheel. 'Waiting for someone, I presume? I suppose you can wait here, as an old staff member. But just to make sure there isn't any trouble I'll stay with you until your business is finished.' He opened the back door of the car and climbed in beside her. 'I'm sure you don't mind if I join you.'

'I do mind, very much.' Fran drew away from him into the far corner. Thinking furiously, she decided that attack was the only form of defence. 'But it's so fortuitous that we've met like this.' With an effort to keep her voice level she said, 'I was about to write to inform you that my dog sustained a fractured skull and brain damage. I'm taking legal advice.' As she spoke Fran snatched a glance out of the window on the other side of the car, terrified that Jez would appear at any moment with the folder under his arm for all to see.

'That was ages ago. Anyway, his fall had nothing to do with me.'

'You know perfectly well you pushed him down the stairs. And you were trespassing.'

'As I said at the time, it was an accident.'

She ignored the remark. 'If I hadn't recently been on holiday I would have chivvied my solicitors. They should have served a writ long ago. My mental trauma was considerable.'

'You can't prove it had anything to do with me. You've got no witnesses.'

'On the contrary. Mr Singh, who keeps the local shop, saw you hanging round my house several times. He also helped me take the dog to the vet after you left. Healthy dogs don't just fall down stairs. He wanted to call the police at the time but I was more concerned with my dog. I think . . . if you have any sense, you'll stop concerning yourself with my presence and go about your own business.'

Jackson stared straight ahead and made no move to get out of the car.

During the whole exchange Brenda had said nothing. Now she turned round and in a voice quite unlike any Fran had heard her use before, said, 'Will you introduce me, Fran?' The American drawl was pronounced; she must be practising for California.

'Certainly. This is Mr Algernon Jackson.'

'Jackson? I think that was one of the names I heard discussed. Of course my company . . . I mustn't say anything yet . . . it's still under wraps.'

Jackson sat forward, unable to keep the surprise out of his voice. 'What's under wraps?'

'Oh, haven't you heard about it? You soon will. It must be all round the place by now. We've been interested in the company for some time.'

Fran noticed his jaw go slack as he spluttered, 'An American company? A takeover?'

Brenda looked inscrutable in an obvious way. 'Come now, you know one can't say anything until it's in the bag.'

Through the fence Fran glimpsed Jez emerge from the front door and start to make his way towards them across the asphalt, his coat open now, held by one hand, his briefcase in the other. 'That's right,' she added 'I think I see your colleague coming now, Brenda.' With her heart pounding she turned to Jackson and forced herself to smile. 'Perhaps you would like me to introduce you? I'm sure he would be most interested in a Nonsec staff member who has such talent for harassment.' She climbed out of the car. 'Do come with me,' she called over her shoulder as she started to walk towards the gate.

Jackson followed her out of the car. From the corner of her eye Fran saw him look at his watch as he murmured, 'Another time, perhaps. I have an appointment . . .'

She walked slowly on, keeping her head turned away from the bad-tempered man on the gate. She didn't look back.

As Jez came up to her she asked under her breath, 'Did you get it?'

'In my poacher's pocket.'

'Walk normally and don't say anything unless you can do an American accent.' As she turned she saw Jackson sidling away in the opposite direction. They reached the car and Jez turned to give a wave to the man at the gate before getting in. 'Drive slowly,' he said. 'Don't rush.' By this time Jackson was out of sight.

Brenda manoeuvred the car out of the park. Fran looked through the back window expecting some sort of alarm to be raised at any moment, but everything behind them was peaceful in the weak sunshine. She giggled. 'I had no idea you could do accents like that.'

Brenda smiled. 'I do speak several languages. It helps.'

Once they were round the corner and out of sight of the building Jez took the folder from inside his coat and passed it back. 'I only looked at the first page. It has your husband's name on it. I could see no other brown folder in the safe so I hope it's the one you're after.'

Fran recognised it at once and opened the front cover. She saw Paul's name, written in his neat capitals. Then a title: 'Clinical record of the effects of increasing doses of PRONTOSIN (PN180)'. Below she saw a date, 17/10/01, and further down, in a hand she didn't recognise, 25/11/02. She stared at the date of his death, her mind paralysed.

Brenda's voice reached her as if from a great distance. 'Wait till you get home before you read it.'

Fran glanced up, caught her eye in the driving mirror and nodded. The small movement of her head felt enormous, as if it would crack open the shell that enclosed her.

'Drop me off at the bus station,' Jez said. 'I'll go home from there.'

Fran tried to say thank you, but the sound she produced came out between a sob and a croak. Jez reached back and touched her knee. 'Don't try and say anything. It all went fine, no problems. We'll talk later.' Then he was gone.

Brenda drove on. They didn't exchange a word until she pulled up at Fran's front door. 'Ring me when you're ready to talk about it. Take care now,' she said.

Fran climbed out, clutching the file. As the car drove away she realised she hadn't offered Brenda a word of thanks.

Without thinking, she headed for the attic and propped herself up on the narrow bed with two pillows behind her back. Then she pushed the ant and frog cushions on either side of her body, as if to wedge herself into safety.

The sheets of paper were in chronological order, each with the date written in the top left-hand corner. The first corresponded to the date on the outside of the file, 17/10/01. Below that there was a figure for body weight and a blood pressure reading, then a brief description of a crude exercise test. 'Three flights of stairs climbed in 35 seconds. Tachycardia 100 per min. Very slight breathlessness.'

Her eyes swept across to the right-hand side of the paper to a column headed *Dosage of Prontosin*. On that first page the dose was

2mg o.d. She knew that o.d. meant once a day. She flipped the sheets between her fingers and discovered that the dosage climbed sharply to 15mg twice a day, and then by stages till it reached 30mg t.d.s. Abruptly, on April 24th the space was empty. The room swirled around her and she clutched at the cushions. That was the day after the specialist told them that Paul had cardio-myopathy.

It was not a coincidence – the date of his death on the outside of the file and the sudden withdrawal of the drug at the time he had discovered he was seriously ill. She had to accept the truth she had denied. He had not faked his results; they were all too true and accurate. The identity of the trial subject was the secret he had kept hidden. This was a clinical record of his own illness. He had been experimenting on himself, treating himself with the new drug, one that was untested and unlicensed: it had killed him.

She was consumed with fury. He had no right to leave her. It wasn't his life to risk on some crazy whim. He was her husband, Sylvia's father. How dare he? Her hands clutched the papers as if to strangle the life out of the story they told.

She flopped back on to the pillows and stared at the ceiling. If only she were dead too. If his love for her was so puny that he could throw his life away, there was no reason for her to go on living. The desertion was complete, far worse than an affair with another woman. Fran had begun to believe his love for Brenda was bound to his love for herself, love that generated love, as she had mouthed to Sylvia. His self-destruction was the opposite of love, it was searing hate turned inwards, a bullet that found its target with such force that it rebounded into the centre of her being.

She went back to the papers, turning them over one by one. As the weeks and months went by, the record of his symptoms on each page got longer. Now his breathlessness made him stop after two flights of stairs, then one. He began to speculate on the possible causes. Anaemia, or perhaps a malignancy in his lungs. (He'd inserted a note to the effect that he hadn't smoked since the age of seventeen, when he had bought three packets but given most of them away.) Here was his first visit to his GP, who had arranged blood tests, a chest X-ray and an ECG. A few pages later the results were recorded in all their detail. He must have persuaded the doctor to give him copies. She couldn't help admiring the detachment with which he made his observations, his writing as neat as ever. Only towards the end did it become straggly. He was trying to make a daily record now, but some dates were missing, covered by the next entry with short sentences, evidently gasped out between one breath and the next.

'Dozed most of the last three days, propped up.'

'Stood by the window yesterday with Fran's help. Breathing easier near the air.'

'Ankles less swollen. Diuretics having effect. PU five times in the night.' How well she remembered those nights when she had slept on the sofa cushions, ready to empty his bottle when it became so full that he was in danger of spilling it.

'Very weak today. Must get well enough to take these to the office.'

'Stronger – a bit. Must talk to Fran.'

The pages slipped from her hands and lay scattered on the bed. She had no energy to read on, or to do the things that had to be done. Brenda would be waiting for a phone call. Worst of all she had to find some way to tell Sylvia the truth about her father's death.

Something stirred in her mind. At least they knew for certain what had caused the cardiomyopathy. The record proved beyond all doubt that his illness was not due to an inherited weakness. That might make up, in a small way, for his desertion. And he hadn't meant to die. As soon as his condition had been diagnosed he had stopped taking the drug.

She tried to think of words to break the news. Poor Sylvia, her father hadn't loved her enough to keep himself alive to see his grandchild.

Fran pulled the cushions from under her and threw them with all her strength, first one and then the other, across the room. The faded ant burst. Feathers rose in a cloud and started to drift down, settling on the furniture and floor and over the bed where she lay.

She watched until the last one had landed, puffing them away from her nose and mouth. Then she sat up, disturbing a small flurry as she began to pick them off her clothes and out of her hair. Going to the mirror, she searched inside her collar where a few stragglers were ticking her neck. The eyes that stared out at her were surprisingly steady.

Brenda had no child; at least Paul's genes were alive in Sylvia. The other woman had held only a small part of him, not the core of the man who had made this final sacrifice. That action had been taken for no woman, unless perhaps for his mother. Fran blinked, surprised by the thought that Brenda was an irrelevance. He had stuck to his own principles, made the grand gesture, so that at the end he was able to stand beside his father on equal terms.

She turned from the mirror and went downstairs. Brenda could wait. First she had to do what she could to rescue herself and her child from the mess he'd left behind.

TWENTY

2004

By the time Sylvia arrived the next day Fran was more composed. She had decided to create an atmosphere that was as near normal as possible. Taking some mince from the deep freeze, she made a cottage pie. Then she scooped out the centre of two baking apples, stuffing them with some dried-up dates left from Christmas. Driven by an instinct to prepare nursery food, she beat up two eggs with milk for a baked custard. As she lit the fire in the sitting room she worried at the words that had been milling in her head for hours, each sentence driving out the one before. None was adequate for the task they had to do.

'Hi, Mum. You said it was urgent. Whatever's the matter?'

'I'll tell you when I'm ready.' She drew her daughter into the kitchen where she'd laid the table. 'Lunch is all set, let's get started.'

As they ate Fran asked disjointed questions, forcing herself to swallow. How's married life? Are you well? How's Richard?

Sylvia tried to answer with a show of enthusiasm, but her mother's delaying tactics worried her.

'Have some more, darling?' Fran insisted.

'No thanks. It was lovely. Just as good as the pies you made when I was little. What's for pudding?'

'Baked apples and custard.'

'Goody.' Sylvia tried to enter into the pretence but she was tired of it. 'Come on, Mum,' she said, as she scooped out the soft pulp of her apple and put the skin on her side plate. She couldn't play the little girl any longer. Once before, in the days after her father died, she had become the adult to her diminished mother. 'You'll have to tell me about it sooner or later.'

Fran put down her spoon. 'I don't know where to start. It's about your father.'

'Of course. I guessed that. Is it to do with Brenda? Does he have other children?'

'No, no. Nothing like that.' She paused, then started to speak in a rush. 'I thought she had talked him into doing something unethical, something he would be ashamed of. I was wrong.'

'Yes?'

'It's worse than that. Well, worse and better. I don't know which.' It was coming out all wrong. 'I wish I'd been a more effective wife –'

Sylvia put out her hand. 'Don't be daft, Mum, you looked after him wonderfully.'

'I don't mean that. If I'd realised what was going on in his mind I might have been able to stop him.'

'Stop him doing what?'

It was no good. She couldn't protect her daughter any longer. Clasping her hands on the table she said 'He took a company drug . . . experimented on himself . . . to prove it wasn't dangerous.'

Sylvia sat very still, looking at her mother. Then her eyes shifted towards the hall where the stairs led down to the study. 'That book . . .'

'What book?'

'The one with all the pencil marking in the margins. The one about the man who swallowed tape worms and attached parasites to his skin to watch the effects.'

'Goodness, I never thought . . .' Fran half rose in her chair but sank back. 'Brenda took it. I wonder if she guessed.'

'Did the drug kill him?' The direct question was asked in a level voice.

Fran could say nothing to soften the truth. 'Yes.'

'Gosh, how brave,' Sylvia said.

It was not what her mother had expected. Brave? Perhaps he was, but she hadn't seen it like that. 'It's such a waste. He won't see your child.' She couldn't suppress a sob.

Sylvia got off her chair and went to put her arm round her mother's shoulders. 'It's all right, Mum. Really it is. Of course I'm sad he isn't here, that he didn't see me married or have time to get to know Richard. But he did what he had to do.' She smoothed her mother's arm. 'He was a great man, Mum, you must see that.'

Fran didn't know what she saw, except that her daughter wasn't destroyed as she had expected. She hadn't lost faith in her father – on the contrary, she seemed to admire him even more. 'At least we know for certain what caused his heart failure,' she said.

Sylvia's grip tightened as she stood frowning by the table. 'Do we? Are we sure it was the drug and nothing to do with his genes?'

'It must have been,' Fran said.

Hurrying through from the kitchen into the sitting room Sylvia said over her shoulder, 'I'll look it up on the net again. Last time I wasn't looking for drugs. What was the name?'

'Prontosin. Finish your pudding first.'

'This is important.'

How like her father she was. When Paul's eye had been caught by something that interested him he would follow it like a dog with its nose to the ground, tracking the tantalising scent of a rabbit. Nothing could divert him from the chase.

Fran listened to the tap of the keys as Sylvia found her way into some relevant sites, using her favourite search engine. Eventually she called through. 'Here we are. Yes, dilated Cardiomyopathy, they call it DCM for short. Causes: viral infection, auto-immune disease, excessive alcohol consumption, pregnancy, exposure to toxic compounds ... Here, listen.' Fran got up and walked through to look over her shoulder. 'Other chemicals such as certain anti-cancer drugs. Was it one of those?'

Fran nodded. They stared at the screen for another moment. Then Sylvia pressed the icon to disconnect and turned the machine off. On their way back to the kitchen she asked, 'How do you know he took it?'

Fran produced the file from behind the cake tins where she had hidden it. 'He kept detailed records. My friend Jez got it from the company. He was so brave, he risked a lot for me. Mr Bennett's letter made all the difference.'

'Who are Jez and Mr Bennett?'

'Jez is the friend I met on Christmas Day. I told you about him.' She went on quickly, 'We went to the Algarve to see Mr Bennett.'

'You and this new man?'

'He's just a friend.'

Sylvia looked sceptical. 'I thought you were going to convalesce from your bronchitis.'

'That was a cover story. I didn't want to say anything until I'd found out what Dad had been doing. There was this man Jackson –'

'Slow down. I want to know everything but I can't take it all in at once.'

Fran didn't know where to start. On that CND march perhaps, when she and Paul had rescued a caterpillar together. But her daughter didn't need all that. 'I began to worry at my retirement do, when this man asked me if Dad kept papers at home. He was such a creepy person . . .' She went on to tell her about Jackson's visits to the house, omitting the attack on Bruiser. Sylvia could be a hothead; she might decide to take her own revenge. That would only complicate things.

'Dad wasn't the only one to show courage. You're a bit on the brave side yourself, Mum.' Sylvia stood up and switched on the kettle. 'What if they notice the file has gone?'

'Not many people know it was there. Paul gave the file to Martin and he's dead.'

'Who's Martin?'

Fran said that was another story. They took their coffee into the sitting room and she told it in front of the comforting fire. Every now and then she looked up, seeing the bed by the window and hearing again the rasp of Paul's breathing.

When Sylvia eventually left, Fran had to face the pain of her loneliness once again. Sometimes she thought it would be better if she had no child, then she would not have to suffer the gut-wrenching separation. It was like the trauma of birth, over and over: the stretch of the umbilical cord as she watched the car drive away, the snap as she turned to go inside.

She must accept that Sylvia had to get on with her own life. Although the separation was painful, it was part of a natural cycle. Buds broke on the trees in the spring, leaves grew to a heavy canopy and fell to the ground in autumn. She couldn't argue with a rhythm that was the stuff of the earth. But Paul's death, before his time, was a rupture; a violent tearing away that had left her to dangle unsupported.

As she drifted aimlessly round the house she could no longer comfort herself with the fantasy that her marriage had been perfect. It had only been adequate, possibly as good as most; but it was over now.

She put on her coat and went out into the garden. The last plank of the tree house had fallen to the ground. There were no fish to be seen in the pond; they must be sheltering at the bottom. In the end, Paul had done what he wanted to do. His death hadn't been planned – it had overtaken him as a side effect of his actions. Like a mountaineer, who defies the dangers for love of the mountains.

For her it had been different. She didn't have any personal mountains to climb, just people she needed to please. Torn between rebellion and a wish to conform she'd satisfied neither her mother nor Paul. She paced on round the garden, thinking of how she had read in some book that the recipe for a good life was not only to make others happy but also to be happy oneself. So often people ignored one or the other.

The phone was ringing as she went inside.

'Hi, it's Brenda.'

'Oh.' Fran didn't want to be reminded of Paul's mistress at that moment.

'Have you had time to read the file yet?' she asked.

'I think you have an idea what it contains.'

'Some account of his illness?'

'If you knew, why on earth didn't you tell me?'

'I didn't know. I just couldn't believe, like you did, that he'd fiddled his results or something. He couldn't have done anything so wrong.'

God, how self-satisfied she was. 'Wrong, right, who is to judge? He deserted us.'

'What did he do?'

'Took increasingly large doses of Prontosin. It killed him.'

'So that was it . . . He died of heart failure, you said. Was the underlying cause cardiomyopathy?'

'What makes you ask?'

'The drug is known to cause it. There have been a number of deaths.'

Fran swallowed twice and hoped her voice didn't betray her distress. 'If that risk is known, why did he do it?'

'It wasn't known until the last few months. His evidence would have saved lives if it had been published.'

'So then he wouldn't have died in vain?'

'I can never forgive Martin for suppressing Paul's work. I suppose he thought he was protecting the company. He must have read the record, because he did take some action. I heard he reduced the starting dose. Despite that, there were still deaths. If the doctors who were doing the trials had read Paul's notes they would have known what to look for and monitored the patients more carefully.'

'What do you think we should do with the file now?'

'I'm not sure. If we expose the company they'll put all the blame on Martin, and nothing would be gained by blackening the name of a dead man. There's no way we can get that Jackson –'

'I'm thinking of sending a copy to Mr Bennett. Although he's retired, he may be able to alert someone to the fact that the man is an unscrupulous bastard who shouldn't be promoted any higher.'

'Do you want to try to make the company pay? After all, if the research protocols had been slower and safer Paul wouldn't have been forced to do what he did. I don't think they would give you financial compensation, though.'

Such an idea had never crossed Fran's mind. Paul had taken the drug of his own free will, stolen it to do so. Of course they wouldn't pay her any money. All she hoped for was that his sacrifice hadn't been completely wasted. 'I don't want revenge.

The choice was Paul's. If the information can still be useful then I suppose it must be published, but I'd rather the company wasn't drawn into it, if possible.'

To her surprise, Brenda agreed. 'I'm not sure what we would gain by exposing them, and there's a lot we could lose.'

Fran relaxed, as if the puppet master who held her strings had laid them down. She had been bracing herself for a passionate argument in favour of using his work to expose the pharmaceutical world. But the company had been a good employer and provided her with the two pensions on which she lived. She didn't want newsmen round her door, the story shouted from the headlines. 'Do you think I'm weak, not wanting it made public?' she asked.

'No. I can understand. I feel the same. After all, he was someone special to me too, and I don't want his memory dragged about in public, even if he was a hero, of sorts. Bigger issues have to be fought, and I'm already *persona non grata* at the company. I can't risk compromising my ongoing campaigns for one small cause. It's better if they never find out about the missing file.'

Fran was stung that Paul's life had become 'one small cause' to the woman who had been his lover for so long. She certainly had moved on. It was easy for a mistress. Not like a wife, who was bound to a man in death as well as in life. For her the problem still remained: to salvage something useful from his death. 'Would there be any point in giving a copy to the specialist who looked after him?' she suggested.

'That's a brilliant idea,' Brenda said. She sounded relieved, as if she wanted to sever her contact with the business as quickly as possible, so as to be free to take part in the next global drama. 'If he feels it adds to the present knowledge of the condition, he can publish it in a medical journal, as an anonymous case history. It might catch the attention of doctors taking part in trials. Warn them to look at the quality of the basic research more carefully.'

'I'll do that, then.' Fran wanted to ring off but felt something else was required of her. 'Do you want to see the file?' Her voice wasn't welcoming.

'I'm leaving for California next week. Jez is coming with me.'

Fran felt choked. 'So you're going to take him away from me, too.'

'Don't be silly. I've had enough of picking up the leavings from another woman's table. It I ever fall in love again it will be with a man for whom I'm special.'

'Weren't you special to Paul?'

'Not really. I think he only fancied me because he felt shut out by you in some way. As I said, you always came first.'

Fran had a ridiculous feeling that she should apologise. 'I don't know what to say to Jez about the file.'

'That's something you have to decide.'

'Of course.' Silence fell between them. Fran shifted her feet. 'Thanks for your help, anyway.'

'I did it for myself too. I needed to know what he'd done. It was very brave, wasn't it?'

'That's what Sylvia said.' Although Fran had been trying to block out the picture of Paul and Brenda together she found herself curious about the depth of their relationship. 'Did you know Paul's father was in Changi gaol in the war?'

'No, he never mentioned it. Why do you ask?'

'Oh . . . it's not important.'

There was another silence. Then Brenda said, 'Despite everything, you knew him better than I did. Perhaps you loved him more, too.'

Fran sighed. She'd had enough of the conversation. 'We can't measure love like the ingredients for a cake. Have a good trip, I may see you when you get back.'

'Shall I put the book in the post to you?'

Oh yes, the book – she must have that back. 'Yes, please. I want to read about the role model for his crazy behaviour.'

'It wasn't crazy, it was noble. I just wish Martin had –'

'What's the use of wishing?' Fran interrupted.

'You sound bitter.'

'I'll get used to it.' Although she knew she was being unfair, she couldn't throttle a final swipe at her old rival. 'I guess part of him was still trying to impress you. I hate you for that.'

'I'm sorry.'

As Fran tried to think of something to take the sting out of her words a bell rang. 'I must go, there's someone at the door.' She replaced the receiver.

Jez was standing on the front steps. 'May I come in?' Fran stood aside, then followed him into the sitting room. 'I need to talk to you.' He walked across the room to look out at the garden. 'You've got a wonderful show of snowdrops.' Turning, he asked awkwardly, 'How are you?'

Fran shrugged. 'I've just been talking to Brenda on the phone. She says you're going with her to California.'

'I haven't agreed to go yet.'

'She spoke as if it were all settled.' Fran pulled at the neck of her jumper before going to throw open a window. 'Would it just be the two of you?'

'She's managed to raise enough money to support four activists. The plan is for two people to stay in a tree, for at least a month, while the others provide backup from the ground.'

'You'll play one of the dramatic roles in the tree, I suppose.' She smiled, trying to lighten the atmosphere. 'Aren't you a bit long in the tooth for that?'

'Hey, steady on. I said, I'm not sure if I'm going.'

Fran couldn't bear the constraint between them. 'For God's sake, let's sit down. Do you want to know what was in the file?'

'Only if you want to tell me.'

She perched on the edge of the sofa and he sat down in a chair opposite, his elbows on his knees and his head in his hands. 'Actually, I would like to know,' he said. 'I've promised not to tell a soul. But the wretched thing has made you so unhappy, I want to understand what's been going on, how it fits into the way your life works.'

Fran remembered their time in the Algarve, before they visited Mr Bennett. Surely the warmth between them hadn't been entirely the product of her own yearning. 'Do you really want to know about me?'

He nodded. She turned away, unable to bear his searching look.

Slowly, she began to tell him. The bare facts were easy, but she found it harder to explain her understanding of what Paul had done. 'When he was very ill he said he'd tried to make me happy and to be a good father. Then he added that even if he'd been more devoted, family life alone would never have been enough for him. I felt hurt at the time, but it makes sense now. He went on to say it wasn't enough, perhaps it never was, for any man. As a woman I could leave another human being as a legacy but men needed to make their mark on the world. He said he had been looking for a purpose all his life.' She paused, but Jez didn't take his eyes from her face. 'I was furious that he was making the traditional assumption that women were only good for reproduction. I too would have liked to do great things. But as I was sitting by his bedside my envy drained away. All I wanted, at that moment, was to cradle him in my arms.'

Jez sat still for a moment. 'I think you loved him very much.'

'I suppose I did. I had trouble showing it.'

He got up to sit beside her on the sofa. She glanced at him, hoping for some sign of affection. His hands lay clasped in his lap, as if he was afraid of what they might do if he let them free. 'Thank you for telling me.'

She longed to reach out, to let the feel of his body chase away the sterile years.

He stood up again. 'Will you sit for me? I've got my clobber in the van. Though what I'd really love is to see your paintings.'

Fran was surprised to hear herself say, 'OK, if you really want to. I'll try to find them while you bring your things in.' She went upstairs and let down the wooden steps leading to the loft. The number of empty suitcases seemed to have doubled since she had last looked. A leather trunk that had belonged to her mother caught her eye. It held old dresses, shoes and long strings of cheap jewellery that Sylvia and her friends had used for dressing up. She could almost hear the tap of high heels as the small feet had flopped about in the silver satin pair or the black sandals encrusted with paste diamonds.

At some time, her wedding dress had joined the other clothes, devoid of the dustsheets her mother had wrapped round it after the ceremony. She lifted it out and held the cream brocade against her body. The full skirt, that had failed to hide her pregnancy, still fell in creased folds from the tight bodice. Each time Sylvia, as a little girl, had taken the crumpled garment out, declaring she would wear it when she was married, Fran had flinched. On an impulse she hurled it down the steps. As she turned to the two canvases against the wall she smiled, remembering how lovely her daughter had been in her simple grey chiffon and matching hat.

Without looking at the pictures she carried them to the opening in the floor and called to Jez to take them from her. Then she climbed down, folded the steps away and swept the old wedding dress into the wastepaper basket.

In the sitting room she saw he'd set the unfinished portrait of her on his easel. He took it down and put one of her paintings in its place. Then he stepped back and looked. The scene was of a river with trees on either side, the whole shrouded in mist. Fran remembered thrusting it aside when she couldn't find a colour that would give it life without destroying the mystery that clung to the half formed shapes. Without a word Jez replaced it with the other. The second one, an abstract, had been painted much earlier in her life. She'd tried to capture various shapes from the natural world around her. Hard-edged leaves and branches stuck out at odd angles under a uniform sky. In the middle, tentative russet brush strokes suggested a living shape, drawing the eye towards the one point of tenderness enclosed within a stylised world.

Jez bent and picked up the first painting to hold it by the side of the other. 'These are remarkable,' he said.

Fran felt confused. 'Neither of them is finished. I gave up in despair.'

He looked at the angular shapes and vivid colours in the earlier painting, turning his head to the side as he explored what he thought might be an animal. 'They remind me of Franc Marc.'

'Who's that?'

'He used these bright colours and nearly always painted animals. He did a yellow cow and blue horses. Worked in Munich before the First World War.' He turned back to the river scene.

'This is so different, more mystical, but as if you were afraid to let yourself go.'

'I think, after Sylvia was born, a part of me got frozen up.'

'Have you any idea why?'

Fran frowned as she tried to make some sense of the distance she'd travelled since she started on her quest. 'I tried so hard to be a good mother, but the only model I had was my own mother. She had very Victorian ideas, nothing I ever did pleased her. But I can't blame her entirely. I never really took responsibility for my own happiness. I wanted Paul to turn the key for me, but because of the man he was, he couldn't.'

'I'd like to help you start painting again. If I may.'

Fran shrugged. 'It's too late now.'

Jez put the painting down. Taking hold of her shoulders, he turned her to face him. 'That's not true. It's never too late. Are you going to let your life peter out, without making an effort?'

He leaned down and kissed her cheek, then took up his palate. 'Now, sit on the sofa as you did before.'

She tried to arrange herself in the old position but found it hard to sit still. The smell of turpentine filled her nostrils. After working in silence for a few minutes he said, 'I have to decide whether to go with Brenda. If I do I shan't have time to finish this before I go. What do you think?'

'About what?'

'My going with Brenda.'

'Would you carry on with the painting when you return?'

'Do you want me to?' The question was not just about the picture and Fran didn't know how to answer. He looked like an awkward schoolboy, his long arms dangling at his sides. 'As I told Mr Bennett, once before I put a cause before the woman I loved. I lost her. I know you need time to get used to the things you've discovered about your husband. And to find yourself again.' He laid down his brush and palate with a fretful movement and sat himself down at her side. Putting his hand under her chin he tipped her face up. 'I won't go if you'd like me to stay. You're more important than any campaign. I know this isn't the time to say it . . . but I've fallen in love with you.'

She looked into his eyes, trying to discern what the word meant to him.

'You're not still in love with your ex-wife?'

'I was for years, I think. But I'm over it now. Ready to love again.'

For Fran, love had been a lifetime commitment. She couldn't expect that again. So many patterns seemed to be on offer in the changed world of the twenty-first century. Geoffrey always had two or three women on the go at the same time. When she gave her love, Fran knew that she gave the whole of herself. Above all else, she wanted to be THE woman in the life of this sensitive man. Even if the affair didn't last for the rest of her life – he was, after all, younger by several years – she wanted to have a stab at her version of love. 'I couldn't cope with being one of a bevy of women. That would tear me apart.'

'It wouldn't be like that. I'm a one-woman man.' He smiled. 'To be strictly truthful, a one-woman-at-a-time man.'

Running her hand over the top of his head, feeling his springy hair, she said, 'I don't know you very well. How can I be sure you won't fall for Brenda, or some other woman in the treetops?'

He laughed. 'Making love in a tree would be uncomfortable, not to say dangerous.' He looked serious. 'But I won't go, if you'd rather I stayed here.'

She jumped up. 'No, you mustn't compromise your principles on my account. We must be free to follow our own path. But if we could walk alongside each other . . .'

He took her in his arms and kissed her with a passion that left her breathless.

When he made to pull away she tried to hold him close. Gently, he disentangled himself. 'I've got to let her know today. Will you be here when I get back?'

Fran nodded. 'You bet I will,' she said.

After he had driven away she stood and looked at her picture of the river. Taking up her new paints, she squeezed some burnt sienna on to the pallet he had been using and mixed it with some white and a dab of lemon yellow. She chose a brush and started to paint a buff shape that could be a sail. Cleaning the bristles in the fluid Jez had left in a jar, she added a white hull. Then, with increasing excitement, she worked on the trees that had stood on either side of the river, so that one bank began to look like a rocky headland, while the other developed the hard edges and corners of a concrete pier. She returned to the hull with its buff sail. The shape lost the lines that defined it as a boat. As she worked the sense of movement became sharper. A creature emerged under her hands, heading away from the constraints of the shore, intent on escaping to a world where it could claim its life in the open sea.